Too Many Gods in the Kitchen

Ben Schenkman

CAFFEINATED TERRIER PRESS

ISBN 979-8-9905133-5-8 (eBook)

ISBN 979-8-9905133-6-5 (Paperback)

ISBN 979-8-9905133-7-2 (Hardcover)

Editing by Katherine McIntyre

Proofreading by Laurie Neilsen

Chapter art by Kat Gruhala (@KinTheCryptid)

Cover design by GetCovers.com

PROLOGUE

God and the Devil shook hands, each smiling as if they had won the negotiation.

"It's settled," Lucifer declared, leaning back in his bistro chair. He stared evenly at his counterpart as if daring Them to disagree.

"Oh, I agree," They said, folding Their hands on the table and returning his look. They sat outside of a small café on Chapel Street in New Haven, Connecticut.

Lucifer finally broke eye contact and picked up an espresso black enough that mortals would've had to sign a waiver verifying they weren't Anish Kapoor. "It's an illusion of choice, you realize?" he said to Leslie, the current moniker God was going by these days.

"Of course," Leslie agreed. "They do love having choices though." They watched men and women walk along on their business, smiling slightly to Themself, and continued. "It would be a shame if we didn't at least let him think he had one."

Lucifer sighed heavily, sipping from the dainty cup. "Your people almost botched the whole thing. I don't blame you for wanting to steal Nick from me. I'd say you need him more than I do, but then I'd have to care about the state of your operation."

Leslie gave a hearty laugh. They drank from Their own mug of herbal tea. "At least we could come to an arrangement. I know you hate it when I step into your business."

"It wasn't the first time, and it's unlikely to be the last. Warn me before you do it again? All the cloak and dagger business almost cost me one of my best agents."

"It was dreadful, I'll admit." Leslie offered a look of genuine remorse. "Hopefully we'll have less of that, given this little joint venture."

"Are you really not keeping Rob?"

"My people were put out by what he did," Leslie said, though no concern was evident in Their voice. "But what about you? Are you still going to hold a grudge against him?"

"I am slow to forgive, if you'll recall. Some time in Purgatory will give him a chance to reflect," Lu replied, his voice dripping with sarcasm. He took a deep breath, fiddling with the napkin on the table. "I am worried about something, though."

The idea of the Devil being worried about anything was enough to make Leslie pause with Their cup halfway to Their mouth. They had known him long enough to wait for him to finish his statement, so Their hands continued Their progress while They made only the mildest, "Hm?" of interest.

"You thought you were clever, trying to poach my employee, but you may have started a chain reaction you aren't prepared for."

"What do you mean?" Leslie asked, genuinely perplexed.

"We've been at this a while, you and I, haven't we?"

"An eternity, and I'm not sure I'm being figurative." Leslie laughed.

"Sometimes," Lu said, drawing out the word, "you seem to forget there are others who have been at this far longer."

"You believe there are other interested parties?" Leslie asked.

"Let's just say I've felt something on the wind. The witch is attracting attention, which means Nick gets involved. Those boys could have their work cut out for them sooner than they expect."

"I suppose we'll have to trust them to make good choices," Leslie said pleasantly.

"You are an idealistic idiot, you know that?"
God sighed. "So I've been told."

Chapter 1

Nick

It was at that very moment I realized I had fucked up.

I stared around the small office, looking across a vast sea of brown boxes littering every surface. I existed at the single point in time when my decisions finally collided and I'd find out whether the crash resulted in a fender bender or a train wreck. Turned out it was, without a doubt, a train wreck.

I had brought a cup of coffee, but I lost it somewhere within the detritus strewn about the room. I stared longingly at what would eventually be a break nook. It currently held nothing but empty metal file racks and dust. Had I really gone from working in a swanky downtown office to whatever fresh hell this was? The problem was, I had no one to blame but myself.

After our last escapade, with Amy and Rob rescuing me from certain human trafficking, I proposed a deal to the powers that be. Both houses, Heaven and Hell, were in disorder, and they needed someone to put the fear of audit into their people. Who was the right person for the job? It wasn't me, but since I was the only one suggesting the changes, they both agreed to give me a shot. It took a while to nail down all the details.

First, my contract with Lucifer was going to remain in place. He agreed to put a rider on it for God, giving Them a certain claim on my afterlife. What was that claim? It was a little fuzzy even for me, but it sounded like I had a choice. As long as I was in good standing with both of them when I finally shuffled off this mortal coil, I could pick between Heaven and Hell. Maybe I would have a time-share in both?

My favorite paralegal did me the honor of reading through my new contract and assured me I was unlikely to do better, so I signed. Since I'd already sold my soul to the Devil, subleasing it back to God was small change.

They granted me my suggested mandate to set up a consultancy and review the deals made both above and below. I would need to be selective. Even with a huge department, I could only do so much. Until we proved ourselves, I didn't have a department. It was me and my partner, Rob. My *business* partner. Not to be confused with my romantic partner, Amy, who was also working for us part-time. Yes, the consultancy had a consultant. That was going to get confusing unless I workshopped some things.

Despite working for the Devil for two years and moonlighting for the other side for a hot minute, this new venture was going to be mostly self-sufficient. I received a modest budget, and they expected me to make do. I could request anything above and beyond if I could justify it, but there were no guarantees. Hence the cheap office. I had free rein over the renovation, but Lu thought it was too good of a location to pass up. It was halfway between Angel and Devil Co. and gave me a neutral place of business. It was hard to say I was impartial otherwise.

"It's perfect," Lu said to me the week before, handing me a folder with the relevant real estate information. "It was an old government building parceled out into office space. If you're going for the 'common man' vibe, you couldn't do better than this." I was excited, looking at the photos and thinking about the potential.

I picked a snapshot out of the paperwork I had brought and held it up against the scene in front of me. Potential, maybe, but reality was shaping up to be more challenging.

Getting what you ask for can be a humbling experience.

Rob poked his head in through the open front door. It had "For Rent" scribbled in chalk marker across the frosted glass.

"This place is great!" Rob had an enthusiasm I couldn't match. He wiped the glass clean with a cloth, then took a rolled decal, applied it to the white pane, and peeled it away to reveal "The Devil's in the Details, Inc."

The name of the consultancy might have been too on the nose for some, but I thought it was perfect. Sometimes a tongue slips on the exact syllable you need and "bam!" In our case, Rob quoted an idiom, and here we were, standing in the middle of a filthy downtown office that hadn't been used since 1962. I was exaggerating. Probably.

"You're right," I admitted, hunting among the piles for my lost beverage. "It's going to be great once we have everything the way we want it. Aha!" I cried triumphantly as I rescued my cup from where I had misplaced it, on top of what would ostensibly be my desk.

"But..." Rob said, with a trailing pause.

"But...I feel like I've bitten off more than I can chew." I sighed, dusting my hands off and leaning against the wall. "Why did I ask for our own office, instead of working out of Devil HQ?"

Rob turned from admiring his handiwork and raised his hands. He opened his mouth, closed it, then finally said, "I have no idea."

"Great. Maybe I'll call in the cavalry to see what we can do about this."

"When do we get started on some of the caseload?" Rob asked while poking around in what was to be his corner of the office.

I gestured at the boxes. "The ones without a thick layer of dust aren't vintage. They're only a fraction of what's going to be sent over when I give the go-ahead."

"Whoa." The sound came out of Rob with more weight than I expected, despite his initial enthusiasm.

"Having regrets?" I asked, smiling at my new partner in crime.

"No, not at all," Rob said, grinning back at me. "You didn't sugarcoat it when you asked me to come work with you. We're two people doing a full department's worth of effort. I just..." he trailed off, looking down at his feet.

"Don't stop now," I said, encouraging him to keep going.

"I'm a little envious."

I laughed out loud. "Of what? Me?"

"Not you, per se. Your new deal." He frowned, lifting the top off a box to investigate its contents. "They couldn't have taken me out of extra super, not-so-secret, probation?"

Rob was talking about his own soul's predicament. He had gotten on Lucifer's bad side a couple of years back by trying to kill me, which sounded pretty bad when I thought about it. Later, he tried to redeem himself by working for God's people but got fired when he used his access to save my ass after I had gotten myself kidnapped by some unsavory folk. Rob's history was...complex.

Neither Lu nor Leslie would admit what the final determination with Rob's soul was. Lu said he'd consider his position, given what Rob did for me. No promises, though. Leslie assumed everything would shake out fine for Rob, despite being fired. We had no idea what that meant, especially with Leslie being a bit of an idealist. There was talk of Purgatory, but I could never tell if that was a concept or actual destination. Maybe it was just their nickname for our office. Regardless, I was empathetic to Rob's plight.

"I'm still working on it. I promise." I didn't know if I was reassuring enough, but Rob grimaced and nodded before shuffling through some more yellowing papers.

My eyes unfocused as I stared across the old space, imagining what it would look like when we were done. An espresso machine and water cooler in the nook, two heavy desks at opposite ends of the room, a small reception desk for the assistant I promised myself I'd hire, and some vibrant color to replace the dated government off-white palette.

I took my phone out and made a quick call to Lester, the Devil Co. office manager and Rob's boyfriend. That was still something I chuckled about. They were an interesting match and genuinely liked each other, but it was a relationship that had formed under odd circumstances.

"Didn't we just get rid of you?" Lester's voice dripped with sarcasm.

"Hilarious. I need a favor."

"Already? Oh, how the mighty have fallen."

I sighed into the phone. "I'm making a command decision. The idea of putting Rob and myself through a personal renovation montage is a waste of time and effort. Lu and Leslie can split the cost, but I need a team in here to get this place in shape immediately."

"How soon is 'immediately'?" Lester asked.

"You completely redid my apartment in less than a day. I think someone can handle it."

"Just because you're right doesn't mean you have to be so loud about it. I'll talk to the boss and see what we can do."

"Thanks, Les, I owe you one."

"Girl," Lester drawled. "You're still deep in the red from me playing getaway driver."

I couldn't help but laugh. "Alright, happy hour this week?"

"You know it."

The line went dead, and I pocketed my phone. "Lunch?" I asked Rob.

"It's like ten o'clock."

"Yeah. But if we go to lunch, we can stop doing whatever this is," I said, waving at the surrounding chaos.

"Sold."

I was gathering up the few papers I had brought with me when I glimpsed a hint of red shining underneath an old newspaper on the desk. I cleared it away to reveal a classic corded phone with a pulsing ruby light. Rob was waiting for me by the door, fiddling with his phone. "Uh, Rob?" I said, gesturing at the antique.

He cocked his head as he approached, then picked up the receiver. Rob held it against his ear for a moment, then pressed "one" on the keypad. He nodded, his eyes widening. After hanging up, he stared at the phone for a long five seconds before turning to me. "We have a client."

"How do we already have a client?" I asked.

"It was a message from someone at the Elephas Group, whoever they are. They asked to meet tomorrow. I'll send you the details." He opened a note-taking app on his phone and started tapping in the information.

"Rob."

"Give me a second, before I forget—"

"Rob!" I hissed, finally getting his attention. "The phone. It's not plugged in..."

Chapter 2

Amy

It was the perfect afternoon for having lunch in a graveyard.

I had the latest true crime novel about a local historic murder, a cheese sandwich, a thermos of tea, and enough time to lie in the sun on a stone bench after eating. The warm rays permeated my black sundress and left me feeling like a contented lizard. The immediate irony in my choice of cemetery wasn't lost on me. I was lazing about in the same place where I'd been held captive in a mausoleum a few years prior.

I shook my head in amusement, considering my more recent history with my former captor. Rob had done a lot to improve himself since that incident, and he had also helped me save my boyfriend from a fate arguably worse than death. I forgave Rob afterward, though it would be more than a little while before I got over some of my more paranoid instincts.

I let the heat wash those unnecessary thoughts away for the moment. My job at the Free Public Library was going well, my latest initiative inspired by our escapades. "Women Get Things Done" was a big hit and near to my heart, given the rescue I orchestrated for Nick. My boss didn't know about the personal connection, but I was happy to let her live in ignorance and smile to myself whenever I passed the front displays.

Graveyards were beautiful expressions of loss. New Haven's were often more ostentatious than most, boasting some gorgeous stonework and architecture. I took my breaks at the Grove Street Cemetery regularly, enjoying the familiar statues and headstones. It was like spending an hour with a distant relative you were surprisingly fond of.

Add the lack of other people, since there weren't many others who found solace in macabre places, and I had a recipe for a wonderful getaway from my daily grind. Occasional visitors passed by or cut through, but today, it was only me and my tea. I sipped the Lady Grey I'd brewed in the break room before I set off for my picnic-for-one and turned another page.

The wind blew lightly across my shoulders, giving me gooseflesh despite the warm day. I checked the time, and there was just enough to arrive before my break ended if I left in the next five minutes. I set about packing everything into my black shoulder bag. I kneeled to stow the thermos away when another breeze licked at my back.

"*Amy...*"

I froze, the hair on my neck bristling like a porcupine. My stomach clenched with immediate unease. A voice was on the wind, barely perceptible. I turned slowly, scanning the graveyard for another human being but not finding a soul.

"*Help me...*" The words came as if whispered directly into my ear

I whirled, startled, but no one was behind me. "Who's there?" I asked the wind as if it could answer, but no reply came. The voice had come and gone, but I sat on the bench, trying to stretch my senses. I had to get back to work, so I picked up my things and made a beeline for the gate leading out of the cemetery. No more noises tickled my ear as I left, but something flickered at the edge of my vision as I walked through the campus.

Yale was full of fascinating sculptures built into nearly every archway and was usually a delight to wander through on my way to and from work, but my afternoon walk held none of the familiar pleasure. I passed other pedestrians and denizens, but along with the snatches of their conversations came ephemeral sounds and snippets of what might have been words or phrases. My mind grew anxious as I tried to focus on the noises, but they faded before I could process them.

I reached the library with more than a vague sense of unease but had little to go on besides intuition that something was wrong. I didn't have more than the usual amount of mental illness associated with growing up in a capitalist society, as far as I was aware. My passing worry that I was developing schizophrenia was mostly irrational. The barely audible whispers grew in volume as I approached the door, finally culminating in one word as I passed the threshold.

"Please!"

The sudden silence of the library drowned out whatever was scratching at my brain outside. I sighed audibly, and it was loud enough to alert my co-worker at the circulation desk to my presence.

Cora was middle-aged, with brown eyes and curly, shoulder-length charcoal hair. She wore a lightweight green cardigan over her outfit. The front desk was beneath an air duct, which threatened to freeze whoever was on duty during the summer or boil them in the winter. She worked as a page and had been with the library for longer than me but had always been kind.

"Everything alright, Amy?" she asked.

"Fine, Cora," I replied with the casual air you used when something might not *actually* be fine, but you *definitely* didn't want to talk about it. She had no idea I was a witch, and I wasn't about to make it a conversation of the day.

"I'm going on lunch now, if that's okay?" she said, smiling.

"Sure, I'll watch the desk for a while."

We traded places, and she retreated into the break room. Once she was comfortably out of snooping distance, I took out my phone. My mentor, the owner of a hippy-chic shop downtown called The Beehive and leader of the local coven, was the best person to check in with for supernatural gossip.

AMY:

Hey, Mel. Anything weird going on today?

MELINDA:

Hey, girlie. How did you know Carl was in town and trying to get me to take him back?

AMY:

What? No, I didn't know anything about that.

MELINDA:

I had to remind him I've been a lesbian for over a decade. So yeah, it's been a strange day so far.

AMY:

No, Mel, not that kind of weird. *Weird* weird.

MELINDA:

> You should have been more specific. But no, nothing here. What's going on with you?

AMY:

> I'm not sure yet, but I have a feeling I should talk to you about it.

MELINDA:

> Well, I'm here if you need me.

I met Melinda some months prior under interesting circumstances. I owed her a favor, and she had been hinting strongly about me joining the Union of Witches Underground—UWU for short. I still groaned every time I said the name, but Melinda wasn't interested in changing it despite the modern connotation.

When I put my phone back into my bag, the embossed leather of my tarot card case brushed against my hand. I had been practicing for months, and my readings had only gotten more accurate by all reports. I still didn't know what connection I had to the powers that be. No patron had shown itself to me, but Melinda said I glowed like the sun when we practiced together.

Tarot had become important to my work, but I tried not to use it as a crutch. Some witches wouldn't get out of bed in the morning if they didn't have a good reading to guide them through the day. I gave others the best interpretations I could, to help them take action in their lives, but I avoided reading for myself unless it was about something important.

My prior experience with Nick and his job, which was part of the catalyst for my growing oracular skill, made me shy away from casual use. But...one card couldn't hurt, could it? Something funky was going on, and I didn't have enough information.

I drew the case out of my bag, still admiring the craftsmanship. It was thick leather dyed a deep emerald green and embossed with a pentacle surrounded by leaves. I found it while browsing at the Beehive and it was my first mundane purchase from the store. I had bought Melinda's help with the esoteric currency of a "big" favor. Money was no good in the back rooms of the store.

I glanced around, ensuring no patrons were approaching my desk, and took the cards out for a quick shuffle. I placed the deck on the desktop and laid my hand over it before closing my eyes to concentrate and set an intention. *What the hell is going on?*

I flipped the top card over, and my forehead beaded with sweat, immediately chilled by the blowing vent. The Tower. It depicted a slim stone edifice with flames licking from each open window, and it was not the card I wanted. As a portent, The Tower was less helpful than some of the more specific major arcana. Tumult, destruction, upheaval, take your pick.

"Well," I said to no one in particular. "That can't be good."

I lifted my head to spy Cora coming back from the break room and quickly packed my cards away. We smiled to each other, mine more forced than hers, and I vacated the circulation desk for the comfort of the stacks. Working at the library, I had the luxury of curating our occult and religious tomes. The lack of interest from the patrons might as well have made it my private collection. I often skimmed through the titles and did research or studied from them on the fly. I made my way to that section and leaned against the shelves as I texted both Nick and Rob on our group chat.

AMY:

Heads up, something weird is going on.

NICK:

Isn't there always?

AMY:

Shut up, Nick.

ROB:

We've got our own strange thing here, too.

AMY:

How strange?

ROB:

How does "unplugged antique phones getting voicemail" hit you?

AMY:

Okay, that's odd.

NICK:

What's your "thing?"

AMY:

I'm hearing voices asking for help, and I'm guessing spirits, but nothing's shown itself to me yet.

NICK:

Keep us posted? We'll let you know what happens on our end. We might need you to look into something for us. Have you ever heard of the Elephas Group?

AMY:

No, but I'll poke around.

NICK:

Be safe?

AMY:

I'm not the one you need to remind to be safe.

ROB:

Touché!

I stood back from the bookshelves and closed my eyes, taking a breath to steady and ground myself. I raised my hand and tried to sense the surrounding energy. Sometimes, when I was unsure of something, I would feel for the pull of a particular book or which direction I should turn in. It didn't always work, but it was worth a shot given where I had found myself.

With my eyes closed, I exhaled and reached out with my senses. Like gravity pulling a falling leaf to the earth or a whirlpool drawing everything to its center, I lurched forward. My hand pressed against the spine of one of the larger books in the collection.

Spirits and Symbolism: Iconography and Imagery of World Religions was a hefty dictionary-style tome geared more toward research than the books on modern reconstructionism or revival of old-world religions. I took it down and walked back to the front desk, leaving it where we kept any personal holds. We were librarians, so of course we brought home books nearly every day.

"Doing some *light* reading?" Cora asked, grinning at her joke.

"I have a door that needs jamming," I quipped back.

"You always have the most interesting choices, Amy."

I smiled thinly, thinking about what happened the last time I was drawing catastrophic tarot cards. "You have no idea."

CHAPTER 3

NICK

W e were supposed to meet a representative from whatever this Elephas Group was at a teahouse off Crown Street at noon. The Marrakesh Oasis was a Moroccan café I had visited in the past. They served a delightful assortment of tea and coffee, as well as a full menu of delicacies. I wasn't sure if this would be a full lunch meeting, so I didn't get my hopes up, but my stomach rumbled at the thought of a Turkish coffee and baklava.

The Oasis was a surprising gem, situated among other brownstone buildings on the outskirts of Yale. The area held a mix of commercial enterprises and residential apartments, and the lush green of the Oasis's gardens were exactly that, an oasis amid a bustling city.

Rob and I discussed likely scenarios on the way over. By the time we had parked, I was winding myself up over the lack of information, and Rob wasn't doing much better.

"It could get complicated quickly," Rob said. "I found a few references to Elephas, but they spanned from Asian elephant families to medical imaging. I don't think we're going to learn anything about who we're meeting with until we get there."

"Fair enough. Though at this point I don't think it's possible to surprise me anymore. Let me lead," I said, walking us to the entrance of the shop.

"Sure thing, Boss."

I turned to glare at Rob, but he plastered a grin on his face and was stifling laughter, his chest spasming with the effort. I sighed and went to push the door open when a pleasant voice called my name.

"Nick! Over here."

I turned with my hand still on the doorknob and spied a pair of men sitting at a small bistro table in the café's courtyard. The shorter of the two waved excitedly in our direction. He was balding, somewhere near middle age, and relatively short. He had a kind face and a bright smile. The colorful Nehru-style vest he wore was in a casual floral print with a light linen shirt underneath. Linen pants and sandals completed his outfit, giving him a laid-back look, which surprised me. Not that I knew what to expect at all.

The taller was slightly more formal, dressed in a sharp blue and white windowpane three-piece suit. His jacket was open, and I could see a pocket watch chain accenting the outfit. He didn't smile at all as I appraised them, keeping a neutral expression.

"Good afternoon, gentlemen," I called back as we approached their table. "I believe you have us at a disadvantage. I'm Nick, and this is Rob, but you already know that. And you are?"

"Oh, forgive me, my name is Arjun," he said, standing and offering his hand. "And this lanky good-for-nothing is my associate, Chetan." He spoke with a light British accent, though it held regional traces of elsewhere. Possibly India by the names, but I didn't want to assume.

We shook hands, and Chetan rose to do the same but nodded in greeting without speaking.

"He doesn't talk much?" I asked as we took our seats.

Arjun laughed. "I think of us like Penn and Teller, only the short one speaks."

"I guess that makes sense. We received your...message yesterday. Can you help me understand what we're here for?" I asked, glancing at the table and noting two cups of tea. "Maybe we can order something, and you can fill us in."

"Perfect." Arjun clapped his hands together and waved to get the attention of a server who brought us menus and took a quick drink order. At least I would get my Turkish coffee.

"You are the gods people, yes?" Arjun asked.

I opened my mouth but had mentally glitched, so I closed it. "I'm sorry, what?"

"The gods people," he repeated.

I looked at Rob, and he stared right back at me, shrugging slightly.

"Well," I began, clearing my throat, "we're consultants, if that's what you mean."

"You don't have to be coy, Nick," Arjun said, but paused as the server brought a glass carafe of tea and a set of three cups, plus my small cup of caffeinated mud. Arjun waited until they had moved off again before continuing. "We know your line of business. No reason to deny it or beat around the bush."

I swallowed, trying to clear my dry mouth and wetting it with a sip of my coffee. "I'm starting to think there are no secrets anymore."

"None among friends, anyway, and we hope you'll enjoy working with us."

I blanched, setting my cup down with a slight tremor. "Come again?"

"I think I've kicked off in the middle instead of the beginning. Let me start over." He cleared his throat and took a sip of tea. "My name is Arjun, and I manage the Elephas Group's New Haven branch. Our people may not be as numerous here, but the population of practicing Hindus in the tri-state area is growing every day. We find ourselves in need of some assistance." He paused, leaning toward me slightly with a smile, as if expecting me to continue his train of thought.

"I'm not sure what you're getting at," I said.

Arjun chuckled uncomfortably, sitting back. "You...really haven't heard of us?"

"Not a bit," Rob added.

"Ahem. Well. You represent certain...interests, don't you?" Arjun asked us.

"We consult for two..." I trailed off, trying to find a circumspect way of saying it. I didn't like all the naked talk of what we did for a living.

Rob filled in the blank for me. "Higher powers."

"Yes, that, and we have a new consultancy for dealing with..." I lost my train of thought again.

"Clerical issues," Rob interjected helpfully.

"Exactly. So what does that have to do with the Elephas Group?" I asked again.

Arjun glanced over at Chetan with an uncomfortable look. The taller man shrugged but remained silent.

"I expected the paperwork to have arrived by now, otherwise we wouldn't have phoned for an appointment," Arjun said.

I was getting frustrated by the circular conversation. "What paperwork? You said we shouldn't 'beat around the bush.'"

Arjun opened his mouth, but Chetan held up a hand. When he spoke, his voice was a sonorous bass. "We represent Lord Ganesha, the Remover of Obstacles, and he has authorized the use of a subcontractor for the continuation of our services while we fill our ranks."

"He cuts to the heart of the matter, as always, when he chooses to. Yes, we have hired your services. But do not worry, we still intend to handle the largest matters. This is just to keep our people happy in the interim," Arjun said. "Plus, you'll have my help should you need it."

I looked over at Rob, who had already turned his gaze to me.

"The gods people," we said in unison.

"So," Arjun continued nervously, "what shall we have for lunch?"

"It's all in order," Jessica said, shaking her head as she scanned the document I had given her. She was my favorite paralegal in Devil Co's legal division and had done me many favors over the course of our professional relationship. I owed her so many lattes I didn't even count anymore and just brought one every visit. She sipped at the offering and glared at me flatly.

"How is that possible?" I asked.

She picked up her stylus and chewed the top. "Well...when you messaged me earlier, I started looking into it, and there's a little-used policy about interagency contracting."

"You're kidding."

"Wish I was," she grumbled and peered over her large-framed glasses at me standing next to her desk. "It would make my life easier because you wouldn't be here breathing down my neck."

I stepped back, chagrined, holding my hands up. Jessica was not a person I wanted to piss off. Her pencil skirt and modest blouse were a front for the take-no-shit personality driving her compact frame. "I don't remember anything about other agencies in the handbook," I said.

"That's probably because you slept through half of the training, like every other hopeful idiot that Lu brings into this place."

I opened my mouth to object, but she was probably right. My new employer introduced me to a classic torture method when I joined called computer-based training. There had been so much of it, and I couldn't recall most of the details. "Alright, so what do I do with the request?"

She raised a finely penciled eyebrow at me. "Your job," she said. "Like the rest of us. Don't like it? Take it up with the boss." She turned back to her laptop, dismissing me. Jessica had the art of the last word down to a science.

I did not, in fact, like it. I had my shirtsleeves cuffed and pushed one back so I could look at the tattoo on my left bicep. It was the fifth pentacle of Jupiter, a famous occult seal of Solomon. If I concentrated on it, I could co-locate myself, sharing my consciousness across two places.

It wasn't teleportation. I would remain wherever my body started, but I could interact somewhere else as long as I was familiar enough with it to visualize it and had permission to be there. I received the ability as a perk on my second anniversary with the company and had it permanently tattooed after my last mishap left me stranded without the temporary version.

"Oh, no you don't," Jessica admonished without glancing up from her keyboard. "You're not allowed to barf here. You want to talk to your boss? Use your feet."

The downside of my supernatural power, for most recipients, was nausea and migraines. The more you practiced, the less severe the effects, but it was never a sure thing you wouldn't need a waste bin. I sighed, but didn't argue, and made my way back to my old desk. I knocked on Lu's office door and walked in after a muffled, "Come in."

I strode into the office, noting that Lu was looking more modern in today's outfit than his usual jet-black suit. He wore a black and red pinstripe number with a red double-breasted vest, white shirt, and red-accented tie. His eyes were deep brown-to-black, and his sable hair was choppy and short but styled in that artfully disarrayed fashion. He had a tightly trimmed Van Dyke beard and lithe features, and the suit was well-tailored for a slim fit. He looked up with a smile as I entered.

"Nick! How are you?" he asked, standing up to shake my hand as I reached his desk. We both sat, and I got right to the point.

"What do you know about the Elephas group?"

"No time for pleasantries? It's good to see you, Lu! How are things?"

I laughed and took a breath to slow my roll. "Hi, Lu, it's great to see you. I love the new suit."

"Much better! Thanks, it's a fresh cut from Dominic. The classics are lovely, but sometimes you need to move with the times. Speaking of, I'm surprised they got to you this quickly."

The shock must have been obvious on my face because Lu continued, "I have to approve those work orders, you know. But when Ganesha—by the way, you'd really like him, interesting guy. When he approved the request for his people? I figured it would be at least a couple of weeks before they contacted you."

I managed to close my mouth, swallowing the dry lump there, and composed myself before asking, "What the hell, Lu?"

"Don't worry, it's standard stuff. Who'd you meet with? Do they still have that duo with the one who doesn't talk? Classic."

"I did, and they promised we'd only be handling small stuff, but the whole thing was still a shock."

"I was thinking about denying your request for the fast office renovation and letting you build some more character, but given this little administrative hiccup, I'll push it through. Construction will be done before the end of the week."

"Thanks, Lu. I appreciate it..." I trailed off, staring into space for a moment before snapping back.

"Where'd you go, Nick? You seem a bit overwhelmed."

"No—I mean, yes, I am, but not how you think. It's one thing to be presented with God and Devil, right? Even with whatever's going on with Amy, it's still a bit out in the aether, intangible. I had lunch with agents of another god, from a different religion, representing over a billion followers. My world keeps expanding, I guess."

Lu cracked his knuckles and leaned back in his chair with his hands behind his head. "They're good people. They just need some help, and with your new agency? You're the folks to do it. I've got faith in you. How hard could the job possibly be?"

CHAPTER 4

ROB

I stared across the newly renovated room, trapped somewhere between a dream and a nightmare. My boss—uh, business partner—caught me searching the horizon, so I put on a big, stupid smile and turned away. A migraine lurked in my future, and I rubbed my temples, trying to stave it off.

Nick didn't know about the inner turmoil I was working through, beyond the envy I had mentioned about his deal. He was just happy I had agreed to take the job. I think he understood the broad strokes of what was keeping me up at night, but I hadn't confided in him about my long-term anxiety after everything had gone down at Angel Co.

I recalled the last conversation I had before they threw me out of their office.

"I hope you're happy with yourself because you just blew up any chance you had of redemption, Rob," my boss, John, had said to me after he discovered I had stolen those documents to protect Nick.

"What was I supposed to do, John? Leave him watching over his shoulder for the rest of his life?"

"You were *supposed* to follow the rules," he spat back at me.

"The *rules* were to help people!" I yelled, losing my temper.

"You mistake your personal litmus test for policy."

I had told John, before they took me on, about the question I asked myself when I needed to know if I was making the right choice. I had been the villain once. After the rude awakening Lucifer had given me, I never wanted to be that guy again. Whenever I was about to make a dubious decision, I interrogated it. Was I doing it to be a good person?

In that case, the choices were: Take the information I had dug up and give it to Nick so he could protect himself from *very* bad people, or ignore my discovery and let Nick fend for himself. I obviously chose door A, and I was promptly let go when Angelic IT flagged my account.

I squared my jaw. "I made my decision, and I'd do it again in a heartbeat."

"You'll have plenty of opportunities to reflect on it. Grab your stuff and get out. You're fired."

I hadn't seen John since then. He was right about the time to reflect. I had been doing little but stewing on it since. What I did, though? It led to where I was sitting now, a business partner working to fix both Hell's and Heaven's problems.

"Earth to Rob," Nick said, snapping his fingers in front of my face and breaking my reverie.

I started at the sudden sound, shaking my head to clear away the thoughts I was dwelling on. "Sorry, Boss, I got caught up in something."

Nick dropped a stack of folders on my desk. "I'm not your boss, Rob. But I am your business partner, who has a stack of old files for you to go through. This is only the start of what Lester sent over, but it's some of the oldest cases flagged for review."

Thinking about Lester, my boyfriend, put a smile on my face. One of the least expected parts of the past year was dating. But

Lester was adorable, sweet, and sassy. More importantly he loved the parts of me I had a problem accepting myself.

Living with the office manager did make separating work and home complicated sometimes. Like when he complained about the emergency renovation Nick asked for. It was good-natured, though. Lester liked Nick and didn't mind pushing the favor through for him. He did get a backrub out of it when he whined about spending so much of his day typing up the work order that his shoulders cramped. It was a thin excuse, and we both knew it, but I played along.

The new office was perfect. I was amazed they had finished it in just a few days, down to the coffee nook Nick had insisted on. If I ignored all of the drama and trauma of the past few years, I was at an idyllic place in my life. The new job paid well, I had reunited with friends I was sure I had lost forever, and I had someone who loved me as much as I did them. Why couldn't I get my shit together and stop obsessing about things I couldn't control?

I plucked the top folder from the pile and leafed through it absently. "When will we start getting stuff from Angel Co.?"

"We're waiting on a liaison. John doesn't exactly want to speak to me anymore after the stunt I pulled," Nick said, chuckling to himself.

I had to admit, when Nick said he told my old boss off for firing me, it was a validation I didn't know I needed. It was a long road from the old me, the one who chased dark powers in a graveyard and lost his mind when his friend got an opportunity instead of him.

"Well," I said, glancing at the pile on my desk. "I'll get on it. Tell me if anything else interesting comes in?"

Nick wandered back to his desk and left me to dig into our first batch of cases. I wasn't sure what to expect. Even though Lester and I dated, I didn't get any inside scoops about what they had sent over. He was a hopeless gossip but tried not to talk shop when we were together. The key word was "tried," of course.

I assumed that until some live client came in, we would be going through the archives.

"What am I looking for?" I yelled across the room as I thumbed through what turned out to be a thin dossier on a former client inquiry.

"Lu thinks we'll know it when we see it, but I'd keep an eye out for things that would make an auditor cry."

"Fair enough…" I trailed off as I noticed the stated purpose of the form in front of me. The client was a widow named Mabel Fasler. She was trying to cut a deal to get her deceased husband's soul out of Hell. From the notes, she wasn't sure whether his soul had descended but had some choice words to describe his activities during life. Despite his transgressions, she still loved him and wanted to find a way to save his soul from Hell and even get it released to go to Heaven.

The story was interesting but didn't really seem like something Devil Co. would care about, not that I was an expert. What caught my attention was a red stamp that read "REJECTED" with an interesting note scribbled in the margins on the top sheet.

"Requested soul is in Purgatory, no further action required."

What the hell did *that* mean? I flipped through the file from front to back. It was only a couple pages thick and consisted primarily of the summary in front and the husband's death certificate. "Hey, Nick," I called out.

Nick's head popped up over his laptop. "Hm?"

"Have you ever seen a deal rejected because the request was invalid?"

"What do you mean?" He walked over to lean against my desk.

I turned the folder around and showed him the page I had been reading. "This guy's wife wanted to get his soul out of Hell, but it says here he's in Purgatory. Why would it end up in an audit pile?"

Nick made a noncommittal noise. "Dunno? Maybe the hair-thin files didn't pass some kind of due diligence? I doubt anyone checked them at all, given this slush pile."

"I guess…" I laid the paperwork on the desk and rubbed my temples, light throbbing alerting me to the migraine stalking me in the long grass.

"Can't hurt to look into it." Nick winked at me. "We're paid by the hour, not the case."

"I'm salary, Nick."

"Even better!"

I sighed, and my stomach rumbled at the same time. I cataloged my morning and realized I hadn't eaten more than a bowl of cereal so far. That, plus my antidepressants, made for an interesting cocktail, and I was suddenly aware of why my head was about to go on strike.

"Want to grab some lunch?" I asked Nick.

"I thought you'd never ask!"

We started to converge on the entry when a figure stepped into the doorway. The woman was petite with fine features, her brown hair covered by a burgundy pashmina shawl that draped her head and shoulders. Her alert brown eyes darted around the room, scanning for something, and finally settled on Nick. The light glinted off a nose ring that accented her outfit, a simple dark blue *salwar* or light dress. Nick had barely opened his mouth before she spoke.

"I need your assistance," she said.

"Why don't you come in and tell us what's going on." Nick said, motioning for her to enter the office proper.

We didn't have many chairs for guests yet, thanks to a delayed furniture delivery for the sitting area. I offered her the metal folding chair in front of Nick's desk. "I'm sorry for the state of the place," I said. "We've only just moved in."

"Which is why we're a little surprised to already have a client," Nick added. "I'm Nick," he said, offering his hand. I settled against the nearby wall.

"Meghna," she replied, shaking it. "I was told you would be able to help me with my problem."

"What problem would that be?"

"I need to have a wish granted by Lord Ganesha in the next month, otherwise my family will be ruined," she said with a straight face.

Nick froze with a grin plastered across his face, and I glanced back and forth between him and Meghna, waiting for a punchline.

"Is that all?" I asked.

CHAPTER 5

NICK

I buried my face in my hands with a groan as soon as Meghna left the office. She had nearly burst into tears when I told her we'd do our best, and I had to gently shove her out the door before locking up.

"Was I bad in a past life, Rob?" I asked.

Rob tapped his finger on his lips, considering. "You weren't exactly great in this one."

"Ha ha, very funny."

"But seriously, what the hell is going on?" Rob asked me as he continued straightening his area.

Meghna's story was a complicated one, and not what I expected as the first drop-in from Arjun. Small matters, my ass. Her family had emigrated from southern India decades ago and established themselves in the import/export business. New Haven was a port city with cargo ships coming and going daily, making for a lively commercial hub. Their choice of vocation wasn't the interesting part, but how they got to the States was fascinating. I didn't know much about Hindu deities, but Meghna's tale gave me a crash course.

"It was my great grandfather who started all this mess," Meghna had said, clucking her tongue in disapproval. His name was Vijay, and he was a poor tinker living in a small town outside of Banga-lore, which is one of the large tech hubs now. He married, which was arranged by his parents, and began his life with his wife. He was dissatisfied and sought the counsel of gurus and *sadhus*, wise and holy men, to find a solution to change his station.

This was an earlier time when the caste system was still in place, so short of a miracle, there was little he could do. He'd almost given up hope when he was directed to a newcomer in the area, who had earned a reputation for providing good advice to Vijay's neighbors. He jumped at the chance for a new perspective and approached this man, inviting him to his home for tea.

The man did not claim to be wise or holy, but offered to help Vijay with his plight if he would do three favors for him, to prove his commitment. They were not overly complex or difficult, so Vijay agreed and performed the services with great speed.

Upon completion of the third task, the man revealed himself to be an asura, which was a kind of Hindu demon, and offered to grant Vijay his desire in exchange for a promise. In three genera-tions, the asura would return to claim Vijay's family line, bringing the living members into his service and harnessing the power of the deceased ones' souls for his magic.

According to Meghna, the story told within her family was that Vijay chose to live well with a curse, hoping his descendants would determine a way to break it, instead of leaving them to generations of poverty and struggle.

"But he wasn't going to be around to deal with it, was he? Pretty convenient he would expect his children's children to figure it out for him." Meghna was not enamored with the memory of her ancestor, unlike some of her family.

Unfortunately, no one had come up with a solution to free them from the asura's eventual grasp, and it left Meghna holding the bag as the youngest adult of the family. It seemed there was a lack of concern from the older generations, which she scoffed at as she told me.

The only plan she could concoct was overpowering her great-grandfather's deal with an even greater bargain. In this case, it was going to be a wish granted by Ganesha. Her family had become devout Hindus over the years, specifically worshiping the elephant-headed god. Knowing malevolent powers existed, even if they benefited you, made it easier to believe in higher ones.

Despite the looming threat, no boon had been sought from Ganesha until now. The older generations had more time with no consequences of the curse to dull their worry, whereas Meghna's life had been a countdown to the inevitable. It lit a fire under her, which led to us, by way of the Elephas Group.

"First things first, I need to get in touch with Arjun," I said to Rob, though his attention was less on our conversation and more on the file in his hand. His stomach growled from across the room. "Maybe I can squeeze a lunch meeting out of him. I expect that's the least he'll owe me before this is all done. Are you coming with? You wanted to grab something to eat."

"No matter how much I'd love to witness whatever is going to happen, I think I need to look into this," Rob said, gesturing at the file. "Something about it is making my brain buzz."

"Chase whatever leads you can. We can split up on this for now. I'll text you if I need your help, okay?"

"Sure thing, Boss."

"You're not going to let that go, are you?"

He grinned at me. "Not for a while, no."

I strode into my favorite Lebanese restaurant where I had asked Arjun to meet me for an emergency lunch meeting. I hadn't given him all the details yet, but when I told him we already had a client looking for the mercy of his benefactor, he understood my concern. Luckily, I didn't have to ask twice, and when I arrived, he was already sitting at a small table with two Turkish coffees and a piece of pistachio baklava resting on a plate in front of the empty chair. I sat, glancing at the pastry before leveling my gaze at the man.

"I hope you don't think you can mollify me with honeyed desserts, Arjun."

He smiled, a nervousness dancing behind his eyes. "Consider it a peace offering?"

"Hrmph." I bit into the confection, and my mood was temporarily swayed by a punch of sweetness directly to my taste buds.

"You've seen Meghna, I take it?"

"You *knew*?" I said, biting off my words.

He held his hands up. "We were aware she sought a boon but had not made the time to meet with her."

I slurped my coffee and continued staring.

Arjun swallowed audibly and went on, "Now that we're contracted with you, our administration must have already sent notice to some of our backlogged clients."

"Hence, Meghna," I added.

"Hence, Meghna."

He waved a server over, and we placed a lunch order. The baklava and coffee soothed my rough edges, but until I understood whether Arjun had set me up intentionally, I wasn't going to let go of my worry.

"I guess this means we need to have a more serious talk about what being a subcontracted agent of Ganesha is all about. I checked with our legal department, and there wasn't anything hinky in the paperwork you folks submitted, so we're on the hook to work with you."

"What did you do for your employer before you started the agency?"

"I always thought of myself in the wish-fulfillment business..." I trailed off, realizing I had walked directly into a trap.

"Funny things, wishes," Arjun said. "Everyone wants something, from the mundane to the heartbreaking. They are fired off left and right at the gods, who cannot help but hear the pain and longing of their people. Some are more empathetic than others, Lord Ganesha being one of the most compassionate. Even he has limits on what he can do."

"If I've learned anything," I said, glancing toward my hidden tattoo, "it's that gods aren't infallible or all-powerful."

"Too right," Arjun agreed. "But what is there to do? Even as a metaphysical powerhouse Lord Ganesha cannot be in all places at all times, so the Elephas Group serves a function. We told you and your associate as much in our first meeting, but given recent events you need a more practical primer. You used to be in the wish-fulfillment business, but what are you doing these days?"

"I'm making sure the right people are getting theirs granted and the wrong people can go to Hell. Quite literally." I chuckled.

"And so you see why we chose you for our services."

I opened my mouth to reply, but our food arrived at that moment, sizzling plates of chicken kebabs with rice. The aroma was wonderful, and my stomach clenched from how hungry I was. My mood was stabilizing now that Arjun was getting into some details, so I tucked into my meal and chewed on my thoughts before getting back to the conversation.

"You need me to vet the petitioner, and if they're worthy, I have to...fight a demon?"

"Perhaps." Arjun laughed and wiped his mouth with a napkin. He had a twinkle of mischief in his eyes. "I doubt you will do any battle yourself, but you must determine if she is deserving of our Lord's aid."

"This is what you call a 'small matter,' Arjun?"

"I will admit I don't know the extent of what you must to do for either task, but I have enough experience handling these matters to say I have full faith in you to resolve it."

"You've just met me."

"True, but I have a good feeling," he said.

"You don't want to deal with Meghna and the angry asura."

"I do not," he admitted. "But mostly because I have other more pressing matters. The timing coincides with you being able to take this on for us instead."

"I still feel set up," I groused. "How do you usually test these 'petitioners'?"

Arjun was finishing his plate, savoring the last crisp bite of chicken. He chewed thoughtfully and considered my question. "In some ways, they do it themselves."

"I hope you're going to give me more than that."

"Too close to fortune cookie wisdom for you?" He chuckled but continued, "No, I mean that in a literal sense. The petitioner will often lead you to their own testing. You must pay attention, but chances are, the tools for determining their worthiness will be shown to you."

"So you cold read your clients?"

"I wouldn't put it as crassly as that. We also seek wisdom from Ganpati. He guides our hands and steps, as it were. Sometimes more directly than others, but we try to interpret his guidance from what we experience with our own senses."

My brow furrowed. My own instinct said Arjun was beating around the bush. It was that or my spirituality-o-meter was broken, and I wasn't following.

He sighed, likely seeing the frustration on my face. "Look, I expect this is confusing. I'd ask you to trust in our process, but that's what you're here inquiring about. I believe you have a special mark, which allows you to be in multiple places at one time, is that correct?"

The hairs on the back of my neck rose in a wave of goose bumps. "How do you know that?"

"My employer sees many things. He may not be omniscient, but he is perhaps one of the more observant gods. Will you put your faith in me for something? It will help you understand what I am saying."

I wasn't sure if I could trust the man, given the nature of our meeting, but having my tattoo was both a perk and a security measure. It was unlikely Arjun would have a way to take advantage by asking me to use it. "I suppose. What is it?"

"It is harmless," he said, staring into my eyes with a palpable sincerity. "I swear on my life. I could give you directions to drive there, but this is much more efficient."

I nodded, and he took a postcard out of his pocket and placed it on the table.

The photo was like one from an art gallery. It showed a padded bench in front of a gilded altar set against the wall of a large room. There were multiple statues on the altar, but the largest was an elephant-headed figure in the center. It was seated, draped in cloth, with one hand raised palm-out and the other cupped at its knee.

"If it is not too much trouble, would you go here briefly, and consider Shri Ganesha?" Arjun asked, pushing the card toward me.

I hesitated. "I've never been there…"

"Fear not, it is a public space, and you are welcome there. It is in Milford, near to the shopping mall, an area I expect you are familiar with. Take all the time you need."

I breathed out, steadying myself, and picked up the photograph. It was very detailed, and while I hadn't tried to co-locate to a place I hadn't visited, there was no reason I shouldn't be able to.

I had been practicing regularly, trying to get over the frequent nausea that came from the literal mind-splitting exercise. Lately I was able to sustain it for at least a few minutes before lying down with a wet cloth over my face. I didn't expect to need a bucket, otherwise I wouldn't have agreed to the attempt. I didn't even have to look at my tattoo anymore. I could just visualize it.

It came to me a while back that it became easier to do this when I wasn't trying to actively maintain focus in two places at once, so I closed my eyes. I pictured the shrine in my mind and focused on the sigil inked into my flesh. The mind-bending feeling of dislocation still passed through me, like I was suddenly shifted left of myself, and I was sitting on the bench in the picture. There were other people around, visiting the various alcoves and altars, but no one paid me any mind despite appearing out of nowhere.

The statue of Ganesha was looking at me. The weight of his observation and his presence settled over me. I had not been directly perceived by another god before, and it was...strange. The presence in my mind approached me gently rather than as an intrusion. A warmth spread through me, making my limbs fuzzy. It wasn't unpleasant, far from it. Then a voice spoke from nowhere. It was coming through the statue, I was sure of it, though it was as if someone was talking directly into my brain.

"The asura are my enemies, and if the child wishes to be saved, then she expects someone to fight on her behalf. Will you go to war for someone who does not also stand for themselves?"

A light pressure grew behind my eyes, but I tried to digest the message. I didn't say anything out loud but tried to push my thoughts in response, *"I think I understand."*

"Good," Shri Ganesha continued. *"I will be pleased if you take this task on for us. My people will support you, should you need it."*

Then the voice, and weight of a god's presence, was gone.

My consciousness returned to my body, and I opened my eyes and stared at Arjun. "Did you know what was going to happen?"

"He likes you," Arjun said, smiling. "It is easier for him to communicate with *mleccha* in a place of worship, like the temple you so kindly visited. I hoped the meeting would prompt some wisdom. Did it?"

"Maybe. I still think this is going to be harder than you expect."

"I have faith in you, Nick. Besides, if you fail? We get our money back."

"You're kidding."

Arjun's wink was all the answer I received.

CHAPTER 6

AMY

I opened the door to my apartment and broke into a cold sweat as I observed the scene in front of me. My living room, normally a lovingly cluttered assortment of plants and knickknacks, was in shambles. Dirt was strewn liberally across the floor amidst shards of broken clay pots. Some were tipped over but hadn't fallen and lent the scene the air of a verdant avalanche in progress.

The baseball bat I kept to the left of the door was still leaning there. I armed myself, holding the length of hickory at my shoulder, ready to strike. Plaintive meows came from the bedroom, which made me worry that whoever had wrecked my apartment was still there.

As I stalked through the mess, noting figurines and decorations mixed in with the greenery, the sound coming from the bedroom stopped. I scanned the kitchen, and there wasn't anything particularly amiss there, other than a few dishes from breakfast spread a little farther apart than I had left them, as if they'd been pushed out of the way.

Despite my worries, I felt alone in the apartment. Other than my cat, Pants, that was. I tried to extend my awareness, to touch the energies in the room, but besides my own nervousness, I wasn't able to pick up on anything else. I reached the bedroom and rushed in, hoping to surprise anyone that happened to be in there, but only managed to spook Pants. She scampered and hid under the bed with a squeak.

No one was waiting for me there, so I made a quick circuit of the apartment and locked the door for good measure. As I turned toward the bedroom to try to coax Pants out from her hiding spot, she made an appearance at the threshold. She was a petite, long-haired, black and white tuxedo cat. Well, normally she was. Today she was a black and *brown* tuxedo cat, her white bib covered with potting soil and her normally white feet stained from the dirt scattered on the floor.

"What did you do? You absolute asshole. You scared me to death," I said to her, placing the bat back where it lived within reach of the front door. Pants let out a pathetic mew, and my irritation melted. I sighed, chiding myself for having a temper with her. "Let's get you cleaned up."

Bathing a cat was perilous under ideal conditions. Attempting this with a cat who had absolutely no intention of being washed was nearly impossible. I was lucky that I'd trained her to accept baths as a kitten, but the habit had slowly worn off as she got older. The larger she grew, and the less frequent the reminders that water wasn't acid, the more likely I was to lose a pint of blood during the escapade.

I ran the bath, put the kettle on, and swept away all the soil and pieces of pottery to prevent her from undoing my good work by running wet fur through a dirty apartment. I finished in short order. The damage was less extensive once I was less surprised by the potential home intrusion and had assessed it more thoroughly.

I dressed in a long sleeve shirt and jeans, despite the warmth, to limit my exposed skin and locked us both into the bathroom for an expedient cleaning. Ten minutes later, a miserable Pants was licking her bedraggled self while sitting in the middle of my bed, making a wet patch. I had managed to wash her, but drying became a bridge too far. She wriggled her way out of the towel burrito I had wrapped her in and refused to listen to reason. I had to open the bathroom door to pull the kettle off the stove, and she seized that moment to escape.

I brought my tea into the living room and settled on my green velvet couch with my latest book from the library. It was a large tome and took up a lot of room on my coffee table. I lived a lot of stereotypes as a goth witch, and my furnishings were no exception.

Sometimes I laughed at myself for falling so hard into the tropes, but I loved my Ouija board coffee table so much. I had a thrifting habit and found it at one of my favorite spots. The owners of Witch Bitch Thrift were an adorable couple, and we had become friendly after my last large spell had costuming components they were able to source for me. Needless to say, I took the table home immediately.

Nick had told me about his latest experience with the Elephas Group and how he and Rob had been hijacked by them to work for Ganesha. I thought it was absolutely fascinating but was secretly glad I hadn't agreed to consult with them full-time. I had enough on my hands with my own practice to get caught in another pantheon's problems, but I never objected to some light research.

I had *Spirits and Symbolism* open to the section on elephants and was getting up to speed on the Hindu deity when a trill came from the bedroom. I didn't lift my head from my reading. Pants chirped when she was chasing bugs or dust motes, so I didn't pay the sound any mind. When she escalated to the "ack, ack, ack" of a cat watching prey, I got up to investigate. I had a mouse in the apartment once, and that was the sound she made before the building had one less rodent to worry about.

I poked my head into the bedroom, and Pants was sitting on my nightstand, peering into the corner of the room. There was nothing to see. It was completely bare in that area. Her head was tilted slightly, and she was staring with an intensity I found slightly unnerving. I approached and stroked the top of her head gently, which made her release a small meow, but then she went immediately back to her self-imposed guard duty.

"Keep an eye on those demons for me, okay?" I laughed, going back to the couch. I always joked with Nick that when cats zoned out into the middle distance at walls or the ceiling, they were seeing supernatural creatures we couldn't perceive.

I was making some notes in a journal to discuss with Nick when we met up later that evening when Pants galloped into the room and jumped onto the coffee table. Her tail was as straight as a flagpole and her eyes as big as saucers.

"What's got into you?" I asked, reaching out to pet her again.

Her tail flicked back and forth, and she ducked my hand and turned to the center of the table. She stood stock-still, raised a paw slightly, and lashed out to smack the table. I watched, confused, because there was nothing there for her to play pounce-and-chase with. No lights, no lasers, no bugs or dust. Nothing, but she continued to land on different areas of the table. Bap. Bap. Bap. I watched for a solid minute as her rotation continued, until I realized she was hitting the same three spots on the table. Bap. Bap. Bap. My attention was rapt, and I stared at my cat as the pattern continued. Bap...A...Bap...M...Bap...Y.

"No fucking way."

One phone call later and I was being whisked into the inner sanctum of the Union of Witches Underground. I had a cup of tea in front of me, sitting at the table with Melinda, the leader of the coven. I told her about what happened at the apartment. "And then she started tapping out my name on the coffee table!"

"I guess this is part of the 'weird' stuff you were texting me about?" She leaned back in her chair, considering the state of me. Her strong hazel eyes were intense, though her clear concern for me softened the look. She dressed simply, as she usually did when she was at the shop, in a set of loose cotton overalls. Today's were blue, though accented by her usual assortment of trans pride and other queer pins.

"I wasn't sure what to expect. I didn't tell you what happened because it felt like a bit of a fluke. I wasn't doing anything in the graveyard to attract attention, but it looks like I may have gotten it anyway."

Melinda sighed as she stood, wandering over to the side of the room that held shelves of occult paraphernalia. The large basement used to be a speakeasy, which had gotten walled off after prohibition. She returned holding a black book with a ratty and worn cover. When she placed it on the table, I could read the title *Witch's Familiars* with a subtitle lost to time as it had slowly rubbed away from use.

"How much do you know about the spirit world?" Melinda asked.

"Not enough, clearly," I replied. I reached out to pick up the spell book, and Melinda didn't stop me. I riffled through the pages. It was a compilation of spells specifically for working with familiars.

"You've got some homework ahead of you, girlie. Your trouble lines up with what me and the girls have been seeing. There's a *lot* of spirit activity, and I've had a line out the door of people needing help with their loved ones not being at peace."

"What does that mean? People have been seeing spirits?"

Melinda scoffed. "Seeing them? No, just the usual nonsense restless spirits get up to. Flickering lights, eerie noises, knocking wine glasses over. Like cats, the whole lot of them."

"Anything in particular you think I'll need in here?" I asked, tapping the cover of the book.

"Given what you told me about Ms. Pants, you might find a thing or two in there." She placed a small charm on the table and pushed it toward me. It was a pearlescent cabochon in a silver setting, ready to string onto a chain. "Selenite. Good for communicating with spirits, and you'll find something to pair it with in the spell book."

"What do you know that I don't?" I asked.

"Not much, if I'm being honest." She took a deep breath and let it out slowly, considering me again. "You might want to figure out who your patron is, if you haven't already."

"Not yet, do you feel like it's related?" I reached toward the stone, and as I grasped it, Melinda put her hand over mine, gently but firmly.

"Something big is happening. I'm not sure what, but so far, you're the only one to have direct communication from the other side. It feels connected to whatever's got their strings on you, and I want to trust my gut. If you can fix this, and hopefully before it becomes a bigger problem, I'll call your debt paid."

My eyes grew wide, and I pulled my hand back, clutching the cold pendant to my chest. "Is it going to be that bad?"

"What do you think?"

I breathed out, steadying my nerves. "I pulled the Tower the other day."

"And that tells you..."

"It *tells* me it's going to get worse before it gets better."

Melinda smiled. "Time to work, girl."

CHAPTER 7

AMY

When I got back to my apartment, Nick was sitting on the couch waiting for me with a bag of Chinese takeout. We didn't live together, but we'd exchanged apartment keys shortly into our relationship, so we were comfortable showing up before the other was home. It was just how our schedules worked sometimes. It wasn't that I would hate living with Nick. He was a fantastic partner, but I prized my independence a little too much to want to give it up in exchange for the comforts of nesting together.

Pants was sitting patiently on the coffee table, gazing adoringly at him. I teased Nick all the time about Pants thinking he was her boyfriend. She clearly loved him more than me, and I accepted it because Nick's cat, Odin, loved me more than him. She wasn't staring into the corner or playing chase with invisible mice on the table, which was probably a good sign. My stomach rumbled at the sight of the paper bag, and it must have been audible because Nick grabbed the top and gave it a little shake.

"Keep bringing me food without me having to ask for it, and I'm going to marry you when you're not looking," I said, walking over to give Nick a hug and a lingering kiss. He was breathless when I snatched my prize from him and carried it to the kitchen.

Nick blushed as I passed, then followed me into the next room, making appreciative noises. "Promises, promises."

I unpacked dinner onto the table. We usually ate directly out of the containers to save on dishes. "Did Pants do anything strange after you got here? I hope you weren't waiting long. I had to meet with Mel down at the Beehive."

"Just her usual trying to put her head in my mouth and excessive requests for pets," he replied as the little demon scurried past the threshold carrying a toy for Nick to throw for her. "What did you need to talk to Mel about?"

I paused with my hand in the bag, trying to find a way to explain what had happened earlier in the evening. "I don't know if you saw, but I'm down a few flowerpots."

"I didn't, but your collection of plants changes regularly. I noticed that Pants smelled different, like shampoo. Did you give her a bath?"

"Good catch. That," I said accusingly, pointing at Pants, "little monster broke at least two of my pots and nearly dyed herself brown in the process."

"Oh, wow. How much blood did you lose?"

"Not enough to warrant a transfusion, thank you very much." I was pretty proud of my ability to bathe cats without needing stitches, though he was obviously teasing. "But why she got dirty is also the reason for my visit to the shop. She was chasing something."

Nick laughed. "I knew your rent was low, but I didn't think it was hot-and-cold running rats kind of low."

"No, silly. She was chasing a spirit."

"I hate that ghosts are a more believable answer than a mouse," he admitted.

I told Nick about what had happened, Pants tapping out my name on the table and the subsequent conversation with Melinda. "She isn't sure what's happening, but her gut says it's going to be big."

Nick popped open the containers and handed me chopsticks before putting the electric kettle on to make tea. He knew I loved tea, and we usually prepared something appropriate for the meal when we got Chinese. "That doesn't seem related to the thing we're dealing with at the agency," he said, pulling down mugs to prepare.

"Not off the bat, no," I agreed, "but it doesn't sound like you really know what's going on with your issues, either."

"True." He put two bags of jasmine tea into the mugs and, after the kettle popped, poured the water. "Rob is working on another case too, looking into some of the older files. I think we might be pulling on three different threads at once this time." He settled back at the table with our mugs.

"Speaking of your case," I said, pausing to bite into a juicy dumpling, "I was reading up on your friend Ganesha before Pants played planchette."

"Oh?" He was quietly slurping hot and sour soup. He had picked up from our favorite restaurant, and from the look on his face, the chef was particularly good this evening.

"It's more complicated than what you said. Not all asura are bad, but Ganesha definitely killed at least one of them. I don't envy whatever it is you need to do to make their situation right."

Nick sighed into his soup. "I wouldn't envy me either. But what about you? What's happening with Pants?"

I told Nick about the spell book and the crystal, but I didn't have many more details because I hadn't been able to sit and study the details yet. "Mel was pretty clear I'd find something useful in it, but she wasn't forthcoming about what I should look for."

"Whatever you need to do tonight, love. I'm just happy to be around. I can check in on my own set of growing emergencies while you handle yours."

A warmth grew in my stomach, and it wasn't just the food. I still got all fuzzy when he used pet names, and I eyed him with interest. "I could use some cuddles and...maybe more, after our dinner settles."

"I'll never argue with a lady who knows what she wants," he said, winking at me as he picked up his chopsticks.

We passed the rest of the meal with smaller conversation, catching each other up on our days and chatting about future plans. Eventually we stowed our leftovers in the fridge, and I was washing what few cups and utensils we used by hand in the sink. Nick nestled himself against my back, wrapping his arms comfortably around my waist and smelling my hair. We still wanted to be close to each other, over two years since we'd started dating.

"How soon do you need to dive into that book?" he whispered gently into my ear. The hair on my neck stood up, electrified.

I put the last of the utensils into the drying rack and turned in his embrace, nuzzling into his neck. "I think it can wait a bit," I said, taking him by the hand and leading him into the bedroom. We both laughed as Pants let out an indignant yowl after being unceremoniously locked out of the room. Had you ever tried to do yoga around a cat? The same rules applied. I could ignore my worries for a little while, at least. Nick was a wonderful distraction.

It was some time later when we found ourselves sitting on the couch. Me wearing a towel around my head to dry my hair after a quick shower and resting my legs across his lap. Him in pajamas tapping away at a laptop set atop them. I was leafing through the spell book, trying to find what Melinda thought was so relevant. There were spells to find a familiar, enhance your magic with a familiar, or even banish a familiar. I didn't like the look of the last one and tried to think of what reason a person could have to want to get rid of one and shuddered. Eventually, I came across what Mel must have been referring to, nestled between two spells about using creatures in divination rituals. I gasped when I read the opening paragraph and managed to startle Nick.

"Did you find something?" he asked.

"Have you heard of the Fox sisters?"

"Can't say I have."

"Oh my gods," I said, excitement bubbling up in my chest. "They were three sisters: Maggie, Leah, and Kate, and they became famous in the mid-1800s as mediums. They would hold these elaborate séances to communicate with the dead, but eventually people caught on, and they admitted to being frauds."

"That doesn't sound like real magic," Nick said, scoffing.

"It isn't, but the crazy part is some people genuinely believed they could speak to the spirits, despite the confessions. People still talk about the sisters to this day in occult circles."

"What does that have to do with familiars?"

"I've never read anything about them having pets, and this book alleges the Foxes discovered the spell." I read the passage frantically. "They supposedly used it to add to the drama of their performances, but at least one of them was a genuine witch."

"Seems a little on the nose."

"Maybe, but this is fascinating! If this is legitimate, the ritual will imbue a crystal with energy that will let a spirit possess the animal wearing it."

Nick eyed me suspiciously.

"You work for God and the Devil, and you're going to give me the hairy eyeball about magical crystals?"

"Touché. What does the spell take?"

I scanned the details, and it didn't require anything out of the ordinary. I had everything on hand, which surprised me. "Huh, I could cast it tonight. Sometimes I forget going through the motions isn't enough if you don't have access to any magical power."

"Which you do," he said matter-of-factly.

"And I have to get better at accepting it." I sighed. "Melinda said I should figure out who my patron is, the one funneling me this mojo too."

"I think it's a good idea. I remember you said it wasn't something you owed anyone for, but I'd still feel weird about not knowing where it came from. Do you mind if I watch? I haven't seen you get all witchy before."

I blushed, realizing the last time I had done a large magical working was with Rob because we were on our way to rescue Nick from his latest set of kidnappers. "Yeah, that's okay."

I went to my room and started collecting my gear. All I would need for the spell was my ritual dagger, a piece of white silk I had, despite the entirety of my wardrobe being black, and the cabochon pendant. I used some of my jewelry-making supplies to attach the pendant to Pants's collar before settling down to start. I worked at the Ouija coffee table, which felt appropriate for what I was trying to achieve. Nick sat in an armchair nearby, his attention rapt.

"You're allowed to talk," I scolded.

"You're cute when you're about to use eldritch power."

"Okay, maybe you're not allowed to talk." I set the grimoire on the tabletop, open to the spell, and laid the square of silk next to it. I went to the kitchen briefly to sharpen my athame before laying it next to the fabric along with a sterilized pin. "Seriously though, once I get started, I need complete concentration, so no distractions."

"You weren't complaining about distractions earlier," Nick said wryly.

"*Nick.*"

He held up his hands. "I can't help myself. Of course I won't interrupt you. Did I mess with you when you were summoning the Devil that one time? No, I did not."

I sighed and turned back to my preparations. I added four candles to the tableau to aid in raising a circle of protection while I was performing the rest of the ritual. It wasn't a good practice to leave yourself vulnerable when casting a spell, and I didn't need to take chances.

I lit the candles and intoned the words I knew by heart, spoken so many times. "I call upon the guardians of the watchtower of the east…" and so on until I had raised the four quarters. Nick was staring but silent, true to his word.

I looked to the pages and read the words there, "Spirits beyond, I come as a humble supplicant. I seek your wisdom and counsel but do not have the means to reach you."

"I offer my blood as a conduit." I picked up the needle and pierced the pad of my index finger, squeezing it to drop three globes of crimson blood onto the center of the silk. The circle spread as the cloth absorbed it.

"I offer my familiar as the vessel," I said, placing the completed collar next to the red mark. I used the razor edge of my dagger and cut across the middle of the fabric, bisecting the bloody ring. "Push against the boundaries as I pierce the veil—"

As soon as the last word left my lips, darkness descended on my apartment. All the lights and candles went out at once and I was blind in pitch-black.

"What—" Nick said, but I shushed him.

I wasn't done with the spell yet, and the sudden darkness was unexpected. I waited, listening, my heart pounding in the silence. The candle closest to the book flared to life without warning, and the last line was visible again. I cleared my throat and tried to keep the tremor out of my voice. "Speak with me, spirits, so I may know you."

Nothing else happened, though the stone was luminescent in the candlelight, so I couldn't tell if it was glowing. I wasn't sure what happened next.

Nick was looking at me expectantly.

"Oh, you can talk now, I'm done," I said.

"What the hell was that?" He sounded a little freaked out.

"Magic?" I said, a little questioningly. As I cleared away the trappings, Pants jumped onto the coffee table, and I blew out the lit candle before she singed her whiskers. "Good timing, princess." I picked up the collar and secured it around her neck. I would have said her eyes flashed white momentarily, but cats' eyes did weird things depending on the light.

She looked at Nick and I in turn, then walked straight to the word "HELLO" painted on the Ouija board and placed her paw on it.

"He—Hello."

CHAPTER 8

ROB

"What am I doing here?" I asked myself and checked the address again on the scrap of paper I had brought with me. I stood outside a small blue house on the outskirts of Westville, a suburb of New Haven, unsure of what I expected. The Fasler residence was one of the well-kept properties in a more well-to-do part of the city. Westville had its own charm, and it was partly why I had chosen to live there. My apartment was in a different section of it though. This neighborhood wasn't full of young renters but seemed to be made of middle-to-upper-class families. Sensible people, but they had Lexuses instead of Toyotas.

I wasn't sightseeing because I was close to home. There was work to do. When Nick had left me to review the old files, I had kept the Fasler case nearby on my desk. No matter how many old deals I went through, I kept glancing over at it. Was I stuck on how thin it was? Maybe it was the sparse text inside. Mabel's request and subsequent rejection stayed on the periphery of my thoughts. Like a dripping faucet or a pebble in my shoe, I couldn't shake it. That was why I found myself squaring my shoulders and striding to the front door of this home in a neighborhood I had no other business being in.

I raised my hand to ring the bell, but the door swung open before I could do more than graze the button.

She was elderly and relatively short, though I couldn't have guessed her exact age due to what was clearly an amazing skin-care regimen. She was dressed simply, but the cut of her clothing implied designer sensibilities. Her shoulder-length silver hair was lustrous and well-kept, framing ice-blue eyes. "Can I help you, young man?" she asked with a light but strong voice.

"Mrs. Fasler?"

"Well, no one's called me Mrs. anything in a long time. But yes, that's me. I'll warn you, I don't take kindly to solicitors. I'm too old to put up with your nonsense if you want me to buy solar panels."

I couldn't help but laugh. She had a disarming air about her. "No, I'm not selling anything. Quite the opposite, actually—"

"I'm not putting the house on the market either. Irwin would turn over in his grave if I even thought about it."

"No, ma'am. I'm not here to buy anything either. Let me start over. My name is Rob. I understand you submitted a request to my employer about your late husband's disposition."

"You're far too young to have anything to do with his affairs. It's been nearly twenty years! Don't tell me something could have possibly been stuck in probate court for so long," she said, pinching the bridge of her nose in frustration.

I waved my hands. "No, Mabel. I'm sorry, can I call you Mabel?" I paused until she nodded. I wasn't sure how to say why I was there, so I went with the truth. "It's about the state of your husband's...soul."

Her face blanched, and I worried she would slam the door in my face. She must have thought better of it because her shock turned to anger, and she stepped onto her front porch to get directly into my face. She jabbed a finger into my chest hard enough that I flinched.

"I thought I told you and your people that I never wanted to see *any* of you again so long as I lived."

I backed away and raised my hands in surrender. "I'm not sure who you think I represent, but I believe we've had a misunderstanding."

"You tell Lee Cormick, if he ever sends another lackey to my door—"

I interrupted her with a last-ditch effort to stop this runaway train wreck. "I represent Lucifer!"

She stopped dead with her mouth open. "Well, it's about time. I'll put the kettle on," she said, then turned and walked back into the house without inviting me in.

I followed her down the hall and into the kitchen, glancing into the other rooms I passed on the way. It was an immaculately appointed home. Fine art graced the walls, spotless white furniture was arrayed throughout the living areas, and every room had either glossy hardwood flooring or large format tile that I assumed was outrageously expensive. There was also a large, framed picture on a mantelpiece of a younger Mabel with a man who must have been her husband.

When I caught up with her, she was already filling a gooseneck kettle she then placed on a gas burner before turning to me. She stared me up and down with vague disapproval on her face.

"What took you so long?" she asked.

I was so off balance from her nonchalance that I stared with my mouth open for a moment before closing it with a click. I cleared my throat and tried to start over. "My name is Rob. Were you expecting me?"

"Not you specifically, dear," she said, eyes softening a bit as she seemed to notice my discomfort. "No, I've just been waiting for a visit from one of Old Nick's cronies ever since I got that note."

"Note?" I asked, dumbly.

"Do you know what it's like to receive a form letter from the Devil himself? I suppose he didn't write it, since it was clearly some boilerplate, but still." She let out a huff, then busied herself setting out a tray of china cups and saucers for the tea on the marble kitchen island and brewing into an honest-to-God matching teapot. My mother owned heirloom china, from my grandmother, but I'd never actually seen a human being *use* it in my life.

"About your husband?" I asked.

"Who else? Irwin was a good man—well, he was good enough. For me, anyway. He didn't deserve to have his soul rot in hell for eternity."

"What makes you think he isn't in Heaven?"

She motioned to the stool next to the island, and we both perched. She seemed to be waiting for the tea to steep while I was waiting for this to all start making sense.

"Probably the womanizing. Or the gambling. Maybe the drinking. I assumed it all added up at some point," she said, the blunt tone of her voice making it clear she had long since accepted her deceased husband's glaring flaws. "But I still loved him, the idiot. I had a friend who signed a deal with your employer, which is why I hoped I could submit the request I did."

"But you didn't offer your soul in exchange for his or anything like that?"

"Honey, I loved him, but I'm not stupid. If I could put him to rest without damaging my own shot at the pearly gates, I would have been satisfied. I'm not religious, but knowing the Devil is real? It's enough to make me think twice about a grand romantic gesture. It's all fun and games until you're actually in Hell. Sugar?"

I laughed out loud and nodded, and she poured the tea. I let the silence linger as she went through the motions of a host, fetching a plate of shortbread cookies to accompany our drinks.

I took a sip and scalded my tongue, then stuffed a cookie in my mouth to lessen the sting. "Do you still have the letter?" I asked around a mouthful of crumbs.

She took a cookie off the plate for herself and walked through a different hallway. I didn't follow. My place as a guest was in the kitchen unless she invited me otherwise, and it wasn't more than a minute before she returned holding a framed piece of paper. I raised an eyebrow at her.

"Tell me you wouldn't do the exact same thing," she dared me and placed the document on the countertop.

"Fair point." She was right. It was a short form letter. It was dated five years back, and I read through the pleasantries before finding the meat of the reply.

We have investigated your claim and regret to inform you that your request cannot be completed. The soul of [Irwin Fasler] is not in our care at this time. Please do not submit additional inquiries. If, in fact, [Irwin Fasler]'s soul becomes our concern, we will reach out with any relevant details. Kind regards, Lucifer Morningstar, Esq.

I gave an appreciative low whistle.

"I assumed one day someone would come tell me it had shown up down there, even though I knew better."

"Oddly enough, that isn't today," I admitted.

She sipped her tea and eyed me again. "Then why are you here, Rob-who-works-for-Lucifer?"

"Can we back up? Who is Lee Cormick, and why did you think I worked for him?"

Her face clouded over. This guy had clearly gotten under her skin. "Him?" she asked. "He's a swindler, is what he is. I have no idea how he found out about Irwin, but a year after I got that letter, one of his men showed up at my door. Garret, I believe his name was. He claimed to be a medium, able to speak with the dead."

"And you paid him to contact your husband?"

"Only after he told me things no one could possibly have known if they didn't have access to Irwin, but yes I did." She wet her lips and continued, "But it didn't stop with Garret. Once I had started paying them, they told me Irwin's soul wasn't in Hell but was stuck in Purgatory. That's when I started worrying I'd made a terrible mistake in trusting them."

She paused, but I prompted her, "What happened?"

"They said they could help get his soul to Heaven. Garret was the first, but eventually Lee himself visited me to pitch his scheme. They needed special materials, rare herbs, all sorts of mumbo jumbo."

"I'm guessing they were expensive."

"Exorbitantly. But as you can see, we did well for ourselves, and I could afford it. I expect that's why we were targeted, but it was too late when I realized it."

"I'm sorry. That sounds awful."

She sighed again, snapping a cookie in half in apparent frustration. "They claimed he was making progress, moving into the 'next circle' or some nonsense, but every time I asked when Irwin would be done, they invented another diamond-encrusted hoop I had to jump through. Eventually I told them I was done paying, and they'd never see another dollar from me."

My stomach sank, as I imagined the conversation with this elderly woman and her extortionists.

She took a deep breath and steadied herself, then stood and walked into the other room again. She was carrying something else when she returned. A small, glass figurine. I couldn't make out the details until Mabel placed it on the counter by my saucer. It was a small statue of a mostly featureless man playing golf, crystal clear.

I looked at her, puzzled.

"The problem was, they really were psychics. When I stopped paying them, they brought this here, and I had to watch as they called the soul of my dead husband back from Purgatory and trapped it in that thing. He always did love golf…"

CHAPTER 9

ROB

"Real china? I would have died," Lester said, laughing, as he rubbed my shoulders. The look on my face when I walked into the condo must have been alarming because he immediately sat me down and drew the story out of me while attacking the knots in my back.

Lester owned a townhouse on Blake Street, near the state university. It was a little ironic, because it was my alma mater for my undergraduate degree. We'd been dating for a few months when he asked me to move in. He acknowledged we weren't lesbians but confessed to envying the stereotype and didn't want to wait to rent the U-Haul.

It was nights like this that made me thankful I said yes, when my head was spinning and I needed a lap to lie in and have someone stroke my hair. Lester was much more the type to want that kind of comfort, but the street went both ways. It was a little insane, thinking about the person I was a few years ago compared to who I had become.

The old Rob was metal, seeking power and trying to lead his group of friends. This Rob? He was content to follow and had learned to love softness. He was a lot gayer, too, but I guessed it was all part of the journey. I must have been staring off into space because Lester shook my shoulders lightly to bring me back to the present.

"Sorry. I got lost somewhere," I said. "The conversation didn't go where I expected, I'll admit." I breathed out hard as he hit an argumentative muscle group. "I'm even more surprised she gave me the figurine to hold on to, in case I could do anything to free Irwin's soul."

The hands smoothing out my neck disappeared without warning, and I turned to find Lester rifling through my messenger bag until he came away with the glass sculpture.

"You didn't tell me you had this!"

"I hadn't even finished the story, baby," I complained, pointing at my neck and making pitiful noises.

Lester grinned and put the statue on the counter between the living room and kitchen before returning to the couch, where he had left me, to continue his ministrations. "Please, continue," he said.

I started at the beginning and told him about the whole conversation. He moved from the massage to sitting next to me and holding my hand as I went on. His face passed through the stages of grief as I explained how Cormick and his crew took advantage of Mabel. He looked vaguely sick when I finished and glanced toward where the statue lay.

"That was awful," he said, resting his head on my shoulder.

"You're telling me. I said I would do what I could about her husband's spirit but didn't make any promises. I'll probably talk to Amy about it. Hopefully, she can figure something out."

"What are you going to do about the mystic mafia?"

I laughed, which was a nice bit of catharsis, with how heavy the conversation had gotten. "Really? You've already given them a nickname?"

"Cormick sounds Irish, and I didn't want to stereotype too hard, so here we are."

"Fair point, I hadn't thought of that," I admitted. I kissed the top of his head and leaned mine against it. We stayed that way for a few moments in quiet comfort before I pulled away. "I'm not sure what I'll do, though. I've got some options, but I think I have to start by going through the boxes of files back at the agency. If this guy's been operating in the city for at least a year, there's got to be more of a trail to follow."

"Well..." Lester said, hesitating.

"Now's not the time to hold out on me, dear one. I have the soul of an elderly golfer in the kitchen."

"It might not be random, the files we sent you. I mean," he said sheepishly, not looking me in the eye.

"Les, what are you trying to tell me?"

He sighed heavily and met my gaze. I wasn't mad and tried to soften it to let that show.

"There's someone you should meet, and if I had known there was trouble like this buried in those boxes, I would have said something sooner."

I was intrigued. "Who is it? Do they work for Lu?"

"Yeah, but they're not exactly mahogany row. It's this guy down in the archives, where the oldest stuff goes. It's not all digital, so it has to get stored somewhere. His name is Adam. We usually just refer to him as 'The Archivist,' he's a little eccentric. I think being in the basement for so long has gotten to him."

"What does that have to do with the records we got?"

"He has theories. Some of them are zanier than others, but he sends them all up to the top. Part of my job is politely handling Adam so it doesn't bother Lu, but..."

"But he might not be crazy," I finished.

"Don't be mad?" His eyes were wide, like a doe in the headlights.

"I'm not mad." I took his chin between my fingers and kissed him lightly. "But if you feel *terrible*, you could make it up to me," I said, teasing him.

Lester breathed out a sigh of relief and leaned in to rest his head on my chest. "I mean, I am awfully distraught..."

When I arrived at the address Lester had given me, I was in yet another location that left me questioning whether I was in the right place. I had been to Devil Tower a few times previously, though mostly to Les's floor when I took him to lunch. My visits were infrequent, given the Devil openly held a grudge against me. This was a different story altogether.

The hallway was reminiscent of utility or steam tunnels, deep in the recesses of the otherwise glamorous building. It was dark, dry, and dusty, every step echoing hollowly as I approached the office. The heavy steel was more akin to a blast door than anything else. I banged on it, and a muffled voice said something I interpreted as "Enter."

My shoulder ached as I shoved against the portal, pushing into the room. Damn, that thing was heavy. Hell must have been serious about the quality of their archives. The room was dimly lit by flickering lamps, and a figure in a black cloak, a hood fully obscuring their features, stood behind a massive mahogany podium. My heart tried to leap out of my chest, and I did my best to calm my aggressively beating pulse.

"My—" I gulped, my throat dry. "My name is Rob. Lester said you'd be expecting me."

In the blink of an eye, the room came to life with the chattering of fluorescent lights. The person in the dark garb held a remote in one hand and was unfastening the toggles of his cloak with the other. He was a red-headed man of middle age and grinned sheepishly as he continued removing his outer layer. The short-sleeved button-down he wore underneath the robe was in stark contrast to his earlier appearance.

"Sorry for the theatrics. I'm Adam." He shuffled awkwardly behind his tall desk but didn't introduce himself further. "I've built a bit of a reputation. It helps keep the requests to a minimum. Everyone wants you to find some file we archived ten years ago, but when you go through the trouble of getting it? They suddenly don't need it anymore."

I laughed, though it had an edge given my recent surprise, and moved to stand across the desktop. "That makes sense. I dropped in mostly unannounced."

"Lester said you'd be coming, just not when. What can I do for you, Rob?"

"I'm with the new agency reviewing old cases, and I came across one that turned out to be more complicated than I expected. Mabel Fasler. I'm concerned there's a pattern, and I want to see if there are other similar records in the archive."

"Mmm, the Purgatory problem," he said.

"The what now?"

He smiled again, though it had more than a touch of smug slyness. "What do you know about Limbo?"

"Not much, but it sounds like you can fill me in."

"Rob, I'm your new best friend." His eyes twinkled, and as he spoke, he became more animated. "This isn't just a place for the deals that happen upstairs. I make sure the records of all the souls moving into Hell are on file. There isn't a lot to do down here, though I take the archival process seriously, and over a year ago I noticed something. Fewer and fewer souls were moving in from Purgatory."

"Is that normal? For them to come here?" I asked.

"Yes! Or at least it's supposed to be. That's why I've been trying to run the issue up the flagpole. The dead aren't moving across the threshold like they used to. The one meeting I had with Lucifer, when I explained my concerns, got me a scolding about how things worked around here. He told me to stop emailing him about it." Adam huffed and hunched into a sullen posture.

I didn't want him dwelling on his hurt feelings more than the rest of the story. "That sounds rough. You were only trying to help."

Adam brightened and leaned across the desk. "Purgatory isn't a terrible place, but it isn't a wonderful one either. It just *is*. When people die and they don't objectively belong in either Heaven or Hell, they go *there*. They get to reflect on their lives and eventually float up or down, depending on various criteria. If the data is correct, there should be a steady stream of the disembodied coming our way. It varies over time, but it's still a consistent flow." He paused, staring at me, and then dropped his voice conspiratorially. "About a year ago? It stopped."

"What does that mean, Adam?"

He grinned madly. "I don't know! But it's probably not good, and no one's listening! Nobody cares because it's a spiritual no-man's-land. Everyone's more concerned about literally anything else. It's why I fed a bunch of those files into your team's queue and hoped someone would be smart enough to pay attention."

"Well, here I am."

"Exactly! I'm happy to give you any information I can. It's been driving me insane on top of being stuck in the basement."

"We have a lot of boxes at the office," I said. "Can you give me a handful of people who fit the profile you observed so I can investigate? Mabel Fasler was the one that got me here."

He chuckled, and the sound was unsettling. "Oh, that's easy."

"Why do I get the feeling there's more to it? What aren't you telling me?"

"We've been fielding a ton of requests for intervention, like your Fasler case. They get stamped and discarded to the archives. Inquiries from loved ones about freeing their dearly departed who are 'clearly trapped in Hell.' Except they're not."

Sweat broke out on my forehead as I considered the possibilities. "How many?"

Adam leaned forward and whispered, "Thousands."

Chapter 10

Nick

We were sipping lattes at The Fix. I hadn't worked there in years, but I considered it my "external office" and met clients there regularly. Mark, the owner, would sometimes check in with me about his latest bean acquisitions and plans for franchise. Now that I was a "big suit," he kept teasing me about partnering with him on a new shop. I kept it in the back of my mind as a retirement plan but otherwise smiled and made noncommittal noises.

"Tell me again why no one else cares about this," I said to Meghna.

"I'm the youngest of the extended family and only-child of my parents, who are the last generation to have kids so far. My cousins and I are all busy establishing our education and careers, so we haven't had families yet." Meghna swirled her coffee and wrinkled her brow. "I'm also the single person who takes this literally. The whole family is devout, does *pooja*, makes offerings, but nobody believes my great-grandfather made a deal with a demon for the family's good fortune."

"But you do?" I asked.

"I..." Meghna lowered her eyes, and her shoulders slumped. "I have been in contact with the asura, so I know he is real."

My eyes widened. "That would have been good information to lead with."

"I'm aware, and I'm sorry," she admitted.

"We can't work together if you're going to keep things from me, Meghna."

"I was going to tell you, I swear. But it has been a confusing time for me, Nick."

"Give me the whole story."

She sighed, took a gulp of coffee, and started again. "This asura, a son of Gajamugasuran, offered me another bargain. He said he would extend the terms for another three generations."

"Is that unreasonable?"

"It's complicated," she said, wringing her hands. "Asura aren't purely good or bad. It's a simple solution, but I'm not sure it's the right one. It's why I sought the boon from Ganesha. I would rather my whole family be done with this 'blessing' than make my great-grandchildren responsible for repeating this mess."

The whole situation was getting on my nerves. I didn't know if I was more annoyed at Meghna for hiding how deep her understanding went, or at myself for being unsure of how to move forward. I sipped my drink, letting the caramel notes of the espresso linger on my tongue. She might have hit the mark, considering her family's good fortune.

"What are you going to do, Meghna?" I asked.

"I thought that's what you were here for," she replied, "to help me."

I considered my conversation with Arjun and my subsequent surreal experience with his boss. "No," I said. "I think you have a fundamental misunderstanding of the Elephas group and my involvement with it."

She froze, her eyes shining like a prey animal in moonlight. "What do you mean?"

"Relax." I sighed and drained my mug. "I'm here to assist you but not to solve your problem for you. The evaluation is about whether you're worthy of Ganesha's favor. You still have to figure out what that means, but if I can point you in the right direction, I will."

She relaxed visibly, though her eyes wouldn't meet mine for a moment. "Thank you, Nick."

"Speaking of ideas, I expect you need to consider your family's position again. You were onto something just now, and I doubt you realize it."

Her pupils darted back and forth until they came to a sudden stop. "Be done with it," she breathed.

"Bingo."

Once Meghna had her epiphany, she vacillated between two states. First was excitement at the prospect of not having a generational curse hanging over her head. Second was growing horror, wondering what life would be like after she convinced her family to give up their business. I had asked how she expected to talk them into it, and she said it was clearly one of the reasons Ganesha had sent her to me. I wasn't going to argue because I wanted her to succeed. What I did not expect, however, was to be sitting at a kitchen table across from an older Indian man staring me down like I owed him money.

Aravind had the shrewd look of a negotiator. He was broad, his shoulders stretching the confines of his clothing as he leaned forward to appraise me. He wore a collared shirt made from linen over black pants and well-shined shoes. His flinty brown eyes were hard, though the glinting might have been from his glasses. He drew a breath, then turned to Meghna, who sat next to me at their kitchen table.

"You cannot wed this scrawny white man, beti." There was a note of finality in his voice.

"Baba!" she cried and tsked at him. "I didn't bring him here to marry. Are you crazy?"

"Hold on—" I started to say, but a large hand in front of my face interrupted me.

"Then why are you both here, Meghna?"

"To talk to you, obviously!"

"I do not need whatever he is selling," he said, eyeing my suit.

"I'm not sell—" I tried to speak, again, but this time it was Meghna's hand that shot up.

"He is from the temple," she said. "I was told he could help us."

"With what?" He laughed and leaned back in his chair. "He can't unload containers dressed like that." Meghna stared at him and narrowed her eyes.

I finally got a word in. "I am not scrawny."

They both turned their gazes on me with a kind of pity, then shifted back to each other.

"I have been telling you about the weight great-grandfather has left chained around our necks, haven't I?" she asked gently.

"Oh, yes, the family curse," he said, chuckling. "I know you worry about it, beti, but it's not real. Did you convince this man we are doomed, and he came to your rescue?" He continued laughing but stood. "If we're going to discuss ridiculous things, I'm at least going to make coffee. Would you like one, young man?"

"Nick," I said. "My name is Nick, and yes, thank you."

"Well, Nick. What has my daughter told you?" He started an electric kettle and bustled about the kitchen with a small steel cylinder and a bag of what appeared to be coffee grounds.

"She's explained that your family has been extremely successful in the import/export business her great-grandfather started."

"Accurate," he said, spooning something akin to Turkish coffee into the top of a two-part contraption.

"But she..." I paused, distracted by his preparations. "What is it you're making?"

"Filter coffee," he replied, pouring hot water into the top and covering it. "Did you come here to help my daughter or learn how to cook?"

I blushed. "Apologies, I'm just really into coffee, and that's something new to me."

His mouth cracked open in a toothy grin. He placed a saucepan of milk on the stove to warm and then came back to sit at the table. "At least you have some taste. You still can't marry my daughter."

"Sir—"

"I'm joking, Nick."

I blew out a breath. "The problem is your grandfather made a deal with an unsavory character, and now the asura is coming to collect."

Aravind looked back and forth between me and his daughter. "So you believe her?"

"She hasn't given me any reason not to," I replied. I glanced at Meghna, and steely resolve shone in her eyes, almost pleading with her father to bend. I decided to tip the scales. The last time I had worked with God's people, they gave me a fancy parlor trick. "And some monsters are real."

A glowing nimbus suddenly wreathed my body. Aravind gasped and said something in Hindi that I had no chance of understanding. I let the moment pass, and the light faded as I let go of my concentration. He should have experienced a sense of peace, but he seemed more freaked out than anything. Even Meghna looked surprised by my little show.

"Why don't you show me how you prepare the coffee, and we can talk more," I said.

He nodded, apparently grateful for the normalcy of it, but his hands shook as he got up and poured the coffee. It was thick and syrupy. He mixed it with the milk and prepared three small cups. His tremors were gone before he set the saucers in front of us.

"What, exactly, was that?" he asked.

"I told you he was from the temple, father," Meghna chided.

"No one from the temple has ever done anything like this, child."

I cut in before they devolved into another argument. "I'm an agent, Aravind."

"For the government?"

I opened my mouth to reply but reconsidered and sipped my drink. It was delicious. If you took an espresso but made it less bitter and mixed it with hot milk, you got whatever this filter coffee was.

"It's the chicory," he said, noticing the surprise in my eyes. "New Orleans isn't the only one to blend their powder with the root."

I nodded. "It's fantastic, thank you. But no, I'm not an agent of any government. I doubt they give light shows like that as standard-issue these days. Normally, I represent...a different belief system. But today I'm here as a member of the Elephas Group, which is who Meghna came to for help."

"What do you mean?"

"Unless you can convince Lord Ganesha you are worthy of his assistance, you're going to belong to the asura. All of you." I drained my cup and looked him straight in his shocked eyes. "Could I have some more coffee?"

Chapter 11

Nick

The conversation with Aravind, once he believed it was possible his daughter wasn't crazy, didn't go the way I expected. Meghna pitched her idea for the family to divest themselves of the business built by her great-grandfather, but her father became defensive and shot it down immediately. Some of it was family loyalty. From his perspective, if his grandfather made the deal, it was something he should honor. It wasn't their place to question the decisions of their elders, especially when it had provided the lives they enjoyed so much.

His other rationale was their belief itself. They were devout followers of Lord Ganesha, and he would take care of them because of their piety. Regardless of whether I was sitting in his kitchen as a representative of said god, telling him otherwise.

He was sticking his head in the sand. Meghna had shed some tears, and I became more frustrated until it was clear we weren't making any progress. We gave up and agreed to regroup later.

It was over an hour later, and I was pacing on the Green. The meeting with Meghna and her father wound me up, and I needed to clear my head. Amy had a "talking" cat, Rob texted me about chasing leads on the old cases from Devil Co., and I was neck-deep in a different pantheon. Life had been weird for a while, but this was a little much, even for me. I had driven myself around until I parked near the war monument downtown and started walking. I was on my fifth lap, closing in on the old church, when my phone buzzed.

ROB:

We need to talk. When can you meet me at the office?

NICK:

Hi, Nick. How are you? I'm fine, thanks.

ROB:

Did someone forget to kiss you goodbye this morning? You're in a mood.

NICK:

A hint would be nice.

ROB:

It's hard to explain. Just get here, okay?

I rounded the path to cross in front of the building and jerked to a halt. A man sat on the steps leading to the large, banded doors, looking in my direction. He had the shape of a man, anyway, but something about his face…was wrong. I recovered my forward momentum. He smiled as I neared, which confirmed my suspicion this wasn't a coincidence. He had a mouthful of subtle shark teeth, wickedly pointed. His eyes were a smoky gray. Even from a distance, they swirled like tiny tempests.

I stopped two arm-lengths away. "You must be the asura," I said, crossing my arms. "Your timing could be better."

The grin widened. "Call me Gaja. And you must be Nick."

"Some days, I wish every supernatural being who wanted to reach me would make an appointment. What can I do for you, Gaja?"

"I'm just checking on my investments. I hear our little Meghna has gone crying to Lord Ganesha for help. It won't do her any good, you know." He heaved himself up and towered over me. His black hair would have fallen past his shoulders if it wasn't gathered in a ponytail. He had an imposing build, muscular with a broad chest, arms like thick tree limbs, and dusky skin. "Our deal was made a long time ago."

"I'm just doing my job, and I wouldn't advise threatening me. I'm on loan, but my boss wouldn't take kindly to your interference," I said with bravado, but my stomach tensed.

"*Nick*," Gaja said, his voice a rich baritone. "I wouldn't dream of it. I thought you deserved to meet your alleged adversary, that's all."

"What do you mean 'alleged'?"

"We don't have to be enemies, you and I," he said. "Why waste the effort breaking your back for a god you don't even believe in?"

"It doesn't matter what you're selling, my soul's spoken for."

He waved his hand. "I don't need that pesky thing. No, Nick, we should be past bargains and threats. I want you to consider working with me, instead of whatever it is you're doing now with Elephas. I promise I'll make it worth your while."

"Work with you?" I grinned. "Why does everyone want me to join their team? I know I'm amazing, but seriously, this is getting out of hand."

"You mock me?" Gaja asked with a light snarl. "I have the power of a god, little man."

I was taking a risk, but recklessness had saved me more than once. "The only thing I'm going to do is make your life complicated, Gaja. The good news is now I'm sure there's something I can do to help Meghna's family. You wouldn't be standing here trying to distract me if there wasn't a chance."

His eyes flashed with the brilliance of a lightning strike, momentary but powerful. "This is a courtesy, Nick. I don't need to bother with you at all." He stepped forward and loomed over me. "But this is the only time I'll extend a hand in good faith."

"You're a walking stereotype, with your not-so-subtle threats." I was sick and tired of every challenge I faced being a brooding villain who promised to ruin my day if I didn't do what they wanted.

He growled, low and throaty, and I'd be damned if he didn't sound like a tiger. My stomach dropped, but I couldn't break the facade. As quickly as his temper flared, it was gone.

"What a brave new world, where men stand unafraid before gods." He chuckled. "Forgive me, my friend. I forgot my manners."

"They make pills for that kind of emotional whiplash."

The storm crossed his face again but only for a moment. "I am used to dealing with my people. You are doing a job, and I respect it. I was sincere in my offer. Your talents are wasted working for your Abrahamic overlords."

"I'm going to steal that in my next performance review." Was he planning to do more than give me another job offer? "If you don't mind, Gaja, I'm going to get going."

He stepped aside and gestured broadly at the path. "Perhaps we will speak again."

"If you'd like to discuss releasing Meghna's family from their contract, I'd be all ears."

When I arrived at the office, Rob was spinning slowly in his chair. He took in my appearance mid-rotation.

"Why are you so sweaty?"

I had walked more than my business attire was prepared for and it showed through my shirt. "I was processing," I said, and refused to explain myself further. "What was it you wanted to talk about?"

He pointed at a glass figurine on his desk. "Guess what this is?"

"Rob, I just met the bad guy holding our Elephas client's souls hostage. I'm not in the mood for guessing games."

He took pity on me and brought me up to speed on what had gone down in Westville and his meeting with Adam.

"Holy shit," I said when he finished.

"I know, right? Every time I think nothing can surprise me I'm shown how wrong I was."

"What does it mean?"

"That's the problem," Rob said. "I have no idea. The worst part? Adam's worried about ripple effects from so many souls going walkabout."

"They're not in Purgatory. Did they rise up instead?"

"I need to check. Adam didn't have that data."

One benefit of the agency was access to both Heaven and Hell's records. Maybe Adam's pet theory about souls going missing was based on a lack of information. Most conspiracy theories were built the same way. Chemtrails were a fundamental misunderstanding of contrails, to name one.

I was happy to have something to distract myself with, and jumped at the chance to help Rob run down his list of names. I made a call to the Angel Co. office to request a new liaison, and if they couldn't manage it in the next hour, I needed direct access to their systems. We sifted through the files Adam had given Rob, corresponding with his handpicked examples.

I must have struck enough fear into the hearts of God's administrative staff because they got back to me within thirty minutes. It took another hour on the phone with IT to set up access from our office, but those were just the nuts and bolts of getting the terminal to work. I guessed it paid to have a reputation. I hadn't used the heavenly systems, so passed that particular task to Rob.

He cracked his knuckles and banged on the keyboard until information fell out about a handful of the cases. The first check was whether the people in those files were in Heaven. We assumed it was unlikely and were not disappointed. Not a single soul from the Archive's suggested pile was upstairs. No one was petitioning for the release of loved ones from the "good place," so there weren't any records in God's databases for any of them.

There had to be something connecting all of them, and Rob suggested we cross-reference each name with as many public records as we could find. I recommended he call the families and check whether Cormick or his associates approached them. A pattern emerged as we made our way through the list again. I searched online for the name of our first candidate and found their obituary. From there, I backtracked through as much social media as possible to find public posts by their friends and family.

A delayed wave of inspiration hit me, and I finally looked up Lee Cormick. It didn't take long before I was comparing the poor unfortunate souls we were searching for with negative reviews on Yelp, Google, and other sites. It wasn't a one-to-one match, because a lot of the people we were trying to find were from older generations. They weren't Luddites, but they didn't have the strongest internet skills. There were a significant number of matches, but one in particular caught my eye.

[1 star review] ABSOLUTE SCAM: Lee Cormick and his flunkies are scam artists who are preying on our grief. Do not trust them. They will bilk you for all they can before abandoning you with no results.

Rob made calls as I worked through my short list and came away with similar results. He encountered some hostility until he said we were investigating Cormick, in which case the person on the other end of the line became his best friend. He didn't reach everyone but spoke with eighty percent of the departed's families. Each gave Rob an earful about Cormick, his scheme, and their outrage. His eyes widened as he talked with the families and took notes.

By the time he was done, we had appointments to pick up two more statues, one shaped like a terrier and the other a sailboat. When he finished, we both sat in silence for a solid minute before I broke it.

"What are the chances most of these 'missing' souls are Lee's victims?" I asked across the expanse between our desks.

"I wouldn't bet against it."

"You know what we have to try now, right?"

Rob rubbed his temples before responding. "We go meet Lee Cormick and Associates."

"I hope Amy is doing better than we are."

CHAPTER 12

AMY

Once Pants had touched HELLO on the table, she wobbled and loafed, falling asleep. The book mentioned possession was taxing for both the spirit and the familiar. Communication would be limited depending on the strength of them both. It was one reason some witches chose heartier familiars, based on their intended tasks. Cats weren't as strong as they were stubborn, so I didn't know how much chatting we were going to do. There wasn't guidance on how long it would take to recharge either, so we wrapped up for the evening and left Pants snoozing in the living room.

Nick stayed the night, but I didn't want him wasting his time sitting around while I troubleshot my way through the practicalities of my new telephone to the spirit world. He had plenty to do running down his own problems, and I could handle this myself. I found Pants curled up on the couch in the morning. She didn't stir when I crossed through the living room to make tea in the kitchen, still wrung out from her initial experience. When my cup was ready, I sat next to her, stroking her fur until she woke up and gave a big stretch.

"What are we doing today, bug?"

She showed her teeth with one of those yawns that would snap a human jaw in half and groomed herself on the cushion next to me.

I grabbed the spell book from where I had left it on the table and reread the passages explaining my new familiar. The collar was a conduit, rather than being an on or off switch. Pants should be able to reject the possession if she wasn't feeling up to it, and the spirit looking to take control would need to act in good faith. The ritual had built-in protections to disallow anything like self-harm or putting the body of the familiar in danger. I had to wait for whoever had greeted us last night to be ready for another session, or maybe they were waiting for me to reach out.

"Good morning, spirit." I spoke to the air but oriented myself to face the Ouija board. "Can you talk again?"

Pants paused mid-lick with a long strand of fur stuck to her tongue, and her eyes widened to solid black orbs. She disengaged from her bath with a shake of her head in almost human-like disgust, then looked pointedly at me before hopping onto the coffee table and landing a paw on YES.

Oh shit, I thought and scrambled to grab my phone and start a timer. I wanted to test how long I would have for our next conversation and hadn't planned ahead. My hands shook with adrenaline as I set the stopwatch to counting.

"Hi, I'm Amy. Were you the person trying to speak to me in the graveyard?"

She tapped her paw again. YES.

"Why do you want to talk to me?"

Pants, or the ghost inhabiting my cat's body, walked around the table and stamped her right paw to tap out a word this time. TRAPPED.

"What's your name?"

SIOBHAN.

I checked the clock, and thirty seconds had passed. "You can't cross over or move on, right?"

YES.

"How can I help you?"

PULL TOO STRONG.

"What does that mean?"

PIERCE THE VEIL.

"You're not giving me a lot to go on here."

WATER was the last word Siobhan tapped out before Pants flopped over onto the table, paws stretching. She came to rest comfortably as she gave a little cat snore.

I had gotten about sixty seconds of "talk" time with Siobhan before the possession exhausted either or both of them. One more unclear variable was how often I would get a chance to speak with her. I stroked Pants's side, then went to the kitchen and found a treat to leave on the table for when she woke up.

I still had bills to pay, so I readied myself for work. The day passed in a blur of answering patrons' queries, re-shelving books, and wracking my brain for what to do next. Siobhan's words were confusing but specific. The "pull" was "too strong" and something about water. Did it have to do with the tide? Maybe it was more like a whirlpool. But her reference to the veil made more sense. If she couldn't pass on to whatever waited for her, breaking through the barrier between worlds might help.

Talking to spirits had some inherent problems. First, they were people, which meant they could lie. I had no guarantees Siobhan was who she said she was or if what she told me was the truth. Second, she might not have any better idea than I did about how to help her stop haunting this plane of existence. Ghosts weren't omniscient, and just because they were dead didn't mean they had learned the secrets of the universe. She had better educated guesses than I did but still couldn't be sure of the answer, unless a more knowledgeable hand guided her.

Mel had suggested my patron was involved. I hadn't done any spells or rituals to get in touch with them. Maybe it was time. I was still a solitary witch, despite the offer from the coven to consider me for membership. Walking a fine line between being a self-sufficient badass and an avoidant recluse was hard. I could rely on people at work when I needed help. Why was it so hard to decide if I wanted to join up?

I had also brought my research to the library that day. Nick knew about the connection between the Elephas group and Ganesha. I owed him and Rob any information I could find. I was looking through *Spirits and Symbolism* when Cora arrived at the circulation desk with a stack of holds for one of our patrons.

She dropped the pile with a thud and wiped her brow. It was a hot day in the library, despite the air conditioning. "I'm out of here in fifteen minutes, Amy. I've got a coffee date."

I didn't have any intimate details about her life, but through casual conversation on the job, I had learned she was divorced. She didn't have a regular partner, as far as I could tell. "Who's the lucky suitor?"

She blushed furiously. "I'm not seeing anyone right now."

"Oh, I'm sorry. I misunderstood when you said 'date.'"

"It's more like a girl's night out," she said as she shuffled through the books, ordering them for pickup. "After my ex and I split, I fell in with this group of middle-aged divorcees. We have a group chat, meet for coffee, and support each other. I never knew I needed a group of women in my corner, but it's honestly better than any relationship I've ever been in."

"That sounds nice."

"It makes me question the quality of my choices, that's for sure. I picked some real losers. Now I have friends who give me their honest opinions about the people I'm spending time with." She looked at my conspiratorially. "You wanna know what we call the group?"

"I hesitate to guess."

"Everyone's been through the wringer, and we joked about all the clowns we've dealt with. So it's the '*Cirque du Oy Vey*'."

"You're abusing two different languages, but I'll allow it for how good that is."

She chuckled. "It's true, but we couldn't help ourselves." Cora finished sorting and dusted her hands off. "I'll go get my things. Have a good night, Amy."

"You too, Cora. Enjoy the ladies' night."

Cora sauntered to the break room with a satisfied smile on her face and left me with my research.

The gnawing in the pit of my stomach had nothing to do with hunger. I took a moment to assess, coming off the conversation with my coworker. I was envious, which surprised me. Of what? Cora had found a community that not only supported but protected each other. Did I have anything to be jealous of when I had an offer on the table from a coven of presumably like-minded women? One I hadn't taken them up on? I shook my head and settled myself, letting the discomfort flow out of me. I knew I'd keep mulling it over as I worked.

Nick had messaged me with some details he received from his client. My book was thick but couldn't possibly fit all of Indian folklore in one place. I augmented my digging with some Google-fu and put a more comprehensive picture together. A maddening bit about Hindu mythology was the limited amount of information available if you weren't diving into the more well-known deities, and even those sources were relatively brief.

My effort paid off, and I made a connection between Ganesha and the asura after collating my sources. One tale spoke of an asura named Gajamukhasura who received a boon from Lord Shiva, a principal god of the Hindu pantheon. Shiva was called "The Destroyer." The photograph in the book was of an imposing four-armed statue in one of his less benevolent guises. Shiva blessed Gajamukhasura and made him invulnerable to weapons. The asura repaid Shiva for the blessing by going on a destructive rampage with his new power.

Lord Ganesha faced him, and after a time, the asura turned himself into a mouse to evade the elephant-headed god. Instead of continuing to attack, Ganesha rode the mouse and taught him humility. In the end, the demon redeemed himself and became a mount for Lord Ganesha.

I texted Nick about what I'd gathered.

AMY:

I didn't find much on the asura, but there was one in particular Ganesha fought with.

NICK:

Gajamugasuran?

AMY:

No, but you're oddly close. Hold on a second.

I went back to my searching and looked up the name Nick had provided. It was an alternate spelling of the same asura I found in my book. I shouldn't have been surprised at an inconsistency caused by both regional differences and Hindi to English translations.

AMY:

Never mind, same one.

NICK:

Great. Send me what you have, this particular demon is a son of his. I had the displeasure of meeting him on my way back to work.

AMY:

YOU MET A DEMON, AND YOU DIDN'T TELL ME?

NICK:

It happened on my walk to the office. I was going to tell you.

AMY:

It's okay, you surprised me. Be careful, his father is invulnerable. I don't know if he could inherit it, but I'd assume the possibility.

NICK:

Speaking of danger, I'm going with Rob to meet a psychic con man. There's a situation brewing, and I need to bring you up to speed soon.

AMY:

Like a fake medium doing séances kind of psychic?

NICK:

Oh, no. He's really psychic, and that's part of the problem. There's a whole clan of them, and they're extorting people to get their deceased loved ones into Heaven. When the families stop paying? They're trapping the souls in glass figurines.

My heart skipped a beat, and I nearly dropped my phone.

AMY:

I thought you said they were psychics? That's a lot more than what mediums do.

NICK:

It's what their website says. Lester called them the Mystic Mafia.

AMY:

That's more accurate, if generic. I need so much information about this.

NICK:

Let's meet tomorrow, I may be out late.

AMY:

Be safe.

NICK:

Aren't I always?

AMY:

No.

NICK:

Touché. I love you.

I love you, too. Try to be less reckless than usual. If they ask, "Does this rag smell like chloroform to you?" Run.

As you command.

I gave up haranguing Nick. He was doing better at not jumping headlong into every problem without looking both ways first to make sure there wasn't a metaphorical bus bearing down on him.

He had said one thing that stuck in my mind immediately, that the psychics "trapped" souls. Siobhan had used that exact word, which was what stood out so clearly. Maybe these threads were more braided together than we thought.

The last thing I did before my shift ended was look in my spiritual guidebook for references of a "veil." There were multiple mentions, especially regarding Samhain or Halloween. The thinning of the "veil between the worlds" was a common trope in folklore. The most interesting piece of information, however, came from a single sentence in the section on Irish mythology. It referred to a sea god named Manannán mac Lir as the "keeper of the veil." Trapped. Pierce the veil. Water. An icy shiver ran down my spine.

Nick wasn't the only person making a surprise visit that evening.

CHAPTER 13

AMY

I arrived at the Beehive five minutes before closing to find it bustling with activity. Melinda was behind the counter, counting out her register and making notes when I walked in. A group of women browsed the store, and as far as I could tell, they had no intention of leaving.

"Amy!" Melinda cried and came around to pick me up in a bear hug. I would swear she enjoyed my feet dangling as she swung me gently back and forth in her embrace. Eventually, she set me back down and held me at arm's length. She was wearing her usual cotton overalls but had an open black robe over them. Her makeup was also more elaborate than usual, which was usually nonexistent. A bright red lipstick contrasted with her pale skin; eyeshadow and eyeliner accenting her features.

"Hi, Mel. I needed to talk to you about something, but it looks like you're busy."

"Nonsense! These are my girls!" She gestured expansively to the rest of the store, and the "girls" in question stopped whatever they were doing to wave in our direction.

Realization struck me. "Oh, are these your coven members?"

"It's a full moon tonight, so we're having a little get-together after hours."

"I should have called first—"

"Hush now. I've been telling them all about you since we met! It's a shame you haven't joined us for an open ritual before."

"Is tonight a public event?" I asked.

"No, no. We only do those for our introductory lessons and beginner rites. This is just for the inner circle." She had a mischievous air about her. "But I bet I could convince them to let you stay. We can handle your business, too."

"I guess that's okay, since it's all people you trust."

"Trust? Girl. I'd take a bullet for these women."

"It was *one* time," called a voice from the other side of the shop.

Melinda gave a laugh that shook the room and yelled back, "And you learned your lesson about nighttime walks. It was a priceless trip to the emergency room."

I cocked an eyebrow in her direction. "If it's not a bother, I'd love to sit in."

"Ladies!" Melinda yelled to the rest of the women standing throughout the store. "I'm inviting my good friend Amy to join us tonight. Any objections?"

An asynchronous chorus traveled back to us with no dissent.

I waited patiently for Mel to go through her routine and flip the door sign to "closed" before leading us downstairs. The Beehive held a secret in its basement, accessed through a hidden door. It was an old speakeasy-turned-storage area, walled off from the neighboring building. They converted it to a large ritual room, complete with an engraved pentacle on the floor. I envied the space and loved every visit. Unlike my previous visits, Mel set chairs in a circle around the symbol with a small table in the center, waiting for the participants.

Mel showed me to a seat next to hers, but as the rest of the group took their places, there didn't appear to be assigned seating.

The room glowed brightly with candles of all shapes and sizes. The comfortable chatter died out as we settled in, and Mel finally cleared her throat to speak.

"Welcome, sisters, on this night of the full moon. We have a guest." Mel gestured to me, and a number of small waves and excited giggles came from the others. "Amy has a concern she wished to bring to me, and I've made it a coven matter for the evening." There was nodding as she spoke, and no one seemed bothered by the situation. "It's only fair we introduce ourselves. Let's go around the circle."

I met Lacey, Amanda, Alex, Jaminda, Nix, and Sprite in turn. The group was diverse in both makeup and appearance.

Lacey was young, plump, pale skinned, and short with curly red hair. Amanda was skinny, black, middle-aged, and had beautiful braids. Alex was svelte and had a prominent nose with a slight olive complexion. I couldn't have guessed her age beyond "old enough to drink." Jaminda had brown skin, a brilliant smile, and extremely frizzy hair. If I had to guess, I would have said she was in her thirties. Nix was androgynous and had black hair with a heavy undercut. They were also the youngest-looking there. Finally, Sprite had the peaceful grace of an aging hippie, blonde hair tied back, and a dreamy expression on her face. A cane leaned against her chair, though I hadn't noticed her walking in with it.

I was happy the coven wasn't just a group of thin white witches, but given their leader was a transgender woman, I wasn't expecting a homogenous bunch.

"I'm pleased to meet everyone." I turned to Melinda. "You said this was the inner circle. How many members are there?"

"Active?" She looked up in thought and tapped her index finger against her chin before answering. "Twenty, all told. We've been around a long time, but we're a picky bunch." This drew a few laughs from the small crowd. "We seven are the dedicated core of the coven though." She held her hand up to forestall any more questions, then clapped once, the sharp sound echoing through the chamber. "Let's begin!"

The tone of the room shifted instantly from a light affair to a solemn event. The speed of the change surprised me, and I settled my hands in my lap to observe. Amanda and Jaminda rose without prompting and set themselves at opposing cardinal points outside the ring of chairs. The two turned their backs to each other and raised their hands, calling out to invite the spirits of the north and south to guide and aid the ritual. They stepped clockwise in unison and repeated this for the remaining two quarters. Both made one more complete circle around us each with an outstretched finger, scribing the air.

The pair returned to their seats, and everyone closed their eyes. I followed suit, and the colors and afterimages from the candles danced on the backs of my eyelids. I matched my breathing with the group and waited, unsure what was next.

Melinda's voice cut through the stillness. "Sisters, we gather once again as the moon waxes full. Meditate for a moment on your intentions for the coming days."

The pop of a wine cork startled me, and my eyelids cracked open. Mel had stood and was pouring wine into a glass she must have placed on the table. She caught my gaze and winked at me, and I shut my eyes again.

She continued, "Hold the image in your mind, focus your will, and fill your body with the energy Luna rains down on us. Breathe it in and let it flow through your limbs, warming your belly. Now, open your eyes."

The smiles on everyone's faces were joyous, but even more surprising was the gentle glow emanating from each participant. A unique color or pattern suffused each of them. Nix's was a golden-hued light, dancing like glitter around them. Sprite's was a glorious silver and covered her like a mirror glaze. The rest were just as fascinating, and a pang of jealousy stabbed at my heart.

Melinda was staring at me. I held my arms out, and scintillating faerie fire wreathed them, amber waves licking across my body. She grinned and nodded to the rest of the group. "Speak your goals, wants, or desires into the circle and charge the libation so we may join our wills together. Alone, we are powerful. As one, we are unstoppable."

"I'm going to get the job," Lacey said, determination ringing in her voice. She nodded to Amanda.

"I'm asking for a raise."

Heads nodded as each spoke.

"The farm," Alex said. "The one I've been telling you about for weeks? Tony and I are going to make an offer on it. The bank will approve the loan."

Progress around the circle stopped as the entire group cheered for Alex's declaration. She smiled, her cheeks burning red, but gestured for Jaminda to take her turn.

"I'm going to dump his ass."

The whoops and choruses of "Girl!" were deafening, and my cheeks ached like they were going to split.

Nix patted Jaminda on the thigh before they spoke. "I'm going to ace my next math exam."

Sprite shook her head heavily. "I was never any good at math. You will do wonderfully! Me? I'm finally asking that girl out. The one at the co-op I've been crushing on for six months." The din following Sprite's statement was as powerful as Jaminda's.

Everyone's eyes turned to me. Some were expectant, some wide and hopeful, but all were welcoming and bright.

"Oh!" I chuckled nervously. "I wasn't sure if I should take a turn."

Mel nodded encouragingly, along with the rest of the group.

What did I want? Everything was happening so fast with what was going on in the spirit world. I had a new familiar who communicated with the dead and a task set before me to help this trapped soul. But when I focused my thoughts on a wish for myself, I came back to these women I met tonight. I had work to do, but at that moment I knew what I needed.

My throat was dry, and my voice cracked when I spoke. "I—I'm going to ask to join the coven."

Energetic murmuring broke out as the women glanced at each other and at least one smug "I told you so" before everything settled down again. Melinda was beaming at me, and I didn't catch any disappointed faces as I surveyed the room.

"Is that okay?" I asked Melinda.

"Last but not least," she said, and cleared her throat. "I am going to have a new seeker!"

Excited cheers erupted around me, but as Melinda rose and grabbed the wine glass, silence descended once more.

"I join my power with yours," she intoned and took a swallow of wine before passing the glass to Lacey, who echoed the words and drank. This continued round-robin until the glass reached me, and my hands shook as I held it.

"I join my power with yours," I repeated and drank a mouthful of wine. It was rich and heavy, but even more so, my mouth tingled from the energy electrifying it. My eyes widened, and nearly everyone laughed, though kindly.

"It gets us all the first time," Melinda said.

She and the rest of the coven closed the ritual and dismissed the invited spirits while I sat in a giddy stupor. The power lingered on my tongue and danced between my fingertips, and I was oblivious to the room until everyone was standing and embracing each other. I rose, and each waited for a turn enveloping me. They hugged me tightly, some swaying back and forth, others more loosely. I worried for a moment, but when I paid attention, it was how they hugged the others. I couldn't parse being accepted by a group so quickly, but the warmth in my chest, unrelated to the wine, was good.

Melinda clapped her hands again and directed us to return to our seats after offering cookies and small cakes from a platter materialized from nowhere, now on the table. I grabbed an adorable tea cake enrobed in dark chocolate with a flower piped on top before sitting. I bit into it, the white cake and raspberry filling a delicious counterpoint to the earlier wine.

Melinda finished her own treat and wiped her hands before continuing. "Now, let's talk about your problem."

I hastily swallowed my mouthful. "Well, I used the spell you gave me and Pants—that's my cat. She acted as a conduit for the spirit trying to contact me, communicating through my Ouija board like one of those talking tables you train animals with." I backtracked and explained the earlier encounter in the graveyard leading to my first genuine contact and informed the group about Siobhan and her warnings. "Melinda suggested I contact my patron, and with everything happening, now seemed to be the right moment."

There were a few "ahs" of understanding, and Jaminda raised her hand. "I won't step on your toes with a new seeker, Mel, but my experience might be helpful."

Mel nodded enthusiastically. "Jaminda had a hell of a time getting in touch with her patron, despite having clear access to their magic. Go on, honey."

"I was working at it for, like, a month to reach mine. I had a good idea who they were, from signs and signals they were putting out, but they were reluctant to show themselves. Finding your patron is unique to each witch. It doesn't happen exactly the same way for any of us. I used the hints and crafted a small personal ritual to tap into their magic and ask them to appear to me. I hope you have better luck and find them more quickly than I did."

I thanked Jaminda and turned to Mel. "Do you feel like I've got enough information to go on? There are plenty of other sea gods, and even though it seems spot on, I don't want to chase the wrong rabbit."

"There's trouble brewing, and we've all felt it." Mel paused and took stock of the heads, nodding in agreement. "Something is wrong with the spirit world. No one else has had the direct communication you have, and I'd bet there's a reason for that."

"What is it?"

"Sweetie, if I knew, I'd have told you already. No, I think someone's pushing you in a direction and if you were on the wrong path, you'd know by now. I suggest you take Jaminda's advice and plug yourself in with what you've got. I have a feeling it'll come to you. As always, I've got a book for you to borrow."

"Thank you, Mel. This—" I hesitated, and my eyes were suddenly wet. "I didn't expect this, but thank you for inviting me."

"Synchronicity, little one. Something brought you exactly where you needed to be. I'm glad it was with us."

I was still buzzing the next morning, my skin charged with the energy from the night before. The party lasted another hour after the ritual, though some members stayed longer to chat with one another. Mel had walked me out, putting a small book about Celtic deities into my hand to "help fill in the blanks."

I spent the morning paging through the loan from Mel, deepening my understanding of Manannán mac Lir. The mythology was confusing, if not outright contradictory. He was a god of the sea but also allegedly an ancient king from the Isle of Man. He may have been one of the *Tuatha Dé Danann* on top of that. The Tuatha were creatures of myth and legend who either became faerie folk or were their ancestors.

It wasn't only the Celtic pantheon that theorized their gods and goddesses were living beings, often from whom humans descended. The Norse deities weren't immortal and interacted heavily with regular people. Egyptian Pharaohs became gods after death, though their bloodlines were distinctly mortal.

As a deity, Manannán held sway over the mists, which were a pathway from the physical to the spirit realm. This had to be my focus, with his connection to the veil between worlds. Pants lay on the bed with me as I read, her tail flicking back and forth. I wanted to talk with Siobhan again, but given how exhausting the experience was for both of them, I would wait until I tried to contact Manannán. It was better to save the spirit's energy for when I needed it. There was no guarantee she would have any more information for me, anyway.

The next step would be to make an attempt to commune with my patron. A plan was forming in my head, but I would have to make some modifications. Magic was about intent but also powered by symbolism. When I summoned Lu, I changed the ritual because of the urgency. This would be similar, in some respects. If I had an unlimited amount of time, I would wait for a properly foggy day to bring me closer to Manannán's domain. I checked my phone, and the forecast for the day was a thirty percent chance of rain showers. It would have to do.

I laid my little grimoire on the bed next to the book. It was a gift from Melinda during our first meeting, and I smiled at the memory. Instincts were also important for spell-craft, and the warmth in my chest hinted I was on the right track. Group ceremonies had a lot of speaking, choreography, and other performative aspects. Some covens sang, others chanted, and many variations existed in between. I was going to be alone, so I didn't need all the pomp and circumstance. The key would be to cast as strong a line as possible from myself and hope it pulled him in.

An hour later, I had my satchel packed with all the ritual items I'd need and was driving to the shorefront. Despite being on Long Island Sound, there weren't a lot of public access beaches in New

Haven. Access to the water was primarily for shipping. Warehouses littered the shorefront you could see from the Q Bridge driving in and out of town to the East. More were available in East and West Haven, but I didn't have a connection to those cities. Dover Beach was too thin a strip for what I planned and was on the Quinnipiac River rather than the Sound itself.

Fort Nathan Hale was another option but was too close to both the Coast Guard station and the Army Reserve for comfort. I was pretty sure I'd be trespassing no matter what I did, so the fewer eyes, the better. I settled on Long Wharf, the nature preserve to be more precise. It was closer to the industrial parks and shipping than I cared for but had some secluded spots where I could get my witch on.

I arrived in short order and parked in the small lot across from the elbow in the road where Long Wharf Drive meets Sargent Drive, not by the beach itself. It was the middle of the day, so I was unlikely to draw attention simply by existing, but I wanted my car outside of the area in case I ended up being pursued by a park ranger. It was funny to think of a tiny spit of nature preserve having its own ranger, but it seemed to be a requirement.

I walked the path that started across the street until I was well into the park itself. Signs showed the trail was a loop, and I ambled along the sandy lane, which curved toward the water. I hadn't decided exactly where I intended to set up for my little ritual, but I would know the right spot when I saw it. Animal trails cut through the brush at irregular intervals. Eventually, a larger one heading straight for the water caught my eye. I followed it, ducking through bushes and over scrub plants growing there.

I emerged from a thorny thicket and had to rescue my skirt from its embrace, wheeling sharply once I was free. The curse on my lips died as I took in the beautiful scene in front of me. I stood on a bed of loose stone, some of it partially submerged by the thin finger of water running up from the shore. It was only slightly wider than

I was and had lush grass growing thigh high on either side as it swayed sinuously in its path.

It was perfect.

My plan was simple, but it required commitment. I laid my bag to the side on the stones and removed the two items I had prepared. The first was a small vial, the second a length of white silk a handspan wide. I checked my surroundings and no one else was in this part of the preserve with me. I hoped being off the beaten path would keep it that way.

First, I removed my boots and socks, placing the ampoule at my feet. I fixed the blindfold around my eyes, then groped for the glass on the ground until I managed to pick it up. Sweat immediately beaded on my face in the warmth. Setting my intention was critical, so I took a minute to calm my breathing and focus on summoning a sea god.

"My patron, I call you," I said to the air. The grass rustled as the wind whipped along the shore and tugged at my clothes. "I seek your counsel and move closer to your realm." I stepped forward into the water. It was warm and shallow, but the stones under my feet were sharp and hard.

"Show yourself so I may sit by your side and gain wisdom." I opened the vial and drank the contents without hesitation. The salt water made me gag, but I fought to keep it from coming back up. I pocketed the empty vessel and walked in what I hoped was a straight line. The water rose to my calves, then knees. I waded up to my thighs when the sound around me changed. The lapping of the small waves on shore drowned out the noise of the city behind me.

Something sharp bit into the sole of my left foot, but little pain followed. I wanted to examine it, but I had no choice but to continue or I would lose my momentum. Magic was also about improvisation.

"I mingle my essence with yours, sea god, to bring you forth and bind us together."

I strode forward, reckless in my movements, my dress soaked with brine. I moved deeper until my chest was submerged, my clothes weighing me down.

"Unfetter my vision. Help me see clearly."

I plunged myself into the water, then removed the blindfold and opened my eyes to look through the murk. A few shapes, hopefully fish, moved in the depths, but it was mostly the serene nothingness below the waves.

I held my breath for as long as possible, which seemed an eternity but was probably only thirty seconds. My chest burned as I emerged, gasping, wet hair plastered to my head and rivulets running over my face. I was wiping my eyes and shaking droplets from my head when a whistling tune drifted to my ears. I turned back to the shore, and a man sat on the thin beach holding a fishing rod in his weathered hands.

"Fucking fish aren't biting today, are they? Seems I've caught something else though. Hello Amy, I heard you were looking for me."

CHAPTER 14

ROB

The word "psychic" conjures various images. On one hand, there are neon palmistry signs, dark curtains, and cultural-ly-appropriative costumes complete with poorly done Romanian accents. On the other, there are TV specials with white-clad visionaries cold reading their audiences to massive applause. There were variations in between, but none of those expectations were met when we rolled up to a funeral home on Chapel Street. The sign outside of a beautiful two-story colonial building read "Cormick & Sons, established 1888."

"Are we in the right place?" Nick asked.

I pulled out my phone and checked the map. "We are, but I think you missed something when you were looking Lee up." I tilted the screen so Nick could see and pointed at two pins nearly on top of each other. "You were searching for Lee Cormick and Associates but didn't notice the other business name hiding underneath it."

"Well, this feels even weirder now."

I laughed and poked Nick in the shoulder. "You're not chickening out, are you?"

"Of course not. We've got a job to do. Even if I don't know what that job is at the moment."

We got out of the car and approached the front door. The stone walk and entryway were immaculate. Intellectually, I understood death was big business, but I had forgotten just how big. We walked right in, since it was business hours, and found ourselves standing in front of a reception desk. The interior was much more modern than I expected. It was an updated design full of white marble and bright lighting.

A middle-aged woman with red hair shot through with silver greeted us. "Welcome to Cormick and Sons, gentlemen. What can I do for you?"

"We're here to see Lee Cormick," I said.

"Yes, he's expecting you. Down the corridor. It's the first office on the left."

I locked eyes with Nick, and he seemed as surprised as I was. We didn't waste time asking questions and moved through the hall to the specified door. I knocked, and after a muffled "come in" came from inside, I opened it.

The man standing behind a plate glass desk beckoned for us to enter. His long auburn hair was pulled back in a ponytail. He wore a full black ensemble of T-shirt, jeans, and blazer, like an emo startup CEO. A crystal statue of a terrier sat next to his laptop. A chill ran down my back, but I kept the sudden revulsion off my face.

"Good to see you, gents." He spoke with a warm Irish accent. "I'm Lee. Cole, this is Rob and Nick. Have a seat."

Two chairs were in front of him, and one more to the side, which held the man Lee introduced as Cole. He was an imposing figure, even seated. The bruiser had a similar style as Lee's but more colorful. Sort of. Brown was a color, wasn't it? He raised his hand to tip the front of his flat cap to us. His fingers were broad, each digit like a sausage, with various tattoos across them.

Nick was the first to speak after we settled. "You were expecting us?"

"I figured you might come around," Lee replied with a grin.

"Because you're psychic?" I asked.

"No, because a little birdie told me. I'm well informed, not prescient."

My mouth compressed into a thin line. "Do you know why we're here?"

"I wouldn't exactly say that. I *have* heard you've been chatting up some of my less satisfied customers."

"Your reviews aren't exactly glowing," Nick added.

"Pfft. You can't please everyone. We provide an important service to the community. More than one, to be precise. There are always going to be disgruntled people when you've got a reputation like we do."

"What reputation is that?" I asked.

"My great-great-grandfather started this business when he brought the family over from Dublin. He scrounged up enough money to get out before the Land War and worked himself to the bone to establish the funeral home here. We're a fixture in this city, roots as deep as anyone."

"What about the psychic side of the house?"

Lee tapped his temple. "Runs in the family, always has. Cormicks were some of the best mediums, and it made sense to offer that service as well once folk understood we weren't full of shite."

Nick shook his head. "That feels like double-dipping in grief to me."

"Come see me when a loved one passes and you didn't get to say goodbye, and we'll have another conversation. Enough about me and the business. What can I do for you two?"

I was pretty sure he was giving me the runaround, so I went straight to the heart of the matter. "Why are you interfering with Purgatory."

Lee glanced at Cole, and they shared a chuckle. "Have you ever been there?"

I shared a look with Nick but answered the question warily. "I haven't had the pleasure of shuffling off this mortal coil yet, thankfully."

"Dreadful place. It's like watching paint dry, only it takes millennia, and all the while you're supposed to be contemplating your life choices." Lee shivered dramatically.

Nick leaned forward in his chair. "Why do you get to decide whether a soul leaves Purgatory?"

"I think you have a fundamental misunderstanding of the services we offer. Let me enlighten you before deciding I'm the bad guy here."

I gestured for him to continue.

"These days we have a subscription model, monthly fee and all that. Had to get with the times. It serves two purposes. First, we allow a family member to converse with their dearly departed through one of our team members. Second, we coach that spirit to help them get out of limbo."

"That sounds too altruistic. What about the figurines?" I gestured to the translucent canine in front of him.

"Fine print."

"Excuse me?" Nick asked.

"Once we engage with a spirit, they're...marked, for lack of a better word. There's a distinct serenity to the void, waiting to see whether you float up or down, but our service brings a higher level of self-awareness, which doesn't normally exist. If they don't get into Heaven or Hell within a certain amount of time, well..."

My sense of horror grew as I interpreted what Lee was telling us. "You're saying if the family stops working with you to get the souls of their dead relatives out of Purgatory, they go insane?"

Lee shrugged, a sheepish smile on his face. Cole's grin was less savory. "Calling up their spirits and placing them in the statues puts them in a kind of stasis. It's a mercy. If the families want to keep working with us, we can summon them out of their vessels and continue the process."

I was almost impressed. "That's diabolical."

"That's business. Speaking of which, what sort do you have with us today?"

"Think of this as a cease and desist," Nick said.

"What you're doing is throwing the natural order out of whack," I added. "We're not even sure what the repercussions are for the number of souls you've trapped this way."

"Do you have something on your official letterhead?" Lee asked with an innocent air.

"Of course not—" I tried to speak, but he interrupted me.

"We're done here, gentlemen. My company provides a respectable service to people in deep distress. I won't have you limiting our ability to help them, unless you've got an official cease and desist from the powers that be."

Nick tried this time. "We represent—"

"Cole, show them the door."

Cole stood, and what he lacked in height, he made up for in muscled width. I eyed Nick, and he shook his head slightly. As we turned to go, I swept the glass dog off Lee's desk, and it fell to the floor with a loud clink as it hit the tile, but not so much as a chip broke off it.

My face must have registered surprise, and Lee smiled as he stooped to pick it up. He brushed it gently but didn't bother inspecting it.

"Thought you'd be clever, did you? I'm guessing you haven't tried that with the ones you've collected so far."

"We—"

"Don't bother. You're not likely to break them. Something about the endurance of the human spirit when it's introduced to its new home. I considered using bricks instead. It'd make one hell of a house." Lee's gaze turned to us both, a malevolence in his eyes I hadn't seen until now. "But the wailing, I doubt I could bear it. Cole? These gentlemen have outstayed their welcome."

We let ourselves be escorted out of the building by the walking refrigerator and were back in the car before I knew it, both of us fuming.

"What do we do now?" I asked Nick.

"Regroup and call in some backup, but I have no idea who that would be."

"Maybe it's time to try Heaven?"

"Can't hurt. Hopefully."

CHAPTER 15

ROB

I hadn't been to Angel Co.'s offices since they let me go. My stomach tightened into knots when we stepped into the shadow of the building on the corner of York and Grove Street. I wasn't afraid, but despite that building's prior promise, the place held no good associations for me. When I said trying Heaven couldn't hurt, it turned out I was wrong, though I tried to keep the emotions off my face.

Nick had never seen the office, despite moonlighting for the "other side" for a while, so I had to show him where to go. The operation itself was in an old state building made of imposing white stone with gigantic columns. It was home to multiple attorneys, bankers, and other high-powered individuals. The heavenly host rounded out the clientele.

"I knew it was near the other office, but I didn't realize how close that was." Nick glanced back toward the Green. "John dropping in for a visit when I was walking the paths surprised me, but he could have seen me from a convenient window."

"You expected more godly magic?"

"Maybe..."

"Don't worry, I'm sure there will be even more inside to disappoint you."

We took the elevator to the twentieth floor and entered a pristine lobby. Between joining the agency and dating the office manager, I had gotten a tour of the Devil Co. building. Well, the main floor at least, so I had a basis of comparison. Where Lu's offices were mostly bright, corporate chic, Heaven's digs were much more of a banker's paradise. The design was well executed but dated. I had told Lester about my experiences there, and he was less than impressed. He described it as "your dad's version of a fancy office building." Old school sensibilities reigned, despite an unlimited budget. No one said Heaven had taste.

I strode up to the reception desk, and a familiar smile greeted me.

"ROB!" The voice squealing my name came from a short Latina woman wearing a gray pantsuit with silver accents. She also sported chunky jewelry and had her hair up in a professional bun. Her face split in a wide grin, and her hazel eyes were wide as she rushed around the desk to grab me in a quick hug.

"Hi, Elena." I raised my arms in what I hoped she would take as me returning the hug, but I wasn't comfortable with the physical affection. Elena was the office manager, Lester's counterpart, if you wanted to look at it like that. She was professional, kind, and intelligent. She also had a crush on me from the first moment I stepped into the lobby. There was never any real action behind it, though I believed she would have said yes in a heartbeat if I had asked her out. It was an interesting time for me when I had first come to work for Leslie. I had been mostly dating men, and the sudden attention from a woman had me off-kilter in a way that wasn't conducive to the work I was trying to do.

It was always professional. I never felt pressured to have anything to do with Elena socially, but the subtext was always there in our conversations. It made me at least vaguely uncomfortable, but I couldn't tell if my discomfort ever came through enough for her to tell.

Why was all this bubbling up? I thought. Then it hit me, because Old Rob might have used the situation to his advantage. The part of me that played the villain before I reformed myself would have manipulated Elena into giving us a more positive outcome. I thanked past me for clawing out of his old headspace and for not being that person anymore.

"What are you doing here?" she asked, going back to her chair.

"We need to talk to the person upstairs. This is Nick, by the way."

"Oh, I know who he is. We were trying to poach him, remember?"

Nick nudged me with his elbow. "See? It *was* poaching."

"What's this about, Rob? You can't just barge in here and expect an appointment."

"It's urgent, Elena. It has to do with some of the audit files your team sent over."

Her eyelids disappeared with how wide her eyes were, and the few people in the lobby scattered when I said the "A" word, as if I had thrown a live grenade. You'd think audits were contagious, with how they were acting.

"No promises, Rob. Let me see what I can do. Have a seat." She gestured to a row of chairs against the wall and picked up the phone while we took our seats. Her gaze didn't stray far from me while she made her call, so it looked like her affections were as misplaced as ever.

"What's the play here, Rob?" Nick seemed happy enough to put me in the driver's seat, and I didn't blame him. He had never been here, and I had the advantage.

I took a minute to observe the office in motion. Other employees were coming and going as we had our conversation. Their eyes slid past us, barely pausing as if they noticed us but were doing their best to disregard our existence. It was as if acknowledging us meant something in their world.

I chided myself for being slow on the uptake. We were the bad guys now! Okay, not actually the bad guys, but to Heaven's headquarters, we were the Spanish Inquisition. Nick founded the agency on the idea that Heaven and Hell's books needed to be audited, and we were the people to do it. I wouldn't take advantage of Elena's interest in me, but the fear we struck into the heart of the angelic corporation? I could work with that.

I tilted my head toward Nick and whispered, "Follow my lead?"

He nodded and leaned back in his chair.

"Did you hear about the Smith case? I was so disappointed," I said, loudly enough to carry through the lobby but keeping a conversational tone.

"How do you think it's going to play out?"

"How could it go any way but badly? They missed every piece of due diligence possible."

Nick gave a low whistle. "Someone's getting fired."

I nodded and glanced over at Elena, who was trying so hard to not stare at us she failed completely. She picked up her desk phone and punched in some numbers, cupping her hands around the receiver to speak into it. It looked urgent.

"I doubt it'll be just one once we get into the details." I reclined in the chair like I was sitting in my own living room, really owning the space. "We'll have to review the entire *department* before this is over."

Elena stood and cleared her throat. "If you two gentlemen will follow me, please?"

I turned to wink at Nick before standing. "Of course."

We followed Elena down the hall to a conference room used for clients. She ushered us in with an enormous forced smile before shutting the door too firmly. There were plenty of rooms on this floor, but she sequestered us in one of the swankier setups. They stocked it with healthy snacks and bottles of water, things you would put out to impress customers.

I snagged a drink and an energy bar, then plopped into a plush office chair. "How'd I do, Boss?"

Nick laughed and grabbed a treat for himself, settling in next to me. "Quick thinking. But how do you know they're not going to have us cool our heels in here until we get bored enough to leave?"

"I don't, but it was worth the gamble. Did you see how everyone looked at us as they passed through? We're radioactive. No one wants attention from auditors, especially if they're good at their jobs. We represent a time sink for them at best and a pink slip at worst."

"Sounds like a good bet. And hey, free food."

The crinkling of wrappers and cracking of water bottles were all the sounds that filled the silent room for a few minutes. I was about to pick Nick's brain about how we would handle the conversation with Leslie, if They deigned to see us, when one of the swivel chairs creaked.

"Who are we waiting for?" Leslie said pleasantly from the head of the table.

I hadn't missed the miniscule warning that we weren't alone anymore, but Nick clearly did. He started in his chair and clutched at his chest. "Jesus Christ, Leslie. You nearly gave me a heart attack." He must have realized what he said, too because an intense blush colored his cheeks.

Leslie was the name God went by since meeting Nick. When I encountered Them, it was Matthew, but They liked to change names as often as outfits, to suit Their presentation. It was what you got when you found out God was non-binary. The one constant was the pair of Doc Marten boots They wore in any guise I'd seen. I hadn't expected to sit face-to-face with God again, though many people would have cut off their right arms for the privilege of meeting Them once. I had the answer to one of the ultimate questions: "Is there really a God?"

Was it okay to still be bitter about Them letting John fire me? Nick and I were in similar boats. He held a bit of a grudge against Lu for his days of confinement and torture with Bryan Albescu. I was holding mine because the "good guys" let me go after citing a ridiculous company policy for digging up dirt on one of Nick's clients. Maybe Leslie knew something I didn't about the future, like me landing at the agency, but I didn't want to give so much grace. My chest grew warm, and my jaw tightened.

"Hello, Leslie," I said.

"It's so lovely to see you, Rob." They gave a small wave from where They sat.

Nick ran his fingers through his hair and sighed heavily. "We need your help. Rob can explain. He's the one running this job down."

A pang of anxiety hit my stomach hard. I hadn't expected Nick to hand the conversation over to me so quickly. "Tell us about Purgatory, please."

"What's there to say?" Leslie stood and paced along the short side of the room as They spoke. They wore a mismatched ensemble of a colorful peasant skirt and flowy top. As They swayed, it was clear They chose the outfit for the way it moved rather than how it looked. Every turn was an accentuated spin designed for maximum flounce. "I don't really spend much time thinking about the place. Would it surprise you to hear God say it's boring?"

I opened my mouth but closed it again, opting to rub my temples. "Let me start over, it was too broad of a request."

Leslie paused by the window of the conference room to stare out at something below. "Take your time!"

"There's a problem with Purgatory. Well, with Hell too. We're here because I'm worried it's affected Heaven as well. We need to understand the extent of the problem." I explained the situation to Leslie, about the souls missing from Purgatory, Cormick and his associates imprisoning souls stuck in Limbo, and our concerns about the same thing happening to those expected in Heaven.

Leslie nodded along and turned to Nick. "Isn't this what we hired you for?"

You could have started a fire with the flint in Nick's eyes. "Technically, you're right, but we still need your support. We aren't sure how far this problem goes."

"That's the issue with Heaven, if you'll remember. We're still regaining our footing, getting some equilibrium. I'm working with the agents on their outreach, but they're focusing on the middle-tier people."

"The middle-what?" I asked.

"You should remember this from orientation, Rob. We help people stay on the path. The folks you're looking for in Limbo? They're very middle of the road, you know? Strayed a little too far from the flock for us to keep tabs on but not so distant we send a search party."

"You mean they sort themselves out?"

"You wanted to hear about Purgatory. That's what it's for." Their eyes lit up perusing the snack basket, and They grabbed something, which was promptly opened and stuffed in Their mouth as They talked. "It sounds like you've got petitioners trying to get dispensation for their loved ones, to get them out of Hell. We don't really do that here. No one is lobbying for souls to be removed from Heaven. Well, there is one guy, but we don't talk about him."

"But someone has to be making requests, right?" Nick added.

"True. Prayers for entry to Heaven, filed correctly, go through a process. First, the agent checks whether the soul is already there. If they are, we answer and put the requestor at ease. No form letters, though that's funny to think of. No, they only experience a sense of peace. Like a voicemail, but better."

"Then?"

"Provided the soul is in Purgatory, we answer in a much vaguer but hopeful way. It feels like a get-well card. We won't say they'll get here, because they may end up in the other place, but it all depends on how each soul uses their time in Limbo."

"That sounds less appealing," I said.

"Certainly. It's more like being put on hold. Anyway, if the soul isn't in either Heaven or Purgatory, we forward the request on to Lu. Silly, really, because it's not like he's going to give up their souls. He earned them fair and square. But we send the paperwork on and close out the file. Further inquiries go into the aether, like a phone ringing off the hook."

I was processing everything Leslie had said and ran headlong into a metaphorical brick wall. "I don't even know if Cormick is aware of this, but he has a perfect con."

"What do you mean?" Nick asked.

"Souls in Purgatory are fair game for him because no one cares about them—"

"Hey now—" Leslie objected.

I raised a hand, trying to hold onto my thoughts. Give me a second, Leslie. I need to get through this. If Angel Co. doesn't find the soul in Limbo, it sends a query to Hell, which will never get answered. If Devil Co. receives a request for a soul not in Hell or Limbo, they assume it's in Heaven."

"Oh, dear," Leslie said.

Nick one-upped Them with a "Holy shit."

I pivoted to Leslie. "What can we do about it? Do you have any control over Purgatory at all?"

It was Leslie's turn to look uncomfortable, Their face scrunching in thought. "Hm, not really. It's like a demilitarized zone or a no-man's-land. Neither side goes there. I'd say it was an entirely metaphorical place, except it isn't, but the only residents are the souls trying to decide if they're contemplating forgiveness and floating or doubling down and sinking."

"Seems like we've found an exploit that's been mined for the last couple of decades," I said.

"Good thing we have you two to fix it," Leslie replied, with a sincerity I found infuriating.

"Goddamn it, Leslie," I complained.

The meeting only lasted a few more minutes once Leslie understood the problem. It was maddening once I grasped how devious Cormick and his scheme were. I had to believe he didn't know the details or why it worked so well for him but simply reaped the benefits. It wasn't that he was an idiot, but his plans existed in a weird confluence of metaphysical shipwrecks he likely wouldn't be aware of.

Nick and I left Leslie with a promise to dig into the situation further and would reach out if we needed help but understood They could do very little to aid us.

"What now, Boss?"

"I think it's time to call it a night. We learned a lot, but I'm not sure which door to kick down next. I saw Elena making eyes at you. Would she tell you if everything wasn't on the up and up?"

"It's Heaven, Nick. You think Leslie is keeping something from us?"

He deflated with a sigh. "Not really, no. Couldn't hurt to ask though. What is it with you and office managers, anyway?"

"Hey. *They're* attracted to *me*. It would be better to ask what's with me being the universal type for office managers. It wasn't anything I was interested in, anyway."

He grinned and let it drop. "Fair enough."

It was early evening by the time I dropped him at home. He needed to compare notes with Amy, and I wanted a long shower and to have Lester put his arms around me and crush my soul back into my body.

Something about meeting the mystic mafia drained me. It might have been the threatening auras and knuckle tattoos. I chuckled out loud, recalling Les coming up with the moniker. I pulled into the parking lot of the apartment, and the dark windows informed me I was the only one home. Lester often worked late—the perils of being the person in charge of making the operation function. It was his townhouse, so he got the small garage to himself. I parked in a resident space and leaned back for a moment of silent contemplation before getting out of my car.

I was walking up the driveway when a heavy footfall on the pavement caught my attention. I twisted, and a stocky blur was approaching at speed, something large and cylindrical held high in one hand. There wasn't more than a moment to take in the scene before pain exploded in my head, and my vision swam in and out of focus. I fell toward the pavement and brought my hands up to shield my face.

I guess it was only a matter of time, I thought groggily as I rolled onto my back. The assailant stood over me, backlit by the streetlights. I raised my forearms to protect myself as the pipe rose and fell again.

Shit.

CHAPTER 16

NICK

I spent the night alone after Rob dropped me off, as expected from my earlier texts with Amy. I didn't mind the silence, punctuated by chirps and meows from Odin, my one-eyed cat. He was my constant companion and cuddle buddy when Amy wasn't at the apartment. He liked her more than me, so I lost top billing whenever she was there. I had adopted him during a tumultuous time when I'd tried connecting to the world around me while contemplating Lu's original offer. It was funny when I recalled it hadn't been three years since I made my deal, but Odin was a big reminder.

I was exhausted and wanted to do my thinking while horizontal, so I got myself ready for bed. I was worried about my approach and whether I was getting reckless. Gaja was nearly a god, and I didn't know what the limits of his power were. I probably should have assumed he could squash me like a grape if he cared to, but the arrogance of celestial beings was wearing on me.

I was thankful Odin wasn't pouncing after spirits the way Pants was. The situation with Lee Cormick was unlike anything I'd dealt with before. My work so far had been relatively tangible, with some supernatural assistance here and there. Cormick's threat was entirely incorporeal, and we didn't understand the extent of the problem yet. The threads Amy, Rob, and I were holding onto were tantalizingly close, but I couldn't tie them together.

I needed some fresh perspective and to catch up with Meghna on my other problem. Sleep would help with the former, and the latter would keep until morning. I stroked the soft fur between Odin's toes and drifted off to the vibration of his rumbling chest.

The night passed in a snap where I closed my eyes for a moment and opened them to the sun streaming through the windows. I left my purring paperweight where he snored and faced the day, putting on my usual coffee while I dressed.

I hadn't spoken with Meghna since the encounter with her father. It had been demoralizing, and we both needed the time to regroup mentally. Where did this leave me? I wasn't the one making the choices, for once. Meghna's plight, while relatable, wasn't mine. Elephas brought me in to do a job, and if she couldn't convince her family to make a change, it wasn't my place to decide for them.

I picked up my phone while my caffeine delivery system dripped, planning to send a text to Meghna only to find hers waiting for me.

MEGHNA:

Can we talk?

NICK:

I'm about to head out the door. Meet me at the office? Half an hour? How do you take your coffee?

If I was having a morning meeting, I'd need another pick-me-up. I was never above having coffee with my coffee and figured I could get one for her too.

Sounds good to me. Cream, two sugars. Thank you, Nick.

See you then.

I arrived at the agency in record time, procuring a latte for myself and a regular brew for my expected guest.

I walked in the door and nearly dropped both cups when I found Rob lying on the floor. I hastily stowed them on whichever desk was closest and rushed over to his prone form, kneeling next to him and reaching out to take his pulse. As I touched his neck, his eyes flew open, and he jerked away from me.

"What the hell, Nick. I was asleep."

I sat back on my haunches, breathing a sigh of relief. "I thought you were dead, stupid. Why, in the name of all things good in the world, are you sleeping on the office floor?"

"It's complicated..."

"Oh shit, are you and Lester fighting? You moved in really quickly—"

Rob waved a hand and levered himself onto his elbows. "Nothing like that."

"I'm pretty sure we pay you well enough to get a hotel if you couldn't stay at home." I glanced over to the couch we had for visiting clients. "And why didn't you use the—" Whatever words I had on my lips died there as I took in the room, and the tableau in front of me finally came into focus.

"Rob?"

"Yeah," he said through a yawn.

"Why is Cole tied up in my office chair?"

"That's the complication." He rubbed at his head to flatten his hair from where it had pressed against the decorative pillow he borrowed but winced once he reached the back of his neck. "And I didn't sleep on the couch because I didn't want to get blood on it."

"What happened last night?"

Rob took a deep breath and let it out in a huff. He pointed at the imposing form of Cole strapped to my desk chair with some kind of rope and gagged with a gray handkerchief. "This idiot ruined my night. I wanted a soul-crushing hug and a shower, and instead I ended up here because I wasn't about to stash him in my hall closet at home. Now was I?"

"That explains almost nothing," I chided.

"Do we have any ibuprofen here? I'm lucky I noticed him coming. He didn't hit me in the head, but my neck is killing me."

I moved into the kitchenette and rummaged through the first aid kit until I came away with two tablets for Rob. Cole was awake and staring, his eyes following me as I returned with a cup of water and pressed the tablets into Rob's hand.

"So, this brick shithouse," Rob said, pausing to pop the pills and wash them down, "came after me last night. I can only assume it was at Lee's behest. I don't know if he wanted me dead or alive, but a glancing blow from a pipe rocked my world for a minute before I pulled myself together. Those self-defense classes kicked in, and I managed to get back to my car and grab the baton I keep in the driver's side door."

"Christ, Rob. You're lucky to be alive."

"Yeah, and he should be thankful I practiced my swings with it, otherwise I might have caved his head in." Rob glared pointedly at Cole.

"Oh, my God!" Meghna cried from the doorway.

Oh shit, I thought as I lunged for the door. I caught the knob before it opened fully and stood in front of Meghna as she tried to peer over and around me.

"Excuse me for a moment." I herded Meghna through the door, shut and locked it, and turned to Rob. "I'm going to take care of her. We're supposed to be having a meeting now."

"This'll keep." Rob made a dismissive gesture in my direction.

I grabbed the coffees from the desk where I had left them and opened the door far enough to squeeze my body through into the hallway.

Meghna stood there with a shocked look on her face. "What was that about?"

"Client," I said, refusing to elaborate. "Let's talk outside. It's such a nice day."

"I recognize him from somewhere—"

"Unrelated, I assure you. Please, come with me." I gestured back toward the entrance, and we made our way out of the building.

I bustled her down the hallway and out the door until we were standing on the sidewalk, leaning against the building. I handed her the coffee with only a slight tremor jostling the cup. She accepted it with a suspicious-looking side glance but relaxed when she took a sip.

"You said you wanted to talk?"

"Yes, thank you...are you sure everything is alright in there?"

A headache was growing behind my eyes, but I couldn't do anything about it until I dealt with Meghna. "Yes, it's fine. You trust me, right?"

"Of course, Lord Ganesha sent you to help my family."

"You're still only kind of right, but he did send me. Or you were directed to me by his people. So yes. Mostly."

She had a sad look in her eyes and had a few false starts before she finally spoke again. "I keep getting it wrong, don't I?"

"Why don't you tell me what you mean?"

She sighed heavily and slumped to sit on the pavement with her back to the wall. She was suddenly much smaller than the fiery woman I had met who was hell-bent on breaking a generational curse.

"I've been expecting you, a literal agent of my god, to solve my problem. But it's not your task. You tried to tell me in the beginning, but I was waiting for you to point me in the right direction."

I slid down until I sat beside her, holding out my cup. "Cheers. You're getting it."

She tapped her own cup half-heartedly against mine with a "thunk." We both laughed at the ridiculousness of it.

"Ugh," she whined. "Why do I need to be the one to do this? You'd think my father would have jumped at the chance to save the family, but he's sticking his head in the sand and assuming we will be saved because—why? Positive thinking?"

"Some people believe everything will 'work out' if they've done their best. Your father, who makes a mean coffee, by the way, has only ever known this life."

"But you glowed and everything! He's seen that it's real, and we're in danger!"

"The human mind will rationalize a lot of things away, efficiently too. Just ask my therapist."

Her eyes widened in surprise. "You have a therapist?"

"Pretty sure we all do. If there's one thing I've realized in this business, it's that sometimes we need to ask for help. Mine just happens to take insurance."

Meghna drank her coffee in silence for a minute. "Everyone else will listen to him, if I can change his mind. But what if I don't?"

"Can you handle an uncomfortable conversation right now?"

"They're all uncomfortable, Nick."

"Touché. If you don't earn Ganesha's favor, what are your choices?"

She held up a hand and counted them out. "First, I could let a demon enslave our souls."

"That sounds like a great start."

She glared at me under furrowed brows. "*Second*, I commit to another deal with the asura and promise another three generations of my family to his service."

"So what you're saying is you've got options."

"Nick! What kind of options are those?"

"The non-zero kind. I'm not saying any of the possibilities are risk free, but they're there."

"Because I could give my descendants a chance to free the family from our cursed blessing."

I nodded. "You kick the can down the road, but it doesn't all end here. I can't say whether Ganesha will like the fact that you've made the agreement, since I haven't worked with him long enough to know how pragmatic he is."

"Oh god, Nick. I'm getting a headache."

"Me too. Take some time to think about it. You've got a couple weeks left at least, but I agree. If your father isn't willing to be convinced, you could spend that time bashing your head against a metaphorical wall."

Meghna rose and offered me a hand. She was strong despite her stature and pulled me up easily. "I don't like my choices, but you're right that I have them."

"It's what I'm here for. Good luck. I think you'll do the right thing."

"What makes you say that?"

"I'm returning the trust you have in me. Someone had faith in me, once, when I was agonizing over something like this. Call me when you decide what you're going to do."

"I will. Thank you, Nick."

Meghna walked away, toward where she had parked her car, and I went back to the office. Rob and Cole were where I had left them, though Cole's face was more bruised than before. The purple was developing where Rob had struck him with the baton the night before.

I needed to ask about something that had been stuck in my brain. "Why did you have rope in your car?"

"Don't ask questions you don't want the answer to," Rob replied.

I opened my mouth to reply, but Rob held a hand up in warning.

"Anyway. What do you plan to do with him?" I gestured to the stocky man bound in my chair.

"I was hoping you'd have some ideas."

"That's a common theme today."

"What?"

I wandered over to my desk to pop some ibuprofen myself. The headache hadn't gotten any better since my return. Everything was escalating at the same time, which was alarming. There was good news, I supposed. Cole had intended grievous bodily harm to Rob, so he wasn't likely to report us to the police for his kidnapping. "Never mind. Let me rephrase. How can we benefit from the predicament he's put us in?"

"We need more information about Cormick's operation."

"True. Do you think he'll talk?" I was maneuvering my end of the conversation to be the "good cop" and hoped Rob would take the hint.

Either Rob was on the same wavelength, or he was irritable enough from sleeping on the floor that he fell into his role naturally. He cracked his knuckles and popped his neck, leaning it from side to side. "It's in his best interests."

Cole continued to glare, but didn't make an effort to speak around the cloth in his mouth.

"I'm going to remove your gag now, Cole," I said, approaching the chair. "I don't think I have to remind you that you assaulted my colleague, so we're all in a bit of trouble if you try to call for help. Do you understand?"

He nodded. I held my hands up as I stepped closer and gently pulled the fabric away from his mouth. Cole sighed in obvious relief, stretched his jaw, and moistened his lips.

"Do you want some water?" I asked. A sound of disgust came from Rob's direction. "Now, Rob. Cole is our guest for the moment." I was toeing the line between good cop and patronizing, but the whole thing annoyed me, too.

"You two haven't done this before, have you?" Cole's voice was a light tenor, which was at odds with his stature and stocky build. He spoke with a similar accent to Lee's. Maybe that's why he hadn't talked when we met him. It was hard to be intimidating when you didn't sound tough.

Rob's laughter broke the silence that followed his question.

"Do you represent the lollipop guild?" he asked before doubling over, wheezing.

"Now you're being hurtful. You don't see me insulting your knot-tying skills, do you? You overgrown boy scout. And how long was that kerchief in your trunk?" Cole spat to one side, trying to clear his mouth.

"Hey, now!" I walked over and grabbed a napkin from the break area. "We just had this place renovated."

Cole's voice was full of sarcasm. "My apologies. If you don't want a different puddle to clean up, I'd suggest you get me to the bathroom. Genius over here is lucky I have a large bladder."

I eyed Rob, who was wiping tears from his cheeks. "Your problem."

He grumbled but nodded. "I searched him when he was unconscious and found this!" Rob brandished a taser, pushing the button so it arced and buzzed, brightening the room for a few seconds.

Cole shook his head and rolled his eyes. "Yes, yes, if I make the wrong move, you'll drop me like a sack of hammers. I understand. I thought we were all professionals here."

Rob looked from the taser to Cole and back again. "Why didn't you use this on me? You had to hit me with a pipe?"

Cole shrugged without offering an explanation. I held Rob's baton while he untied our captive. I followed them to the washroom, standing guard until Cole finished his business. Cole returned to his—*my*—chair and rubbed his arms and legs as we continued our conversation. Rob picked up the rope, clearly intent on restraining Cole again.

"If I promise to be a good boy, could you not tie me up again? Plays havoc with my joints."

Rob stared at him for a second but coiled the rope instead as he talked. "Why did you come after me?"

"Orders. You know how it is."

"Do you remember who we work for?" I asked.

"Sure. Why do you think I was kidnapping him instead of killing him?"

My mouth compressed into a thin line. "Alright, but why did you want to do that in the first place?"

"Why does anyone do anything? Leverage."

His casual demeanor had me off guard, but at least I was getting information. My phone chose that moment to buzz. It was a message from Arjun, who I knew I was going to have to catch up with soon, anyway.

ARJUN:

> Let's talk at your earliest convenience. I'll buy you a coffee at the Oasis.

I wasn't sure it was a good idea to leave Rob alone with Cole. But I had too many irons in the fire, and this was Rob's problem.

"I'm sorry, Cole. Rob's going to have to tie you up again. I have an engagement elsewhere."

"I'll be on my best behavior," he pleaded with an innocent tone.

"Just because we haven't abducted anyone—"

Rob cleared his throat.

"Just because *I* haven't abducted anyone before doesn't mean I'm stupid."

Cole chuckled and held up his hands in surrender. "It was worth a try, wasn't it?"

"Points for trying. You'll have the time it takes me to run this errand to tell Rob how your operation really works, and why we should trust letting you go."

"Or what?" Cole asked.

"I let Rob get creative," I said, and Rob's eyes lit up in a way I didn't enjoy, but I assumed it was part of the show. His acting was a little method for my taste. "He's grumpy without his beauty sleep."

CHAPTER 17

NICK

It was a solid ten minutes before Rob finished tying Cole up again. We had given him a glass of water and left the gag off so he could speak. Satisfied that Rob was unlikely to have the tables turned on him while I was away, I took myself to the Marrakesh Oasis.

Arjun was already there with a cup of Turkish coffee and baklava waiting for me. He had an identical order in front of him with a bite taken out of the pastry. He rose and shook my hand before we sat. "You look worried, my friend."

"I've got a lot going on, not the least of which is our shared client."

"That's what I wanted to talk to you about. How is it going?"

I sank my teeth into the crisp dough of the baklava, pistachio dust falling to the plate. My eyes closed, nearly involuntarily, from how delicious it was. A sigh escaped my lips around the mouthful, and I slumped back in my chair. I must have needed a break more than I thought. The coffee was dark and rich, perfumed with a hint of rose water. Arjun waited with a patient smile as I sipped.

"It's complicated," I said.

"She must be close to a solution at this point."

"I wouldn't say that." I straightened in my seat, resting my elbows on the table and steepling my fingers against my lips. "She knows she needs to make a decision, but this is a heavy burden for someone her age."

"I have every confidence she'll find a way to satisfy our Lord. That being said, we want to ensure you're prepared for dispensation of the boon."

"What makes you so positive she's going to figure it out?"

"Nick, in my culture, we have a word. *Tathastu*. It comes from Sanskrit. In English, it translates roughly as 'let it be so.'"

"I get the English words, but I have no idea what you mean."

"There's another in Arabic, *inshallah*, 'if God wills it.' But they're not the same. I could look at young Meghna and say, '*Inshallah*, she will make her choice if God wills it.' But it removes the burden from her and puts it on God. Instead, I see the weight on her shoulders and acknowledge it. But the wish in her heart, what she is trying to do, is also there. So instead, I say *tathastu*, let her wish be so."

"It's a nice concept. Let's hope it plays out your way. I left her considering her options, which included getting into bed with the asura for another three generations." I explained the situation to Arjun, including Meghna's conversations with the demon. He asked a few questions, since this was new information for him, but didn't seem too surprised.

"I don't think continuing the 'blessing' would be an ideal solution, but Ganesha has patience. Perhaps she will make a choice which frees her family. On the other hand, she may pass the problem to her descendants. In either case, it will be done with the wish guiding her."

"I said I had faith in her."

Arjun eyed me over the rim of his cup as he sipped his drink. "Did you mean it?"

"Of course I did!"

"Then we agree. *Tathastu.*"

"What do I need to do to dispense the boon? If she manages to figure it out."

Arjun rummaged in the messenger bag at his feet for a folder, which he pulled and set on the table. He dove into the bag again and returned holding an extremely ornate pen, which he placed next to the folder. "You'll need to fill out this form, and you both sign it."

"It's like I'm closing on a loan."

"Not entirely wrong but definitely not right."

"I was joking."

Arjun shrugged. "I wasn't. It's not as far off from executing a contract, like you would be more familiar with."

I turned the folder around and opened it, glancing over the single page without reading it for content. The signature lines were there as expected.

"I sign first, then have her countersign, and that's it?"

"Precisely, and you'll have helped your first Hindu out of a bind. Feels good, doesn't it?"

"It'll be better when I finally put all the plates I'm spinning in the air down." I twirled the implement in my fingers. It was made from heavy brass and covered in tiny, ornate scrollwork. "Do I need to use this pen specifically?"

"Yes, it's very special. We execute all our contracts this way, so please don't lose it. We expect it back when you're done."

I picked the sheet up and rubbed the corner between two fingers in case a second page clung to it. "Does this need to be filled out in triplicate?"

"The one is fine. Who do you think we are, Nick? This isn't the Stone Age."

Arjun and I made small talk until the desserts and coffee were gone and parted ways. I had to get back to Rob and find out what he'd gotten from Cole. When I arrived, the scene was mostly as I had left it. Cole was still tied to my chair, and Rob looked just as grumpy as he had before.

"Oh thank the Lord, the boss is has returned. Could you untie me now?"

"That depends on whether you've given Rob any useful information. How did our friend do?"

"He told me a lot, actually." Rob's tone belied the statement. It was almost like he was disappointed Cole had been so forthcoming.

It was less complicated than I would have thought. Lee's explanation had summed up a lot of the history of the family and their unique talents, but the extent of their continued operation was surprising. It was multi-generational in the present tense. What I hadn't expected was to find Lee's great-great-grandfather, and his descendants who had passed through the veil, were still leading the family. Speaking with the dead wasn't limited to the spirits in limbo, it seemed.

The elders of the family were passing advice back and forth from the afterlife, and based on my understanding of their particular brand of business, the progenitors of the clan were firmly ensconced in Hell. It made for an interesting mental image, the living Cormicks having a séance with their dearly departed family and business associates. Did someone take meeting minutes? It was a bizarre cross section of the fantastical and the absolutely boring.

"Why so agreeable all of a sudden?"

I had untied Cole, and he was massaging the feeling into his limbs again. "We're in the same line of business, aren't we? The weird stuff no one can explain, and we make the rules up along the way. Professional courtesy, so you knew where we all stood."

"That's all very interesting, but why should we let you go?" I asked.

"Well, if you don't do it now, you will later." He spoke with a calm assurance.

Rob crossed his arms and glared. "What makes you say that?"

"You don't even know what to do with me. Plus, I've still got some cards up my sleeve. How many nights are you going to sleep on the floor, Rob?"

Rob rubbed the back of his neck, clearly contemplating his future.

"I think it's time we get security," I said, pulling out my phone, but Rob held up his hand to stop me.

"No, let me call Les. I owe him an explanation, and he can put in the request for us. What should I tell him?"

"Besides the truth? I would start with 'I'm sorry I didn't come home last night, honey. I got hit over the head with a pipe and had to deal with that.' Keep it simple."

Rob narrowed his eyes at me as he dialed Lester, holding the phone to his ear. He waited for the connection but hung up shortly thereafter. "His office phone went to voicemail. Let me ring his cell." He tried again, but his brow furrowed as the second ended the same way as the first.

"Is he ducking you? Maybe he's mad that you didn't get in touch last night or come home. I'll try him on mine." I dialed Lester's company phone, then his mobile, and had the same results as Rob. A wave of nerves passed through my stomach, and when I looked at Cole, he had a sly grin on his face. "What did you do?"

"Those cards up my sleeve?" He leaned back in his chair and winked at Rob. "Leverage."

CHAPTER 18

AMY

"Manannán mac Lir."

His head snapped around, looking behind him. "Where?" Then he turned back to me, grinning. His clothing was simple, what you might expect to see on a random stranger fishing along the shore in the summer. Cargo shorts, sandals, and a tank top in colors that blended with the sand and the sea. He stood, leaving his fishing pole where he had sat, and approached me.

I was still knee-deep in the water, having waded closer to shore. "For a King, you don't seem very serious."

"And you're too young to be this much of a grump. Nice to meet you, Amy." He held out his hand.

I splashed the rest of the way to dry land and shook it. His grasp was warm and strong, contrasting the chill of the breeze on my wet clothes. Calluses scraped at my palm as we disengaged. I couldn't help but note this was the second deity I had touched. "I'm sorry. You answered my call, and I'm chiding you for having a sense of humor."

The ginger hair around his mouth split into a wide smile. "You've had an interesting time lately, so I'll forgive you. Do you have something dry to change into?"

I had planned ahead, thankfully, and rummaged in my bag for a towel and spare clothes. One problem—I hadn't thought it through that I might have a guest. "Can you, uh..."

"Oh, right. Of course."

He turned his back to me, and I scanned the area. There weren't any other passersby, so I wrapped the towel around myself and shucked out of my wet things before swapping them for dry ones. Manannán whistled a jaunty tune to himself while he waited. I cleared my throat when I finished, and he faced me again.

"Walk with me?" He gestured to the path leading to the main trail.

He led the way up the sandy terrain until we encountered hard pavement again. My foot hit the asphalt, and I squeaked in pain. The adrenaline had worn off, and the gash I had made in the pad of my foot ached from the hard pressure.

Manannán watched as I limped to a nearby bench to inspect my injury. It was an inch-long cut but wasn't bleeding freely, only seeping and coloring the sand crimson where it stuck to me. He followed, then tutted as he examined it along with me. I pulled a bottle of water from my bag and rinsed the dirt away, poking and prodding to make sure nothing foreign was under the skin. I looked up, and his eyes distracted me through the pain. They were the exact color of the sea. Not any one hue but shifting waves of blue, turquoise, green, and black. They were hypnotic. A person could lose themselves in eyes like those. They were deep set and framed by his full beard and wild hair.

The absence of pain alerted me that something had changed. I looked down and almost missed his hand passing over my foot, leaving unblemished skin behind. There was no trace of the cut. My eyes widened in surprise.

He winked at me. "It was my domain that did that to you. If I want you to finish your task, it's the least I could do."

I fished through my bag for my socks and the towel to clean myself up and put my boots back on. When I rose from the bench and nodded, we set off again on the trail.

"What *is* my task? I'm glad you responded to my invitation, and I'm thrilled to know which patron has been funneling me magic—"

He tsked and shook his head. "It's not exactly like that. The whole 'patron' gods being the source of your power. I can't blame you mortals for using the analogy, but it puts a lot of pressure on us while also stealing your own thunder."

I hadn't expected a lesson in thaumaturgy from the Irish god of the sea, but here I was. The path wound toward a boardwalk jutting out over the water. "So, how *does* it work?"

Instead of answering, he asked, "Can atheists have magic?"

It was a fascinating question. Some world religions had no real deities and were primarily animistic, believing in the spirit inherent in all things. Rocks, trees, animals, the wind, everything held a "soul" if you followed animism of any kind. I hadn't come across the question in my studies so extrapolated.

Atheism was expansive and had one main tenet—there were no gods. Atheists coming from Christianity usually manifested the statement as "there is no God," but for the sake of argument, and the walking proof of polytheism in front of me, I went with the broader option. If atheists didn't have faith in gods but could still believe in the spirit invested in living things, could they hold magic?

"Yes," I answered confidently.

He gave another toothy grin. "Good choice. So aye, I'm your patron. But you were manifesting power before I set my sights on you. It's part of the reason, really. You've got an enormous amount of potential, and I wanted to make sure you had access to the tools you'd need to develop it."

My cheeks burned with a blush. "Thank you."

"Don't thank me. You've been pushing your own studies. Patrons don't make the magic happen so much as they make it a little easier. Like artists, back in the day, who had a wealthy benefactor. They could pursue their passions and build their skills because an influential person who believed in their art stood behind them. That's how it works. Well, mostly. You don't need the fiddly bits, but you've got the gist now."

"I think I understand. But why me?"

He barked a laugh. "Full of yourself, aren't you?"

"No, I—"

"I'm teasing! You're the one who said I wasn't very serious. Just trying to live up to expectations." He guided us toward the end of the pier. "You're not the only one. We get our pick. Your friend Melinda has told you before that you're a bit of a beacon, I'd wager. I just happened to be the first to claim you."

I wasn't sure how being "claimed" made me feel, and it must have been plain on my face because he chuckled again.

"Don't make it weird. You don't owe me anything. You're a seed that's planted itself. I'm just the gardener adding some water and fertilizer now and then."

We made our way to the edge of the walk, our feet clomping on the wooden boards. Manannán sat with his legs dangling over the waves, and I joined him.

"So, what *is* my task? No, wait a second. I summoned you, but you had a job waiting for me and it sounded like I should have already known about it. What gives?"

"Call it a test."

"You'll need to give me a little more, I'm afraid."

He leaned over and bumped his shoulder into mine. Such a casually intimate gesture took me entirely off guard. "I had to know you were willing to dive in."

"Literally? Because that's what I did."

He gave a quick hiss. "Pun unintended, for once. No, I wanted to know if you would take the next step. So forgive my presumptuousness, but once you passed my small trial, I got carried away."

"That helps, thank you. Now, what do you need my help with?"

His brow furrowed, and he took a moment before speaking. "I've got a problem. Well, we've all got one, really."

"Does it have to do with the restless spirit who contacted me? Siobhan?"

"Aye. She's one of mine. I'm glad you figured out a way to communicate. But she's a symptom of a bigger issue."

"What's that?"

"It's part of my dilemma. Something is hiding the cause from me. I'm the Keeper of the Veil, but I'm not omnipotent or omniscient. I can't see everything, and a lot of what happens in this city is outside of my domain."

"Siobhan said she was stuck, and the pull was too strong, but I have no idea what she meant."

He nodded. "I can tell you a few things, but then I need you to be my eyes and ears on this. There isn't a problem with the veil itself, but nothing crosses it, no matter what I do. Souls are stuck on this side, the mortal realm, haunting it. Something is holding them here, but whatever is causing it is in this city. I can feel it."

"If it's like a magnetic field, and it's drawing the souls toward it, then why can't you follow the pull?"

"Because it's not exactly like that. It's a weight, or a pressure. It's keeping things in place. Less like magnetism, more like increasing gravity. If it were so simple, I'd like to think I'd have already solved it."

"Sorry."

"No, don't be. It's true I haven't cracked it, and I'm not sure what'll happen with this many souls trapped on the wrong side of the veil for much longer. It's why I need your help."

He took something out of his pocket and held his palm out to me. In it was a small seashell. He pushed it toward me until I picked it up, examining it closely. It was iridescent, a perfect spiral.

"You know how you can hear the ocean if you hold a shell up to your ear? If you speak into it, the sea listens. If you figure out what's causing this, speak my name, and I'll come."

He started to rise, but I grabbed his arm and held him there. "Can I ask you for a favor? It's not related to Siobhan, as far as I'm aware, but it's probably in your domain."

"No promises, but ask and I'll see what I can do."

"There are souls trapped in crystal statues. Can you tell me how to free them."

He cracked his knuckles and smiled ear to ear. "Oh, lass, now you're speaking my language. I can give you some ideas, but you'll need to experiment and find out what works."

"There's no universal 'free the spirits' spell? I'm shocked."

"Now there's the sense of humor I knew lurked in your heart. Tell me what you know, and I'll do what I can."

I didn't have a lot of information, yet. Nick owed me a much longer conversation than the one line text telling me about the statue dilemma. I shared what I had, and when I mentioned the name Cormick, his eyes darkened.

"The look on your face tells me you know something about the Cormicks."

"They're not mine, even though their family immigrated from Ireland. It's not where you're from, or whose blood you've got in your veins, but what you believe. I'm not sure belief is the right word in their case, but they pledged themselves to the church a long time ago."

"Good to know, I guess."

"It doesn't mean much to you, but the fact that it's the Cormicks tells me the talent they're wielding isn't going to respond to my usual methods. It's why I can't simply hand you a solution, otherwise I would."

"It's alright. Anything you can give, please."

He ran his hands through his wavy hair. "You've got a few choices. First, the tried-and-true method: destruction. If you break the statue, it's likely the spirit will be able to escape."

"Is there any chance I'd harm the soul trapped inside it?"

He raised an eyebrow in what looked like appreciation. "A kind concern but you don't need to worry overly much. When someone dies, they lose their tether to the physical plane. Whatever the Cormicks are doing to house them in a statue isn't likely to give them enough of a connection to be harmed."

"Okay, what are my other options?"

He shrugged. "Well, you say they're glass, so hopefully that does the trick. Nothing like a good smash 'em up. But if that doesn't work, you may need to call the spirit out in order to free it. Might be a combination, like a one-two punch. If you draw the soul far enough from the figurine, you may be able to break it and finish the job."

"I've never summoned a spirit like that. I'm not sure where to start in this case."

"What you did to call me up worked a treat, but I'll give you one hint. Sacrifice is powerful magic. It doesn't have to be large, but it has to be meaningful."

"So destroy the vessels or summon the spirits out and *then* break the statues? Those are some limited choices."

He spread his hands in apology. "If that doesn't work, go for variations on a theme."

I groaned. "Make it up as I go. Got it."

CHAPTER 19

AMY

I left Manannán staring out across the water. I guessed even gods had a lot on their minds sometimes. There was plenty on mine, and I needed the rest of the information Nick had promised me. We all owed each other some explanations, and it was high time I checked in with the boys. We still had our group chat from when I rescued Nick, so I texted while I walked to my car.

ROB:

Ouch. Burn.

NICK:

I love you too. We've got a lot of irons in the fire. I'll explain. See you soon.

It was a short trip back to my parking spot, and I was on my way to the coffee shop. It was funny, thinking about where Nick had started. I never visited him when he worked as a barista. We weren't as close back then, and I usually saw him in company at Rob's. I had spent more time at the café since Nick changed careers than I ever had before. It was like a touchstone—a reminder of where we had all come from.

I didn't mind when he used it as his "second office." It wasn't a nostalgia trip but a space he was comfortable in. I liked the way Nick had evolved. He took the best pieces from his experiences and layered them together to make a new whole.

I arrived before they did, so put in our usual order before scouting a table in the corner. Mark waved at me, poking his head out from the back as I picked up our cups. I wasn't in the mood for small talk and was thankful when he disappeared as quickly as he had materialized.

Rob was the first of the two through the door, and his expression made my stomach clench. It was an uncomfortable mix of two Robs. One part was worry, the kind of concerned look I expected from him. The other was anger, which I hadn't seen for a while. His clothes were rumpled, and his body was tightly coiled. He scanned from side to side as if trying to decide where to launch himself.

Nick followed on his heels, looking around until he spotted me waving from my perch. He didn't seem nearly as bedraggled as Rob, but he also had a distinct hint of panic driving his features.

"What happened to you two? You look like you slept in your clothes, Rob."

Rob pulled the collar of his shirt to the side and exposed a purple bruise where his shoulder met his neck.

"Holy shit. I'm sorry, what happened?"

Rob opened his mouth to speak, almost lunging forward with the energy of an adrenaline dump, but Nick raised his hand, stopping him.

"It started yesterday. Sorry, Rob, let me handle this."

Rob nodded and picked up his coffee with trembling hands.

Nick told me all about their meeting with the Cormicks, backtracking further to explain the soul statues in detail. Rob placed a glass figurine of a golfer on the table for me to examine. He also jumped in with colorful commentary when Nick got to the part of the story involving the attack until they reached this morning.

"You did what?" I asked.

"We tied a man up in the closet at the office," Nick answered. "How else were we supposed to meet you for coffee?"

"I could have come to the office instead!"

"It's a bit of a mess there right now," Rob added. "Plus, it's better if you aren't involved unless you have to be."

"I get to make those decisions—" I broke off as Rob swept his coffee mug onto the floor. It shattered, and the sudden crash silenced the room. I shared a glance with Nick, who gave a small shake of his head.

"They have Lester," Rob said in a whisper that begged to be a roar.

I reached across the table to grab his hand. "Oh, Rob. What can I do to help?"

Nick laid his own on Rob's arm and squeezed. "We don't know yet, but we're working on it. You've been busy too. Why don't you give us an update on where you're at?"

I gave an abbreviated version of my side of things, including my new status with UWU and the conversation I had with Manannán. "I didn't have a lot to go on, but I asked him about freeing souls trapped in physical objects."

"What did he have to say?" Rob asked.

"He had an old-fashioned approach starting with 'smash em', but I—"

Rob took hold of the statue on the table and tossed it over his shoulder. It spun end over end until it crashed to the ground and…didn't break. I scurried over to where it had landed and inspected it. It didn't have so much as a scratch, and when I brought it back to the table Rob's expression was dour.

"The enduring human spirit," he said dryly.

"That's a terrible pun."

"He wasn't the one to come up with it." Nick sighed. "Anyway. Did your sea god have anything else to say on the matter?"

"He did…" I turned the statue over in my hands. "Can I hold on to this? I need to do some experiments."

"Be my guest. We've got a couple more from some of Lee's other victims."

I tapped at the glass but stopped when I wasn't sure if it annoyed the inhabitant like a goldfish in a bowl. "Is it okay if I free the spirit inside?"

"That could be a problem. Cormick said the souls they were working with would go insane the longer they were aware of their existence. The statues are like little stasis pods. We need a plan for what happens after they're free before you go ahead with it."

I nodded. "I'll try to develop a method without actually releasing it. No promises, this isn't an exact science. What are you two going to do?"

"I have an idea," Rob said, turning to Nick. "But you won't like it."

"I'm worried about Lester too, Rob. I don't have to like it. It just has to work." Nick rose and knocked back the rest of his latte in one gulp. "We have to go. Too much to do. Guy in a closet. You know, the usual. I'm glad you joined the coven. It sounds like it'll be good for you. I'm sorry we don't have time to celebrate."

"I understand. Rain check. I'll keep you posted on my progress."

I walked out with Nick and Rob, giving Nick a quick hug but a longer kiss before heading back to my apartment.

It was nonsensical, but I buckled the glass golfer into my passenger seat before taking off. Rob's example made it abundantly clear he expected them to be indestructible, but I didn't want to take any chances. Plus, a human soul was in there. A little care and courtesy was the least I could do, handling that kind of precious cargo.

When I arrived home, I made quick work of a few necessary chores. Pants needed to be fed, and I had to check on whether Siobhan wanted contact. I got no response when I asked if she could talk, and Pants continued to inhale her bowl of kibble, so I moved on to my primary task of the night.

It was time for some science. Well, magic, but I had a hypothesis to test, so the concepts still applied. If I couldn't destroy the vessel, I needed to find a way to draw the spirit out. First, some destructive testing. Rob may have thrown the statue around, but I doubted he exhausted the possibilities. My landlord had a fire pit in the yard, which I was free to use, so I laid a quick fire and brought a notebook with me to keep track of my efforts.

I helped myself to some tools and materials lying around the maintenance shed. Glass was made of melted sand, wasn't it? I wasn't sure how effective heat would be at destabilizing it, but I tossed the statue into the fire once it was roaring. Rob said not to do anything permanent yet, but I didn't have high hopes. I figured ruling out the unlikely methods was safe enough, and I'd be pleasantly surprised if it turned out otherwise.

There weren't any visual changes to the figurine as it lay in the fire, so I fished it out with some fireplace tongs and set it on a cinderblock I had pulled from beside the steps. "Smash em", I said to myself, raising a hammer and bringing it down with as much force as I could muster. I flinched when I made contact, and a loud crack echoed through the yard. The statue stared innocently at me, now wedged between two broken halves of the gray block.

"Fuck." I was fairly sure it wasn't going to work, so I didn't know why I was disappointed. Unless there were explosives hidden on the property, I wasn't likely to make more progress than this first test. I had planned on rolling over it with my car, but at this point I was positive I'd get a flat tire for my efforts, and it wasn't worth the trouble.

I put out the fire, wrote a note in my phone to buy a replacement block before anyone noticed, and started cleaning up my mess. To add insult to injury, or injury to insult in this case, I sliced my palm on a jagged piece of stone. The pain cut through my frustration, and I hissed, cupping my hand to examine the wound.

I grabbed the figurine and tucked it into my armpit before walking upstairs and back inside. I left it on the coffee table before going into the bathroom and tending to my hand. I had washed it and was applying disinfectant and a Band-Aid when I sensed a presence behind me. I turned, but no one was there, not even Pants. It was the feeling you got when a puff of air moved your hair, like someone walked past you.

When I returned to the living room, Pants was on the table, rubbing her face against the statue.

"What are you doing, bug?"

She turned to regard me, and it wasn't Pants. Her expression was more human. She pawed at the golfer and jumped immediately to the Ouija board to tap out a message.

"WA—"

"I know, Siobhan. Water."

She shook her head and hissed, which startled me, then spelled a single word before collapsing to the table. WAR.

I picked Pants up, because the possession was clearly over, and set her next to me on the couch. Our conversation was nowhere near as long as the previous ones, but maybe an agitated spirit used more energy. I examined the statue, and a small red blotch was smeared on it near to where Siobhan had been touching it. I must have gotten a drop of my blood on it when I carried it inside.

"Are we at war with the Cormicks?" I asked Pants and stroked her fur as she slept. "I hope not. I'm not sure what Rob has planned, but if Nick isn't going to like it, then I probably won't either."

I lifted my hand to examine my bandage, then glanced back to the dot of crimson on the figurine. "Well, Siobhan, at least you gave me an idea."

CHAPTER 20

ROB

"Is this a felony?"

"Well, Adam, it's not *not* a felony," I said, tying the last knots restraining Cole in an old-school metal office chair in the basement of Devil Co.

"You're not reassuring me in any meaningful way."

I hadn't planned on involving the archivist, but after discussing my idea with Nick, we decided to stash Cole somewhere while my plan played out. The Cormicks might try to waltz into the agency and liberate their family member without freeing Lester. Transporting Cole wasn't a job I relished, and Nick went green when I grabbed a canvas shopping bag to use as a makeshift hood. Our adversaries might be aware of the office, but they might not, and there was no reason to take chances. He left this part to my skilled hands. I didn't blame him, given his prior experience with his last client...and with me.

Cole was thankfully agreeable, understanding his situation and complying with professional grace. I didn't know if I should have been worried about the trajectory of my life, but at the time I was just happy I didn't have to use force. Given the anger boiling just below the surface of my thoughts, I would have, but it would have made everything messier. I had placed his chair in a corner of the room, so he couldn't see anything other than the cinder block walls even when he craned his neck as far as it would go.

Nick walked around, inspecting my handiwork. "It's temporary. No one is going to come looking for him. We need somewhere secure to keep him while we're working out a few things."

"What Nick is trying to say is this guy's a professional heavy. His people would be in just as much trouble with the law as we would if anyone went to the cops about it. Nobody wants that, and he's confident his family has enough leverage to get him back in an exchange of some kind."

Cole said something, but the bag covering his head muffled the sound. I removed it carefully, keeping my fingers away from his face. I trusted him as far as I could throw him, which wasn't far at all. He attempted to survey the room, but I had done a good job with his restraints, and he quickly settled again.

He chuckled and flexed his shoulders to test his bonds. "You should've seen your faces. I expect the boys'll be in touch soon about a handoff. Can I have a drink of water?"

"Does this happen to you often?" I asked.

"I wouldn't say it's been frequent, but it's nice to be nicked by amateurs this time. You got lucky. I'll give ya that. But it's all over except for the waiting."

Adam's face had a greenish cast, and he shuffled from foot to foot.

"Don't worry, Adam." Nick laid a hand on his shoulder, which made him flinch. "You're not a field agent, and no one's expecting anything from you other than making sure our friend here doesn't leave the room."

"Alright. I'll do it, but you guys owe me."

"Deal." I checked my knots one last time before retreating to the door. Nick and I were in the hallway before either man could say another word. We leaned against the wall and breathed for a few seconds before Nick turned to me.

"What's this idea I'm not going to like?"

I wasn't going to beat around the bush, but I needed Nick on board with my plan, so I had to approach it the right way.

"I know you don't approve of torture—"

"Your plan is to *torture* Cole? I get that you're angry about Lester. I'm furious too, but violating the Geneva Convention isn't the answer."

I cursed myself for starting at the end instead of the beginning. I closed my eyes, blew my breath out, and took another calming one. "No. The plan is...Look. I'm...not that guy anymore. Besides, I doubt it would do anything other than piss off the Cormicks."

"Then what are you suggesting?"

"We might need to ask Lu for something, unless it's in your wheelhouse."

"Spit it out, Rob."

Shit, I *was* beating around the bush. "Have you ever gotten access to the souls in Hell?"

Nick opened his mouth, then closed it abruptly and cocked his head to one side. "You know? I don't think that's anything I've seen before."

"Can we get a meeting with your boss?"

"With his office manager missing, I expect we can squeeze into his calendar. Let me make a call."

"It's a little out of the ordinary," Lu said after resting his espresso cup back in its saucer.

We were sitting in his office, and I had just finished explaining part of my plan. I had never been farther than the lobby before, usually meeting Nick or Lester for lunch. My hands were sweating, and a tightness had settled in my chest. The last time I saw Lucifer, he was threatening my immortal soul, so I shouldn't have been surprised that I was nervous.

What I didn't expect, however, was the appraising look he gave me after I had laid out my idea. Lester didn't share many stories from work while we were together, but he was always envious of Lu's sense of style. It was one of those things Lester tried to emulate, putting himself together for the office every day. Being on the other side of the desk from this immortal figure, dressed to kill in a jet-black suit, was more than a little intimidating.

"What are you hoping to get out of this?" Lu asked.

I glanced at Nick, but he shrugged as if to say "It's your plan."

So I cleared my throat, which was suddenly as dry as Lester's sense of humor. "It's twofold, really. First, we speak with the head of the Cormick family, who's still pulling strings from Hell. If we get him on board with giving up the business, then he talks to Lee. We exchange the hostages, call it quits, and monitor the situation."

Lu steepled his fingers under this chin, leaning his elbows on the top of the desk. "That sounds like an overly positive scenario. What happens when Old Man Cormick doesn't agree to tell his descendants to stand down?"

"This is the part I'm not sure how comfortable I am with," Nick added.

A flush of anger suffused my body. Nick was my greatest supporter. He gave me my job, moved past me trying to kill him, and was a good friend. That being said, I would have slapped him across the face if it wouldn't destroy any chance I had to make this work. "What if it was Amy, Nick? How comfortable would you be, then?"

Lucifer raised one eyebrow, then inclined his head toward Nick, who was absorbing the impact of my question.

Nick took a breath and huffed it out. "I'd probably act first and worry about the implications later."

The tightness in my chest let go, and I flexed my hands to relieve some of the tension there. "Okay. So if our cease and desist request falls flat, we would have to bring in the bigger guns." I turned to speak directly to Lu. "This is where I need your assistance, uh...sir?"

"Look, Rob, I know I make you nervous, but you can relax with the 'sir' stuff. Lester's been bending my ear about your situation for a while now. I haven't made any decisions, but we're a long way from the crypt on the Green. Aren't we?"

The relief that washed over me nearly knocked me to the floor. It wasn't forgiveness or absolution for what I'd done to Nick, but it was something. "Thank you. It—it means a lot. Okay. We need your help because we don't understand how your operation works once the souls are in your possession."

Nick jumped in. "It's new territory, even for me. I've only dealt with the living side of the house, so I couldn't answer any of his questions when he was briefing me earlier."

"I hold the two parts separately most days. Our ground operations here interface with living people who want to entrust their souls to me in exchange for certain dispensations. We monitor the 'bad' eggs, but don't do much beyond keeping tabs. Once they're off the chessboard, as it were, they slide directly into my possession."

"You're doing it again, Lu," Nick said.

Lu sighed and rubbed at his temples. "Forgive me, Rob. I get wordy when I'm in lecture mode. There aren't levels of hell, per se. Dante was a little too creative putting his story together. The good-to-gray ones, they mostly just exist. The differences between the lower boundaries of Heaven and the upper ones of Hell are not stark."

What Lu said was interesting, but we hadn't hit the parts relevant to the matter at hand. "But the darker souls? I'm expecting Mr. Cormick to be in that lot."

"Here's where it gets complicated. Once a soul is in my possession, I can do what I like with it. I told Nick a while ago, Hell isn't fire and brimstone but a loss of free will. That's true, but I left out some salient details about the worst of our inhabitants."

Nick leaned forward in his seat, looking extremely interested in where this was going. I couldn't blame him. If I had signed my soul away to the Devil and hadn't gotten all the details, I'd be worried about what loopholes I missed.

Lu must have noticed, because he waved his hands at Nick. "This won't affect you, unless you're planning on a much different career path than the one we've talked about. Calm down."

Nick's hands unclenched from the arms of the chair, but he was clearly still on high alert.

"The more problematic souls," Lu continued, "get individual attention. I have a division that creates specialized programs for each of them. They might relive the bad choices they made, to reflect on them. Some experience their actions from the perspective of their victims. That's a popular one, let me tell you."

I couldn't help but ask, "Why?"

"Hell isn't a place of torment, but it's also not an opportunity for forgiveness. If the worst of the souls there can learn empathy and accept the harm they did while they were alive, they can earn a spot in the less restrictive parts of Hell. Think of it as a rehabilitation program. It's challenging, and they have to want to do it, but in the end it's effective."

"What about the Cormicks? Are they repentant?"

His eyes flashed white, like a screen. "Not a single one. They're hard men and mostly keep to themselves."

Nick had a quizzical look on his face. "Wait a second. Why can't you stop them from communicating with their kin? If they're in perpetual time-out, how are they getting contacted?"

Lu had the grace to appear uncomfortable. "There are rules for everything, including this. What the Cormicks are doing is old magic. It's intertwined with this belief structure, but it's got roots. I can't stop Lee because he's got the free will to ruin his afterlife. I can't keep him from his great grandfather either because it's an area outside of my control."

Nick and I had talked about the limitations of gods, and how weird that was. I hadn't experienced it in person until now. "Alright. Last question before my official request. Are there limits to what you can or can't do with a soul in your care?"

"Other than not destroying them, I have a wide latitude."

"Great. We can worry about the details later. For now, can you please arrange a meeting with Great-great-grandpa Cormick?"

Lucifer snapped his fingers.

CHAPTER 21

ROB

Before the snap registered in my ears, we were somewhere else. I had a moment of disorientation, which settled into my head, dropping through my stomach like a panic attack. My heart raced, and sweat broke out across my forehead as I took in my surroundings. I was sitting in a chair, similar to the one in Lu's office, but there were six set around a wooden table. The room itself was nondescript, decorated like a conference room from the seventies.

Nick sat to my right, looking as uncomfortable as I was. This was new for him too. There was no precedent for what we were experiencing. Lu sat at the head of the table, grinning slightly at the two of us.

"What just happened?" Nick asked, before I could pry my mouth open to speak.

"Welcome to Hell." Lu gestured with wide arms at the room around us.

It was surreal to imagine this was Hell. I couldn't help myself. "Why is it so brown?"

"It's not." Nick and Lu responded simultaneously and stared pointedly at each other.

I stood and walked to the wood-paneled wall, knocking it with my knuckles. "Seems brown to me."

"We're in a liminal space between the worlds. You're on the edge of damnation, really. The precipice, not the pit."

"That still doesn't explain why brown isn't brown, Lu," Nick said, echoing my own thoughts.

"Your minds aren't comfortable with the concept of nothingness. This is an entirely incorporeal place, and what you're seeing now is a coping mechanism. Given your simple, human brains—"

"Hey!" Nick and I both called out.

"Fine. Your *meat processors* keep it simple, because of your three-dimensional thinking, so you each conceive of something mundane or boring. Harmless. In Rob's case it's a brown conference room he had stashed away in his gray matter somewhere."

My stomach was queasy, and Nick looked only marginally better.

"So we're here," I said. "Now what?"

Lu snapped his fingers again, and a man was sitting at the end of the table opposite him. "May I introduce Eoghan Cormick."

The man nodded to Lu, as if acknowledging an equal. This guy had some balls. He wore a deep umber double-breasted suit, the jacket open to expose a vest sporting a gold pocket watch chain. The navy tie around his neck was immaculately done, contrasting with the crisp white of his shirt. He didn't seem like a penitent or a prisoner but had the air of a shrewd businessperson or mafioso.

His appearance fascinated but also surprised me. "I didn't realize you had a dress code in Hell."

Lu's grin hadn't faded. He seemed to be getting a kick out of having Nick and me off our game. "We're not without dignity, even here. This is how Eoghan sees himself. Unless there's an intentional reason to do otherwise, this is how he'll appear to us."

"Much obliged, Scratch," Eoghan said in a deep baritone. His accent was thicker than the one his descendants retained. "I appreciate any diversion these days. What can I do for you gentlemen? I assume my host here isn't looking for my counsel."

"I have some grievances to lodge against your family," I said.

"How is it my business? I'm dead." His tone was innocent, but he couldn't keep a sly grin off his face.

My pulse quickened, and I wanted nothing more than to wipe the smirk from his lips. Lu leaned back in his chair, a neutral look on his face. It was clear he was leaving this to us and likely me specifically, since it was my request that got us here. Nick must have noticed the clouds descending over my head.

"I can appreciate a game of cat and mouse as much as the next guy," Nick said, "even though I expect you think you're the predator in this situation, and we're the prey."

"What can I say? It's been a while since I could spar with men who had a bone to pick with me. Old habits die hard. Why don't you lay out your grievances, and I'll respond to them."

"Seems fair," Nick replied, nodding to me with an obvious cue.

"First, your kin have kidnapped my boyfriend. We have one of yours in custody, as well."

"Did you owe them money? You should be able to handle the trade yourselves. I doubt you'd have come all the way here to speak with me for such a small matter."

My face grew hot, and I had to close my eyes and take a few deep breaths instead of spitting nails at Eoghan. Eoghan was right, Lester was a symptom of the illness but he wasn't why we were there. I had to resolve our problems holistically, with Lester as a piece of the whole. If that was all we needed, I'd have already given Cole over in a hostage exchange and been done.

"It's part of a larger problem, yes. Your family business is disrupting the natural order of ours. And don't play coy. We know you're in contact with Lee and the other mediums."

"I don't see how a little commerce would disrupt—"

I interrupted him, spittle flying from my mouth as I spoke in a rush. "You've been extorting families for years, preying on their grief. You're keeping souls from going where they're supposed to go!"

"No matter how much the family heeds my advice, I don't control them. I've lost my free will, but they haven't. What do you want from me?"

"I want you to tell them to give up that part of the business. No more 'shepherding' souls from Limbo. They can act as mediums and help loved ones communicate with the dead, but no more pyramid schemes—"

"What's a pyramid scheme?"

My mouth hung open as I considered how to explain a modern con like that to someone of Eoghan's generation. It was an innocent enough question, but I wasn't planning to get into the weeds with my demands. "No more extortion, and they have to agree to never trap another soul again. Not in a statue or otherwise."

"So, in short, you want me to tell my family to abandon one of the most lucrative parts of our business?"

Nick's surprise was evident on his face. "They must be aware you're in Hell. Is it worth damning the rest of your family to an eternity of suffering—"

"It's not exactly suffering," Lu added.

I gave Lucifer a withering look, and he winked at me. I nearly lost my mind. "Whose side are you on?"

Lu spread his hands and shrugged.

Eoghan smiled broadly and nodded again at Lu. "Milton said it best, 'better to reign in Hell than serve in Heaven.' I vowed to ensure my family and our descendants are taken care of. If each of us must accept an afterlife here, it's worth it to maintain the safety and comfort of the Cormicks. Forever."

Nick's face fell, knowing what was coming next.

"Last chance," I said. "You can choose to call off your family, keep to the 'honest' work, and we exchange Lester and Cole. Then we're even."

Eoghan had a dark twinkle in his eye. "Or?"

A cold calm descended on me, and I locked eyes with this man who was the progenitor of our current problems. "Let me tell you how this is going to go."

An hour later, we were sitting in Lu's office again. The disorientation from the shift in and out of that liminal space had given me a headache and from the looks of it, left both Nick and me queasy. Though in his case it might have had more to do with the direction our conversation with Eoghan Cormick had gone.

Finding him both unrepentant and unwilling to advise his family to change their business model was unsurprising. I didn't expect anything else, if I was being honest with myself. The fact I didn't care was a little concerning. I needed Lester back, and I would have done more than interrupt the already uncomfortable afterlife of a mystic mobster to make it happen.

"I hope that was helpful," Lu said.

"We'll find out. It would have been easier if he had agreed to plan A, but plan B should work just as well. It relies on Lee Cormick exercising his free will in a direction we want him to, but I'm not giving him much of a choice."

"Well, I'll leave you both to it. Let me know if you need any more assistance, but I expect you to handle the rest of this negotiation yourselves. What am I paying you for, otherwise?"

Nick and I had the good grace to laugh at his joke, even if we were feeling a bit lackluster.

"But seriously though, it was some good out-of-the-box thinking. I'll be curious how it all plays out."

Lu dismissed us, and we returned to the archives. We found the door cracked open when we arrived, so we made our way cautiously inside. The figure we had left tied up in the corner was still there, but Adam was nowhere to be found.

"Adam?" I called out, heading to the corner to make sure my knots had held. Something was wrong with the picture in front of me. It was at that moment I found our problems had multiplied in our absence. The person bound in the chair wasn't Cole.

"Goddamn it, Adam!" My voice rose and my mind raced. "What happened?"

Adam tried to speak, but only muffled noises came out around the handkerchief gagging him. I pulled the cloth out of his mouth, and he sighed in obvious relief.

"Just keep an eye on him, you said!" Adam blurted, as I loosened Cole's handiwork. It turned out his knot-work was better than mine. "I was working at the desk for an hour. He was shifting in his seat, but it's not comfortable, so I didn't think anything of it."

"We don't need a novel," Nick said.

Adam glared at us both. "There's a reason I'm not a field agent! He put me in a chokehold. I had an asthma attack and passed out! I woke up like this, and he was already gone."

Nick and I shared a meaningful look, concern evident in his eyes. "What now?" he asked.

"We keep going," I said, finishing the last of the knots and freeing Adam.

He stretched and rubbed at his legs. "Ugh, pins and needles!"

Nick grimaced. "I hope we didn't need that leverage after all."

CHAPTER 22

NICK

I trusted Rob to keep his cool, but I didn't need to put more stress on him with even more riding on his plan, so I offered to call Lee and his associates. I didn't have Lee's personal number, so I reached out to their office and was routed through their admin, who dealt with us when we were at the funeral home. She put me on hold for an egregiously long time before Lee's voice greeted me through the speaker.

"Nick! I'd say it's been a long time, but it really hasn't. How are you?"

"We can skip the small talk, Lee. I want to set a meeting."

"What do we need to meet about?"

Despite the strange and supernatural things I'd been witness to, my time with the Devil hadn't given me the ability to reach through the phone and strangle someone. "I think you know, and I don't appreciate being played with. What was it Cole said? Aren't we all professionals here?"

"Yeah, I guess nothing's looking quite how you expected when you started your day. But Nick, please, tied to a chair? Kept in a closet? You're lucky Cole's one of my most level-headed fellas. He only holds grudges when I tell him to, and I haven't decided on your case yet."

"We want Lester back and to talk about your business model."

"Speaking of your friend, there, he's a damn sight better off with us than Cole was with you. Professional courtesy and all. He's been well taken care of. I can give you some pointers if you—"

"Cut the shit, Lee."

"Well, if you're going to be like that. What do we have to discuss regarding my...business model, was it?"

This conversation wasn't going well. Lee must have assumed he held all the cards since we lost Cole. I had to believe he wouldn't want to hold Lester indefinitely and was mostly giving me a hard time. "You're causing more trouble than you realize, and we have a proposal for you. The least you can do is hear us out, unless you plan on keeping Lester as a houseguest forever."

"My ma said trouble was my middle name. It's not. It's Eoghan, after my great-great-grandfather, but if I had a *second* middle name, it'd probably be trouble."

"Lee..."

"Fine, fine. Alright. I don't expect you'd trust us to gather here at the office, so pick a neutral place, and we'll be there."

"Meet us at the Broadway Triangle and bring Lester."

"Why would I do that? You don't have anything—"

"Eoghan sends his regards."

The connection was so silent I worried he'd hung up on me until his quiet, raspy breathing returned.

"What did you say?"

"You forget what business *we're* in, Lee. Tomorrow, at noon. We'll have a table. He'd better be unharmed. You'll regret it if he isn't."

"Hold on—"

I hung up, satisfied I'd flustered him. I needed to bait the hook. He had been smug enough, and I worried he wouldn't listen, but that didn't seem to be a problem. Now? It was in Rob's court, and I had to wait and see if his plan worked.

The Broadway Triangle was a spit of land between Broadway and Elm Street. Over time, it had been paved in brick and established as a picnic and arts spot. Some of the most well-situated businesses surrounded it on the edge of Yale. Staples like the university bookstore and some name brand labels but also a never-ending carousel of restaurants and other businesses rotating in and out of the area. It was where I had met Amy for noodles after I made my deal with the Devil, but even that eatery hadn't survived and was replaced with an upscale taco joint.

We sat at one of the larger built-in tables on the edge of the tiny park. Rob was sweating, and it wasn't from the heat. He drummed his fingers nervously on the table and kept scanning the pedestrians coming and going for our quarry.

"Chill out, Rob. Have a fry." I gestured at the paper cone of fried wedges in front of me. I had insisted on stopping by an Indian street food place two blocks from our meetup to grab something to settle my stomach.

"How can you eat? Aren't you nervous?"

"Of course I am, but an empty stomach doesn't help your nerves. Besides, I'm not saying I'm used to this level of stress, but it's telling when I'm not too bothered by it. Could things go sideways? Absolutely. Will I be able to handle everything better if I'm fed? Also yes."

He sighed and picked a perfect, golden-brown fry from the pile and bit into it. His face changed from sullen to curious. "What are these?"

"*Idli* fries."

"That doesn't explain these." He took another mouthful, clearly enjoying himself. I was glad to give him the momentary distraction, if nothing else.

"Arjun recommended the place. They're rice cakes cut, fried, salted, and spiced. Amazing, right?"

He nodded and was about to have another when his eyes focused on something over my shoulder. I swiveled, and three people were walking in our direction. Lee led the pack, a storm cloud hanging over his head and fire in his eyes. Cole looked much the same as when we had last seen him, but his demeanor was more stoic than Lee's.

I glanced back to Rob, and there was relief on his face. Lester was, to my eye, unharmed, and from Rob's expression, he would have agreed. The hardness that had been present since Cole had tried to kidnap him was gone, if only for the moment where he was taking in Lester's appearance. He made to rise, but I gave a minute wave to keep him seated. Their reunion would have to wait until after we'd negotiated Lester's release.

The steel returned to his gaze as he turned it on Lee. I swiveled to face our incoming guests as they reached the table. Lee sat, but Cole remained standing behind a nervous-looking Lester.

"What did you do?" Lee asked, before I could even greet him.

We were in a public place, but I wanted as many assurances as I could get. The Cormicks were a traditional lot, and enemies respected formalities in certain cultures. I placed a fresh packet of fries in front of him. "Share some food with us. I was trying for traditional bread and salt, but this will have to do."

"A formal declaration of safe harbor?" He grinned, despite his clearly foul mood, and unwrapped the snack. "Perhaps you're not the fool I took you for." Biting into one, he nodded and gestured for Cole to do the same. The broad man swiped a fry and popped the whole thing into his mouth, crunching appreciatively. "Now.

Again. What did you do? I can't reach Eoghan anymore, and I assume you're to blame."

"I'm going to explain our conflict and give you a chance to make the right choice."

"Bold of you, deciding what the right choice is. Don't you work for Satan?"

"We all have our flaws, Lee. That just doesn't happen to be one of mine. Yes, I'm employed by the Devil, but I don't mistreat souls. You didn't build the largest part of your business around connecting loved ones with their dead relatives. No, it's trapping souls and extorting their families until you drain their finances dry."

"I'm still not clear how it's your business."

"We're in the business of souls, Lee. But a different line. We want souls to go where they're *supposed* to go. Not where we *decide* they go. You're playing God, at least a little bit. Taking those decisions out of the hands of the souls in Limbo."

"So, what's the proposal?"

I nodded to Rob, who picked up the negotiation. "First, you stop all communication with souls in Limbo for the purposes of impacting their journey upwards or downwards. Anything that would make them self-aware and spiral."

"*That's* first?" Lester cried, shifting forward to glare at Rob.

Rob kept his calm, to his credit. He glanced at Lester and must have mouthed something at him, because Lester leaned back again, mollified. Rob continued. "Second, you agree to stop exploiting the souls of your clients and never imbue an object with a soul again."

"Is there a third part of your ultimatum?" Lee asked, an insolent smirk plain on his face.

"Yes. Third, you free any of the spirits you've trapped so far and lay them to rest."

Lee tapped his chin, appearing to consider our demands. "Well, unless you boys have an offer for me I don't see why I would agree to any of—"

Rob pulled a glass figurine from the satchel lying at his feet and placed it gently on the table in front of him.

"What the *hell* is this?" Lee spat.

The statue was small, maybe eight inches tall, and held the likeness of Eoghan Cormick in his Sunday best. The detail was exquisite, even better than the statues Lee used. It was obvious who the statue represented, even from a distance. The malevolent look on Eoghan's face was in glorious detail.

"Say hello to your great-great-grandfather, Lee."

Lee grabbed at the statue, but Rob was quicker and swept it off the table and into his possession before Lee could reach halfway across the table. "Careful. We don't know if these are nearly as durable as the ones you've been producing. The process is a bit different, and I wouldn't take any chances." He placed the statue back in front of him when Lee withdrew his hands.

"How can I be sure you're not full of shite."

"How close do you need to be? To talk with him?"

He reached hesitantly and laid his arm on the cold metal of the tabletop, palm out toward the statue, and closed his eyes. It was only a moment before they flew open again, and he recoiled in his seat. "You bastards."

"Now, now, Lee," I said, gesturing at Rob to put the statue away, which he stowed while I continued my conversation. "I think we're beyond petty insults. We're all professionals here."

"Alright, so you've got Eoghan. What makes you think this'll convince us to give up our business? Eoghan took a vow, same as the rest of us, for the good of the family. You've got him trapped in a little knickknack there, but it doesn't change anything."

I didn't believe Lee was serious for a moment. We had him on the ropes and off guard from his reaction to seeing the figurine.

Now that he'd confirmed it was really his ancestor, we would have to seal the deal. I nodded to Rob to take over again.

"We considered it, and I think you're going to be impressed with what we've done. This type of conflict encourages innovation, and we're pushing the boundaries here."

"Oh hell, don't monologue at me," Lee said, rubbing his face with his hands.

Rob laughed, and it was a bitter sound. I hoped whatever resolution we came to would happen quickly, and we could get him back on the right path. I was concerned with the lengths he went to in order to make this happen, but I couldn't blame him, given the stakes.

"Fine," Rob said, biting off his words. "It's not only a piece of glass, Lee. It's an echo chamber."

"Come on, what the hell do you mean?"

"You're a smart man, Lee. You gave us the inspiration for this. The souls you summoned are going crazy, right? Well, for every soul you trap in a physical object, Eoghan Cormick suffers the same. He's resting comfortably now, but if you so much as nudge another soul into the physical world, he'll start experiencing their anguish. It's an amplifier. So, the more you produce, the worse it gets for him."

Lee's eyes were steely, and Cole looked like he wanted to punch something. Lee spoke between gritted teeth. "So you want me to stop helping people because of the harm I'm supposedly doing, but you're fine with torturing my ancestors."

"We all know 'helping people' isn't your goal," Rob said. "So stop pretending."

"Give me a moment. You," Lee said, pointing at Lester. "Stand right there, and don't budge. You'll see your man in a minute if you're lucky." He nodded to Cole who followed him to a corner of the patio, out of earshot. They kept their eyes on us but talked quietly among themselves.

"I hope this works," Rob said. "They could decide one soul is worth sacrificing."

"Did we promise to not do this to any of their other relatives?"

"Well, no. I guess we didn't."

"Then I'd say there's an implied threat represented by that malevolent hunk of glass."

Rob shrugged but did look less worried. He was making eyes at Lester, his brow furrowing. "Baby, did they treat you okay?"

Lester gave an exaggerated sigh. "It wasn't the Ritz, but they were mostly gentlemen about it." There was a hitch in his voice, belying the calm tone he affected. I could see he was eager to be free from his captivity. He wasn't bound like Cole had been, but he was clearly uncomfortable.

Rob's muscles were tense, outlined through his clothes. I knew he wanted nothing more than to jump from his chair and hold Lester, but the necessity of our negotiations prevented him from acting. His relief was evident when Lee finally walked back over and took his seat.

"Well?" Rob asked.

Lee clucked his tongue at Rob but addressed me. "Tsk. A little anxious? Your boy here needs some lessons in parlay, doesn't he?"

"Leave him be. You've got his partner. What do you expect?"

"Fair enough. What kind of deal is this? Handshakes? Paper? Electronic signature?"

"I think we understand each other well enough for a hand-shake," I said.

"So let's be absolutely clear. We don't muck about with souls in Limbo anymore, and you won't design a new line of glass statuary from the Cormicks currently resting in Hell?"

I gave a broad smile. "That's right. We also get Lester back, and no more strong-arm tactics."

Lee nodded, though it appeared to be mostly to himself, as if he was still considering his choices. "What about the souls already out there in the world, resting comfortably in their little vessels? Will those hurt Eoghan?"

"We're not monsters," I said. "Even though this is a little more draconian than my usual flavor of deal. But you didn't give us much of a choice."

"I'll agree to free any of the spirits we're able to, but we get to keep doing the psychic business."

"So long as you're not messing with the ones in Limbo trying to get them to move or imprisoning them, we're not going to stop you from communicating with them." From what Lu had said, it wasn't likely we could have done that anyway without explicit agreement from the Cormicks themselves. It was good he assumed we would have been able to stop them.

Lee nodded, looked at Cole, and said, "It was fun while it lasted, wasn't it?" Then he turned to me and thrust out his hand. "You've got a deal."

I shook the man's hand and felt a familiar flare behind my eyes. Lee startled and tried to pull free, his grip on my hand loosening. He stared from his palm to me and back again, as if expecting there to be a burn or mark of some kind. I tried to suppress my own shock. I'd have to see Lu about what happened, but I wasn't going to betray any of my own surprise.

"What the hell was that?"

"You keep asking that question. We made a deal. Now, let's talk about the existing statues you've got."

He stopped examining his hand, and the smile returned to his face. "What are you going on about?"

"All the souls you've trapped so far. You said you'd free them."

"Wasn't part of the deal," Lee replied.

I goggled at him. "Excuse me?"

"It wasn't. Part. Of. The. Deal. I said we'd free all the spirits we're able to. Well, the number is zero."

I couldn't believe I had put myself in this position. It might as well have been amateur hour. I chided myself as my mind churned on what the next phase of our plan would be. The part I made up on the fly.

"You see," Lee continued, "we can't release them. Never figured out how, and it wasn't high on the priority list. Most of them aren't in our possession, anyway. We don't keep track of them once they leave our hands. If the families didn't want them? Well, people pay a pretty penny for something as precious as a soul."

"You're kidding me."

"Would I lie to you? No, don't answer that. Of course I would. But in this case? I'm not. You did a good job putting us over a barrel on this one. I'm glad to return the favor."

"And we get to clean up your mess?" Rob asked.

Lee smiled and stood. "Well, it's your problem now, isn't it?"

Chapter 23

Nick

Rob and Lester's reunion was sweet, but I wouldn't be able to give them a lot of time before I needed Rob's help again. They were sitting at the table where Lee and Cole had vacated, with Lester perched on Rob's lap. Rob was holding him around the middle, with his head buried in Lester's chest.

"What did you two do?" Lester asked. He looked well enough, but his eyes were haunted in a way I found familiar. Captivity did that to a person.

"I walked into Hell to get you back," Rob said, and Lester eyed him quizzically.

"He's not exaggerating," I said, patting Rob on the back. "It was good work."

"Thanks, Boss."

"It's not like we cut them off from their entire business, only the sketchiest portion of it." I ran my hands through my hair, the fatigue from our encounter settling into my bones. I wasn't going to mention Rob's slide back toward his more ruthless side. That was between him and his therapist. Despite my faith in it being a temporary measure, rather than an indicator of future problems, I filed my concern away for consideration down the road.

Rob turned to me, and as if on cue, a cloud passed over us, casting a shadow across his face. "We solved some of this mess. What do we do with the rest of it?"

I had been thinking about it, and it was possible Lee left us with the bigger part of the problem. It was a stupid mistake, not ensuring the release of any spirits captured by Cormick and associates. Without a clear count from them or enough data from Adam to zero in on a number, we had no idea what we were dealing with. It was an improvement, stopping the tally from increasing, but it was like containing a house fire instead of extinguishing it. It burned merrily in the confines of the box we had placed the problem in, but it was nowhere near out.

It was also still not my only issue, even from the perspective of troubled souls. The pen from Arjun weighed heavily in my pocket, my obligation to judge Meghna's efforts sitting squarely on my shoulders. Rob and Lester were still mooning over each other, forgetting my existence.

"Hey, Rob. Take Lester home. You've earned a break. I've got to deal with the Elephas in the room."

Rob had perked up when I mentioned a break but groaned at the pun and was nodding along by the time I finished speaking. "Okay, thanks. We'll, uh, see you later?"

Despite the sun returning from behind the clouds, banishing the shade, my energy didn't return. This had drained me, and the smile I plastered across my face was all for show. "Sure, I'll text if I need you before tomorrow."

Lester stood, abandoning Rob's lap, and grabbed me around the ribs in a quick embrace. "I don't know what you did," he whispered into my ear, "but you did good. You're being too hard on yourself. I can see it on your face."

"It's part of my charm," I said into his, then pulled back and held him by the shoulders. "It's good to see you."

"Work on it one step at a time. You can't eat the whole elephant at once," Lester said.

Rob grimaced. "I don't think you can say that."

Lester shared Rob's uncomfortable look, then shrugged. They walked off toward Rob's car.

"Don't worry about me," I called after them with as much sarcasm as I could muster. "I'll call a rideshare or something." And just like that, it was me and my thoughts standing alone in the Broadway Triangle.

I sat, closed my eyes, and let the sun bake the ennui from my body for a solid minute. Then I pulled my phone out and dialed Meghna. When she answered, I didn't waste any time.

"Unless you think something is going to change in the next week, it's decision time. Take an hour, but we need to meet, and you can tell me which direction you're going in."

"Okay, Nick. I think you're right." Her voice was soft and resigned.

"One more thing…can you pick me up? I need a ride."

Meghna was gracious enough to drive us to one of the other local coffee shops to talk. It wasn't The Fix but a trendy new place over on Audubon Street. It was full of shiny copper and dark wood and had a gastropub vibe. They served cocktails as well as the usual caffeinated fare, and it had already been a day, so I ordered myself a Kahlua and club soda.

It was a simple drink but cold and refreshing besides being subtly alcoholic. My mother introduced me to the pairing a long time ago, and it was an occasional habit I had picked up from her.

I wasn't much of a drinker, but when you brought coffee liqueur into the mix, you had my attention.

I offered to buy Meghna something, and she chose a green tea blend, declining anything boozy. We sat at a small bistro table, stirring our respective drinks aimlessly. Something in the air told me it was going to be a conversation neither of us wanted to have, but I was running short on patience for other people's problems.

"I'm going to take the deal," she said in a matter-of-fact tone.

I was the one who had suggested Gaja's offer as an opportunity to give herself and her descendants more time, but a pang of guilt twanged in my chest. "I had a feeling that might be the case, but can you tell me why?"

"Going against my parents' wishes, ruining the life my great-grandfather sacrificed for? The idea of it makes my skin crawl. I don't want to condemn my children and theirs to an eventual fate of servitude, but it's hard to deny it's the simplest answer for right now."

"Maybe you can convince them?" I protested, but my heart wasn't in it. I knew the answer as much as she did.

"You don't come from an Indian family, Nick. It may be the modern era, but they don't encourage young women like me to make momentous decisions affecting the entire family. I'll go to school, build a career, but in the end, my father will expect me to heed his counsel, and right now he believes we are on the path Lord Ganesha has set for us."

"But what do *you* think?"

"That I'm stuck in the middle with no good choices. So rather than crying about it and not making any, I'm going to pick the least disruptive one for my family. For now, anyway."

I nodded while sipping my drink. My head was full of the potential futures ahead of her. "I respect your decision. Frankly, I'm not sure what I'd do in your place."

She laid her hand on mine, resting on the table. "Thank you for everything, Nick. You did your best. I'm the one making this complicated. I came looking for help, but maybe it was too late in the game to change course. I'm going to do my best to fix this, but it may not be for a generation or two, if ever. I have to come to terms with it."

We stayed like that for a moment, and if I could read anything in her expression, it was a calm acceptance. At least she was making peace with her choices. Sometimes it was all a person could do.

"I'm glad I could help. Well, try to, anyway."

We finished our drinks, and Meghna dropped me off in front of my apartment. When I got upstairs and situated myself on the couch, Odin came to comfort me. It should have been a triumphant moment, but I was still kicking myself for what happened with Cormick. A rumbling twenty-pound cat does wonders for nerves, and he placed himself firmly in the middle of my lap to shake all of them out of me.

I took out my phone and texted Amy, realizing it had been more than a few hours since I'd heard from my girlfriend. We had spent the previous night apart, and I had no intention of sleeping alone after the day I had.

NICK:

I'd love some company, if you're up for it. I don't know how deep in witchy business you're in right now.

AMY:

knock knock

NICK:

???

I jumped when a key turned in the deadbolt and Amy walked in, a small white box tucked under her arm.

"How did you know?" I asked, standing and rushing over to grab her in a long embrace. The warmth of her arms wrapped around me melted some of the tension from my shoulders.

"Rob texted," she said, breaking away to place her package on the coffee table. "He told me you'd had a rough afternoon, so I brought pastries. I thought you might need some sweets, a cuddle, and a sounding board."

"You're a godsend." I untied the knotted red-and-white string and opened the box to reveal my favorite cookies in the universe. There was something about someone knowing you so well they could bring targeted comfort food. I might have teared up if I wasn't so drained from the day, but the relief flooding through my body must have been evident.

Amy smiled at me and tilted her head to one side. "Did I do good?"

"You did better than that."

The humble rainbow cookie was a sliver of heaven—tricolor almond cake and raspberry filling coated in dark chocolate. I plucked a square out of the pile and took a bite, my lips immediately messy with chocolate. I savored the mouthful, sighing audibly and letting the last of my stress melt away. If I had to pick a last meal, I would be hard-pressed to not end it with one of those confections.

Amy let me have my moment, but concern reflected in her eyes when I finished enjoying my treat. "What happened?"

"It's complicated." I told her how things went down with the Cormicks in excruciating detail. She laid her hand on my arm when I got to the part where I absolutely dropped the ball on ensuring we freed the souls Lee had captured. I went as far as my last conversation with Meghna and the disappointing outcome there. My stomach churned, the sweet in my stomach souring as

I made my way through the tale. When I finished, she was curled alongside me on the couch, her head resting on my shoulder.

"Do you want solutions or comfort?"

I wrapped my arms around her and drew us down to lie on the couch. "Comfort first, then you can hit me with any suggestions you have." We stayed snuggled for a solid ten minutes. I played with Amy's hair, and she traced the stitching on my shirt with her fingers. I always said it was the quiet moments I cherished the most, and that held true. The soft vanilla scent of her hair filled my nose, and our chests rose and fell together, our breathing synchronized.

I was beating myself up for a mistake anyone could have made, and now wasn't the time to wallow in it. Slowing down and letting my mind catch up with the day's events was what I needed, whether I knew it or not.

I took a deep breath and let it out in a resigned huff. "Alright, hit me."

The slap was light but so unexpected it made my brain do a hard reset. Amy sat bolt upright, holding her hands to her mouth in apparent horror. I laid there, brow furrowed, trying to determine how I felt.

"Oh my gods, I didn't mean to smack you so hard. You were so serious and brooding I couldn't help myself."

I touched my hand to my cheek, but it wasn't even warm. "You didn't. It was just surprising. Maybe next time, don't let the intrusive thoughts win?" I smiled involuntarily. "But I understand the impulse. I think it did what you wanted though. I am thoroughly distracted from my moping."

She dropped her hands to reveal a sheepish grin, and we shared a giggle as I levered myself upright again.

"Okay, shoot—" I paused as soon as the word passed my lips. "You don't have a gun, do you?"

She laughed out loud and shook her head. "No, of course I don't. Now you're teasing."

"You're the one showing a sudden penchant for casual domestic violence," I retorted with Amy looking thoroughly scandalized. I took the opportunity and leaned in for a quick kiss. "Yes, I'm teasing. Please, tell me about your ideas."

Her face lit up, and she grabbed her satchel from where she had left it next to the couch. "It's not so much an idea as an update. I told you I had some experiments to run on releasing a spirit from the statues, right?"

"You did. Did you have any luck? Given my screw-up with Cormick, we could use any kind of success right now."

"I'll give you a solid 'maybe.' Look at this." She drew the golfer's statue out of her bag and placed it on my coffee table.

As far as I could tell, it was in exactly the same state as it was the last time I saw it. "What am I supposed to be noticing?"

"Patience, love." She rolled her eyes and continued rummaging in her bag. I was apparently not supposed to take her literally.

Amy pulled a few more odds and ends from her purse and set up shop in front of her. She placed a black cloth with a pentacle in the middle of the space, similar to the one she used to read Tarot. She then put the statue in the middle. Amy sterilized a sewing needle in the flame of a small lighter and set it atop the cloth as well. I kept my mouth shut as she continued her preparations.

"I don't expect anything to happen, but I'm going to cast a small circle to contain the spirit if I manage to mess something up."

"That doesn't sound entirely promising."

"Hush," she said, not unkindly.

She closed her eyes and positioned her hands as if holding an invisible sphere as big around as the circle on the table. I had never been particularly sensitive to the work Amy did, but I could almost perceive something coalescing in the space between her palms. It was like a soap bubble—iridescent, clear, and ephemeral. As soon as I noticed it, it was gone, or at least invisible.

Amy picked up the needle and poked her index finger with it, squeezing a tiny drop of blood to the surface. She was muttering something, a chant of some kind. "Blood...soul...call to you..." I couldn't make out all the words. She extended her finger across the boundary of the circle, and as soon as it crossed the threshold, there was a low whine. It was nearly imperceptible but nagged my inner ear like a painful vibration.

The closer she got to touching the statue, the louder it was, until finally the noise in my ears built to a fever pitch, and I shouted, "Please, stop!"

Amy withdrew her hand, and the sound died at once. "I didn't realize you could hear it too," she said.

"I'm sorry. I didn't want to interfere, but I was worried whatever you were doing was going to release the spirit."

"It's okay, you're right to be cautious. Sometimes I go farther than I should. It's why we have each other, right?" She smiled, then sucked on the finger she had stuck. "I found that blood called to the spirit, and I'm working on a spell to draw the spirit out enough to let us destroy the statues."

I grabbed her by the shoulders, and her eyes widened in surprise when I kissed her firmly. "You're brilliant."

"Thanks, but I don't know what the noise is—"

I didn't let her finish because I knew exactly what it was, and it wasn't good. "It's the screaming," I said, letting the simple statement hang in the air.

She blanched. "Oh. Right. Forgot about that part. Did they explain why the souls they mess with in Limbo go crazy? It didn't make any sense, on the face of it."

"I've given it a lot of thought actually. I didn't have a clue about Purgatory before this case, and what I learned from both Lu and Leslie indicated it was a place for quiet reflection. The souls simply exist, on their own, undisturbed, as they contemplate their lives and either float up or down. Eventually, they're supposed to make it to the shores of Heaven or Hell, right?"

"I guess. But why does it matter if Lee contacts them?"

"You know how you take baths sometimes, and you lose track of time? You've told me about it, where you float and get lost in thought and then an hour has gone by, and the water is cold."

"Okay, I'm following so far."

"I'm going to assume Purgatory is like a sensory deprivation tank. It's constant temperature, comfortable floating, and there's nothing to indicate the passing seconds. Real people often have a problem with those tanks, but for the sake of argument, let's say souls are fine there."

"Assumption noted," she said.

"Great. Psychics can communicate with spirits, including the ones in Purgatory. But for them, it's like a passing conversation or a memory. It happens as a brief interlude and then fades away. Like a single ripple in a still pond."

"But this isn't the same."

"No. It's like throwing rocks repeatedly into the pool until there are enough ripples that they crash into each other. Trying to influence a soul makes it more self-aware. It's reintroduced to the concept of linear time. Except it's trapped in a sensory deprivation chamber."

Amy's mouth hung open. "Holy shit."

"It's why they put them in these," I said, flicking the statue with a finger, "little stasis pods. Somehow it stops the clock and lets them rest."

Amy whistled a low note. "That sounds worse than Hell."

"It does, indeed. I think we've done enough experimenting for one night, but it looks like you're on the right track."

Amy packed her things back into her bag, including the statue.

"We have no idea how many of those figurines exist or where they are right now," I said, settling back into the couch. "But it almost doesn't matter. We can't free them if we don't know how to keep them from going insane. If only we had a fast track…"

"I can smell the light bulb burning out in there," Amy said, watching me as the gears turned quickly in my mind.

"I have an idea, but it's a long shot."

Amy sat next to me on the couch, draping her legs over mine. "Is it something that needs to happen in the next hour or two? Or can we do something totally mundane? Like watching a movie and going to bed?"

I laughed and grabbed one of her feet, massaging it. She let out a low moan and collapsed like a rag doll against the cushions. "It can keep until tomorrow. I have to check in on a project and talk to an old friend."

"Are you feeling more optimistic?" she asked, a glimmer in her eye.

"About more than a few things, actually." I deserved some respite, so for the rest of the night, I didn't think of much beyond Amy and me. Much to Odin's displeasure.

CHAPTER 24

AMY

I had work in the morning, so I woke to the gentle chime of my alarm. I managed to turn it off before it disturbed Nick. He deserved as much rest as he could get. It was rare I got myself up before he even made his coffee. His face was relaxed, mouth slightly open in a gentle snore. So much of his energy turned to anxiety and worry. I savored a minute of him at peace, then did my best to tiptoe out of bed.

"Hey," Nick muttered, his voice muffled by the pillow. "Do you have to go?"

I leaned in and kissed him on the forehead. "I need to stop in at home and check on Pants before I head into the library. Not everyone makes their own schedule." My tone was teasing, and it must have landed well enough, because he smiled.

"Text me later, okay?"

"Of course. Get some more sleep. You'll need it to save the world later."

He snorted and snuggled deep into the blankets again. "Not the world, maybe the city. Like Batman," he said through a yawn. "Or a square block. I'm a low-rent superhero..." His voice trailed off into mumbles, and he was already asleep again.

I chuckled quietly and got myself up and ready to go, splashing water on my face and brushing my teeth before heading out the door. It was a quick ride to my apartment, and I thanked the gods nothing was amiss when I opened the door. Since Siobhan had easier access to me with the spirit collar, she hadn't seen fit to run Pants all over the apartment again to get my attention.

The statue weighed heavily in my satchel, so I placed it on the coffee table for relative safekeeping. It was indestructible, but any glass statuary in a house with a cat made me nervous on principle. Once Pants was fed, I shed my clothes and hopped in the shower. I hated putting on a clean outfit without bathing. It was something I could accept in other people but not for myself. My brain wouldn't allow me to get dressed and leave for work if I didn't, even if it was only a quick rinse.

The near scalding water hit my skin, and I shivered with goose bumps from the temperature change. My mind wandered as I scrubbed myself, contemplating the day. I couldn't go any farther in my experimentation without actually releasing one of the souls if it worked the way I expected it to.

Nick's explanation of why it wasn't safe to free them yet made sense, but my shudder wasn't from the heat. I didn't want to dwell too much on that particular issue when I had problems of my own. What was the next step in finding the source of Manannán's problem? Siobhan had said something about war with the Cormicks, but that didn't seem to be the case.

The shower thought struck me hard, and I rolled my eyes at myself. Maybe she wasn't warning me about a conflict with the Cormicks but was trying to spell something longer. The amount of time we had to "speak" wasn't long. If she was burning through her and Pants's, reserves before finishing? It would explain why I misinterpreted her message.

Time was getting away from me. I was walking between the bathroom and my bedroom, toweling off my hair, when something caught my eye. The statue was gone, and when I stopped long enough to take in the scene, Pants was asleep next to where it used to be on the table.

"Pants!" I rushed over and found the golfer in one piece, lying on the floor. The collar, which Pants had worn since the night I performed the familiar ceremony, hung off a protruding piece of glass.

I had never needed to keep tags on Pants. She was an indoor cat since I rescued her, but it was supposed to be a good practice in case they ever got loose. I tried to keep a safety collar on her for a short period of time, but she hated it so much that she would snag it on anything lying around to rip it off. The one I used for the spell was an older buckle style, so I had to keep it loose enough she wouldn't choke, but tight enough she couldn't slip it off casually.

She looked up and bared her teeth in a gaping yawn before sitting on her haunches, staring at me. She protested slightly when I put the collar back on her, pawing at me, but didn't make any motions to remove it once reattached. "I'm sorry that you don't like it, bug. But you have to put up with it for a while longer, okay?"

I gave the golfer a once-over to ensure it was unharmed. My heart raced despite the fact that I knew nothing could have broken the figure, but better safe than sorry. I checked the clock and swore. I was going to be late if I didn't move my ass.

Traffic was on my side, and I made it under the wire. The day itself was an odd one, and I spent a fair amount of it mentally cataloging where I was while physically cataloging my share of books for the day. It always felt strange when a door closed on a project, and enough balls were in the air that I needed to perform the mental inventory.

I had done what research I could into Meghna's problem, but it was moot at this point, anyway. She was making the best choice for herself and her family, playing the long game, but that didn't make the situation any less disappointing for Nick. I knew he looked forward to the resolution of his cases, and even though this one had a different provenance, he had leaned into it. I wouldn't consider any of it work wasted. We all learned more about the Hindu pantheon, but I didn't need to spend any brainpower there anymore.

The case Rob had uncovered, which led to the Cormicks, was fascinating. The hunk of glass resting on the table at home was proof there was still more to do. I was so close to a solution to freeing the trapped souls, and I was proud of myself for following the breadcrumbs Manannán had left for me. I tried to wrap my head around the fact that an unknown number of lost souls were drawn out of Purgatory for nefarious purposes. It was good they had stopped the mountain from growing, but now it was more like an iceberg. They only saw the tip protruding from the water, but the bulk of their problem hid below the surface.

Then I had *my* problem. The task Manannán had set for me was to find whatever was keeping souls from being able to cross the veil. I had missed the opportunity to question Siobhan about her message, distracted as I was by Pants slipping her collar. I'd have to make that a priority when I got home. Regardless, Siobhan was my only lead so far, and her help had been variable at best due to the limitations of the spell.

The choice was between talking with Siobhan through the Ouija board or through her playing pounce and chase with Pants. The second option was unreliable at best and terminally slow at worst. Possession had limited timing and tired them both out, so I couldn't use a combination of the two even though I'd thought about it.

The returns wouldn't shelve themselves, so after lunch I wandered the stacks with a cart. I was musing on my options when it occurred to me I hadn't told Mel about my run-in with another god.

AMY:

> I'm sorry for not texting sooner, but I took your advice and tried to contact my patron.

MEL:

> AND?!

AMY:

> It worked! You were right. It was Manannán. I'd love to tell you about it and get your thoughts on the next part of the problem.

MEL:

> Welcome to the coven, girlie. It's part of what we do. Come round the shop after work?

AMY:

> Perfect, thank you!

I tucked my phone away with a smile. I had never had "girlfriends" growing up, as the weird kid who wore too much black. Being part of the coven, even as a seeker, was shaping up to be an entirely new experience for me. I had people in my life I could rely on, this wasn't about that. Nick was a rock, and Rob had turned into a great friend despite earlier challenges, but I could admit my background was short on estrogen.

The winding path I had taken passed by my "private" research area, and I traced my finger along the cover of *Spirits and Symbolism*, which I had brought with me to return to its shelf. I placed the book in its spot and ran my finger along the spine. "I guess I won't be needing you anymore. For now, anyway."

The Beehive was closing by the time I made it there after my shift. Tori was ushering the last of the customers out of the shop as usual. She greeted me as I came through the door, the patrons eyeing me suspiciously because I was clearly going the "wrong way" as they exited.

Before I could ask, "Where's Mel?" I was enveloped in a bear hug and lifted off the ground. I did manage to squeak, "Jeez, Mel!" before being muffled by a generous bosom.

"Sorry, dear," Mel said, putting me down with relative care. "I should ask first, but once I know someone's a hugger, I get carried away."

"It's alright," I said, face warm from the short restriction of blood to my head. "Is it only you and me, or is the rest of the coven around?"

"Just us chickens. Tori! Would you be a dear and close up? I'm taking Amy here downstairs for a chat. Lock up behind you. I'll do the final sweep before I head out."

We quickly found ourselves in the study area of the ritual room with the electric kettle on. Mel was one of those people who was forever a step away from making tea, which also fit her personality as a matron and host. She sat heavily with an "oof" while the water boiled.

"It has *been a day*," she said, removing her granny boots and massaging her feet. "Summer is so busy, lots of tourists, and we're the 'weird store.'" She chuckled to herself.

I took the book of Celtic mythology out of my bag and placed it on the table, pushing it over to her. "Thank you for the loan. It was helpful."

"Of course! I'm glad it worked. Tell me everything!" She bustled about, setting a pot to brew but glancing back over to show me she was still listening.

The difference between talking about my magic with Nick and Mel was stark. I started the tale, and Mel's eyes lit up when I got to my ritual. The story poured out of me with that kind of interest, and I went into painstaking detail on the ceremony itself. She even "oohed" a few times, when a bit of symbolism caught her interest. I was particularly proud of it. Her face held an air of contemplation when I finally talked about the task Manannán had set for me.

"Well, that explains a lot," she said, choosing a biscuit from the plate she had brought over with the tea set.

"It does?" I put a few sugar cubes into my tea and added milk.

"At least I hope so. Spirits have been acting weird. I told you when we first discussed all this. If there's a force dragging all the spirits down, the 'gravity' he was talking about, it makes sense."

I sipped my tea. She had made a delicious English Breakfast, and it was soothing my nerves, but I still had an undercurrent of worry. "How am I going to find the source, though?"

Mel tapped at her chin, and we sat in tea-drinking silence for a minute, only broken by sips and slurps.

Something was dancing at the edges of my thoughts, spurred by the company and location. "How was it you found this place again?"

Her eyes lit up. "Dowsing! I hadn't thought of that in this situation, but if there's a single source, it might be worth a try."

"Do you have a dowsing rod I could borrow?"

"*Do* I?" She jumped from her seat and rushed to one corner of the basement. She came back holding a Y-shaped branch, brandishing it above her head triumphantly. "Here you go! I'd say it was the rod that found this place, but it would be toothpicks by now. But it's good quality hazel, and I used it in my last dowsing class, so I know it isn't a dud."

I accepted the stick from her and examined it, but it was exactly as she said. I had never dowsed before, but I understood the concept from books I had read. "Any pointers?"

"Let it guide you. It's like pendulums or Ouija. You can influence it with your thoughts and energy, so it's easy to lead yourself astray. If you trust it to draw you to your target, it should guide you to where you want to go."

"Too bad I can't dowse-and-drive. It's a big city."

Mel barked her usual laugh, echoing through the basement. "I can picture it now, but I expect you'd get pulled over. No, you'll have to do it on foot. You can try to skip ahead, but if you pass whatever it is, you'll end up backtracking. You'll figure this out."

"Thank you, Mel. For everything."

She blushed lightly and took herself back to the table to finish her tea. "Any time, Amy. I'm glad you're with us. I look forward to seeing your progression. You've got a bright future."

"We'll see how lucky I am with this first."

CHAPTER 25

AMY

I wasn't sure where to begin, so I took myself to the Green. It was a wide-open space in the center of downtown. New Haven was bigger than "where Yale is," but it was a reasonable place to start. No one paid you any mind wandering downtown if you kept to yourself. This changed, however, when you were carrying a big stick in front of you and walking around with your eyes closed.

The good news was that most of the attention I received was in the form of judging looks and people keeping their distance. Sometimes it paid to be one of the weirdos. It was hard to clear my mind, but I tried my best to use the meditation exercises I had practiced and let the hazel wand do its job.

Daylight was burning, so I had to come up with a plan of attack. If I found a direction from the dowsing rod, drove a few blocks, and tried again, maybe it would fast-forward what would otherwise be an excessively long evening walk. My self-preservation instincts kicked in enough for me to text Nick and Rob to warn them I'd be wandering into various parts of the city by myself. They told me to let them know if I needed any help but to otherwise "be

192

safe." We said that to each other a lot, but on reflection, it wasn't without reason.

Then I was off. I walked my way to the southeastern edge of the Green and tried for hop number one. I drove to a spot on Brown Street, two blocks farther from the park, and got out to test direction again. Once I confirmed my original heading, I did my best to continue in a direct line, but the streets didn't cooperate. I found myself going under the highway toward Long Wharf and stopped again on Hamilton Street to check my bearings.

That was where it got weird. The good news was I was having an easier time letting the tool do its thing once I had calibrated to it. I was getting relatively clear readings, for something without any indicators beyond the pointy end.

The bad news was instead of pointing southeast, like previously, the dowsing rod swung between northeast and southwest. I took myself to the northeast at the corner of Water Street and East Street for another reading. This time, it pointed directly east.

I pulled out my phone and opened the map app. Something about this was tweaking my brain. I placed pins for my dowsing spots on the map, starting at the Green, and a pattern emerged. Hopping back in the car, I headed southwest along Long Wharf Drive, making two more stops to dowse and make more pins.

In the end, I went analog and grabbed an emergency paper map of the state I kept in my glove box. I must have looked insane, parked along the water at one of the random picnic tables. A map was spread out in front of me, the cap of a pen in my mouth and one hand making marks while the other thumbed my phone. It was getting dark, and Nick texted me, checking in on how everything was going. My hyper focus had me, and all I could message back was, "Busy, come by later and I might have something to show you."

With enough data to go on, my mind extrapolated as I drove home. I took my steps two at a once. The map fluttered wildly in one hand. I barged through the door, startling Pants. There was no time to mollify her until I had run down my current train of thought, so I laid the map out on the kitchen table and fetched a compass from some of my art supplies.

When I finished, a wide circle encompassed most of the ports downtown. It stretched from Long Wharf to Grape Vine Point in Fair Haven to the northwestern part of East Point, where the container ships docked. My face flushed, elated, but I buzzed with frustration at the same moment. I had narrowed my search, but it was still a broad swath.

It was apparently Nick's turn to arrive with comfort food because he chose that moment to walk through the door holding takeout containers of ramen.

"Oh, bless you," I said, throwing the pen to one side and walking over to take a plastic bowl and give him a long kiss. He was still leaning forward, slightly off-balance, when I broke away and brought my bounty back to the kitchen.

"What have we got here?" he asked, coming through the doorway and joining me at the table. He quirked an eyebrow, glancing at the circle I had drawn with big arrows around it pointing inward.

"I found something. At least, I hope so. I went to talk with Mel after work, and we had the idea of dowsing for whatever was keeping everything stuck on this side of the veil. It was easy enough to do, so the signal must have been super strong, but I hit a border, and all the rod would do was scribe a circle. Whatever it is, it's big, and it's somewhere inside this."

Nick had popped the containers and mixed the broth into both of our bowls, setting up for a quick meal. "That sounds promising."

"Yeah, but the center of the circle is over the water, so it's not exact."

"Unless you're going to need scuba gear."

My stomach knotted. The idea of having to dive to the bottom of a bay hadn't occurred to me, and anxiety pulled at my chest. "I sure as hell hope not."

"One problem at a time, and you're probably right. Inside but not at the center, makes more sense. I think Manannán would have told you if a sea monster was causing trouble in the Sound. It's getting late. Why don't we take a break and eat some calories? A little distance from the problem might help."

"You're right." I sighed, folding the map and grabbing chopsticks and spoons from a drawer.

We ate in a companionable silence. My after-work escapades had drained me more than I realized, and my shoulders slumped from the loss of adrenaline fueling my earlier discoveries. When we finished, I was heading directly toward a food coma and curled up on the couch with Nick to rest my eyes.

Something was wrong.

My head was swimming, and my eyes were open, but I didn't remember waking. I had practiced lucid dreaming occasionally, but this was nothing like it. I levered myself off Nick's chest, my stomach lurching and the imbalance in my head nearly bringing my dinner screaming back up.

AMY! a voice screamed in my head.

It was as if I were sitting as a passenger behind my own eyes. My arms and legs were working without my volition, and I tried to concentrate on wrenching control from whatever was moving me like a marionette.

"Amy?" Nick asked groggily in a gentle voice.

I managed to push a muffled "Mmph" from my lips but then jerked to my feet like a scarecrow on wobbly legs.

Stop fighting me! It was a woman's voice, softer this time, and I started to parse what was happening. I clutched Pants's collar in one of my hands, hooked over my thumb, the cabochon radiating heat like a hunk of coal in a forge.

Siobhan? I thought, trying to shake my head like I could force her out of my mind.

No reply came, and my body made its way with quick but clumsy steps into the kitchen. It was as if my limbs were asleep, being thrown around by a force unfamiliar with them. The hand not holding the collar grasped the map and shook it open, then grabbed the pen and stuffed the cap between my teeth, biting down with disproportionate force. Bitter ink flooded my mouth, but my arm kept moving until it was making rough marks on the map. It was haphazard but targeted, as I continued fighting for control.

I rallied my strength and pushed with all my might against the possession, gathering my power and forcing it through my body.

"GET...OUT!" I yelled through gritted teeth before collapsing onto the floor in sudden relief.

The sense of dislocation which had flooded me ebbed, and the heat from the pendant diminished, though the sting from a welt on my hand remained. My breath came in ragged gasps, and as my equilibrium returned, my eyes closed, and I was dead to the world.

CHAPTER 26

ROB

Lester's recovery was swift. Maybe a little too swift. I took him home from the meeting, and after a long shower, he collapsed into bed for the rest of the afternoon. He was in good spirits, smiling at my attempts to engage. I wasn't sure what he needed, but did my best to be attentive. If I learned one thing during my stint as a villain, it was that everyone handled being kidnapped differently. Amy had been pretty nonchalant about it, but I was almost positive she knew I didn't have any intention of harming her.

Nick was different, having been through that particular circumstance twice, though only once at my hand. The first time, he bounced back quickly. The second took longer, mostly because the treatment he suffered at the hands of a Romanian tech oligarch was much worse than what I put him through.

Lester was his usual catty self, first gushing about how much better his water pressure was than where the Cormicks had kept him. Then complaining about having to make his own dinner, which I laughingly stepped in to do for him. One of the benefits of captivity, he said. The food wasn't great, by his account, but it showed up without him lifting a finger.

I asked him, periodically, how he was feeling. His response was always a smile with, "I'm fine, baby." I believed him, because it was what you did, and on top of that, it seemed to be true. We spent the evening cuddling on the couch, watching his favorite drag shows, and eating whatever comfort snacks he wanted. I made multiple trips to and from the kitchen, going as far as feeding him by hand just to be sweet.

We fell into bed together late that night, and after kissing him thoroughly, we curled up with my arms wrapped tightly around his chest and stomach. He was the little spoon. Despite his earlier nap, he drifted off, and the slow cadence of his breathing lulled me to my own slumber.

I woke to a text from Nick. At least he had waited the night before needing me for something.

NICK:

> I'm going to check in on Walt. Do you know where we are with Heaven on his project?

I was taking point on the church renovation. Walt's "deal" with Angel Co. was supposed to have been the first contract we oversaw as an independent agency, to test the changes Leslie's people made to their infrastructure.

They were so paranoid about the issues Nick had pointed out during his own trial run as a "diet angel" that Olivia, the project manager assigned on their side of the house, kept things humming smoothly while we were setting up the agency itself. I didn't have to do much beyond read her updates and make appreciative noises.

Everything was going to plan for the full renovation to be completed in another six months. The original estimate from Devil Co. was a bit generous. Reality, minus all the graft, was more like twelve months, and we were about halfway through. The commercial kitchen was about to go in, since the structural and other large cosmetic changes were complete.

ROB:

We're on track, no issues to report.

NICK:

Great. I need you to do me a favor. We may have to bring both parties to the table for something. I'd love it if Leslie attended Themselves but will settle for Their admin. Can you make that happen?

ROB:

Well, that sounds complicated. I'll do my best. What about Devil Co.?

NICK:

I hate asking so soon, but can you find out if Lester is okay trying to get Lu involved? Or handling it himself if Lu can't?

ROB:

He seems to be doing fine, so I'll do it, but reserve the right to tell you to go to Hell, if he isn't.

NICK:

Noted.

When I finished the exchange and looked up from my screen, Lester was awake and staring at me with a bemused expression on his face.

"And I thought *my* boss was demanding."

I blushed, flipping the phone over onto the nightstand. "I'm sorry—"

"I'm *fine,* baby. Seriously. I was there yesterday, I know you've got work to do."

"About that…"

"What does your over-caffeinated partner want?"

"He wants me to get both sides bought in for a meeting. I'm not sure what it's about, but I'm assuming it has to do with all the trapped souls. I'm going to talk to Leslie, or Their admin, myself but—"

"But you need my help with Lu."

I grimaced. "If you're up for it, I'd love it. I have to know if Lu would attend a meeting, or if he wants you to go instead of him. If it's not too much."

Lester lowered his eyes to the bedspread and took a deep breath before responding. "Once I knew they were holding me to get to you, I convinced myself that I wasn't in danger…"

"But…"

"But…I could tell they'd have done something to me if everything had gone sour. Lee was a polite monster but a monster nonetheless." He played with a corner of the comforter between his fingers.

"I wouldn't have let him hurt you," I said, sitting again and grasping his hands in mine.

"I believe you. You walked into Hell for me, right?" He gave me a wan smile, but it only made it halfway to his eyes.

"I'd do it again."

Lester laid his hand flat on my chest, over my heart. "I believe you. And I'll be okay. But this isn't about me anymore, right?"

"You shouldn't do anything you're not ready for."

Lester eyed me sideways, his mouth compressed in a flat line. "I'm not going to make anyone else deal with my boss. It'll take me a few days to decompress and a solid month or two with my therapist, but I'm well enough to handle whatever you need."

I kissed him on the forehead, then on the lips. "Thank you."

"You thank me properly later." He sighed dramatically, but the seriousness in his eyes belied his playful tone. "But alas, you've got too much to do for me to distract you right now."

I laughed and drew him down to the bed again. It turned out I wasn't so pressured I couldn't take a few minutes, more than a few minutes really, before I had to leave the townhouse. Sometimes you had to make time for something life-affirming when the world felt upside down.

A quick shower and a longer kiss later, I was out the door, heading downtown to Angel Co.'s offices. I told Lester I was going to stop by the archives to talk to Adam again and to text me if he needed anything while I was at the tower. I figured the least I could do was apologize again for what happened with Cole, but I also wanted Adam's take on the statues.

First things first though, I was striding through the lobby up to Elena's desk. She seemed to alternate between happy to see me and nervous about whether I was going to make another scene in her lobby.

"Rob! Hi!" She half stood from her seat.

"Hi, Elena, no time for hugs today."

She settled back down, looking a little disappointed. "What can I do for you?"

"I have to talk to Leslie, or if They're not available, I need your help as Their representative."

She blanched, clearly caught between reaching out to God Themselves and taking on additional responsibility. "Can you give me more than that?"

"Not much. It's a request from Nick. He's got something important going, and he needs to bring the two houses together."

"Like Romeo and Juliet?"

"Hopefully not. Too much underage weirdness and suicide. More like the Hatfields and the McCoys, probably."

Elena stared blankly at me.

"The two feuding families down South?" I said.

She opened her mouth, then closed it again.

"Never mind. I need someone to agree to a meeting with Hell's representatives."

She brightened, picked up her phone, and dialed what I hoped was Leslie's number. Did God have an extension, or would it have been all for show? Some questions would never be answered.

I turned to observe the rest of the room, pretending that there was some semblance of privacy. She spoke into the receiver in a hushed voice, so I couldn't make out either side of the conversation. Whatever they discussed, it didn't take long before she hung up and gave me a pained grimace.

"I'm not sure what you're up to, but you've got Their attention. One of us will be available for the meeting. Text me when it is, and I'll make sure we attend." She handed me her business card with her cell listed there. I added her contact information to my phone and gave the card back to her. I knew myself, and it would have just ended up in the trash.

"Thanks, Elena. I appreciate it." I retreated to the exit, already on to the next part of my mission for the day.

"Don't be a stranger!" she said cheerfully.

It was funny how much of a stranger I already was, compared to the people in the office. I hoped the changes we were influencing would be positive, but I didn't have time to worry about that now.

"Ouch!" I yelled, pulling my hand back from the buzzer next to Adam's door. I tried the door when I arrived and found it locked. A new doorbell hung to one side of it. I had pressed it—because why would I suspect something as simple as a *doorbell*—and received a small electric shock as a reward.

I crouched to stare at the plate holding the button, and with a jiggle, I determined it was loose. My fingernails bent slightly as I pried at it until it came away from the wall with a pop. Upon closer examination, a small battery was attached to the back, and someone had affixed the whole assembly to the wall with double-sided adhesive.

"What the hell, Adam!" No one was there to listen, and the door was too thick for anyone inside to hear me, but it felt good to yell about it. The glint of light off glass caught my attention. A small camera, which hadn't been there before, perched above the entry. I banged on the door while staring daggers into the tiny lens until the door swung open to reveal Adam, dressed in office casual, with a sour expression on his face.

"Come in, I guess," he said, turning and scurrying back inside.

I followed him in, scratching at the tip of my finger where I had been zapped. "I don't work here, but I doubt OSHA approves."

Adam laughed, but it didn't have any humor in it. He sat behind his desk and glared at me. "Do you know how many visitors I had before you came, Rob?"

"I'm going to hazard a guess and say zero."

"Correct! And since then, I've had multiple, plus abetting a felony—"

I raised my hand in objection. "*Probably* a felony." Adam glowered at me, and I lowered it sheepishly.

"Then the goon you stashed here knocked me unconscious."

"We're *very* sorry that happened. I hope you're alright. It's why I came to check on you."

"And another thing—" Adam paused mid-tirade. "You...came to check on me?"

"Of course! You were helping us out with Cole, and it got you in trouble. I was hoping to avoid that, despite it being a bit of our MO."

"Oh," he said through a small exhalation, the wind leaving his sails. "Uh, sorry about the buzzer. I figured it would deter most people."

"I understand the camera, Adam, but maybe skip the electrotherapy?" I placed the button on his desk with a click.

He blushed, chagrined. "Yeah..."

"How are you, though?"

"I'm okay. I freaked out in the moment, but honestly, it's the most exciting thing that's ever happened to me. Other than getting a job working for the Devil, of course." He chuckled to himself. "Imagine working for Lucifer getting old. But here I am."

I smiled at him, happy to have defused the situation as quickly as I did. "I'm glad you're alright. These are the stories we break out at parties." I licked my lips, hoping my next request wouldn't upset the balance I had achieved. "I know it's too soon, after your brush with criminal enterprise, but I could use your help."

Adam's eyes darkened. "I hope you didn't say all that to butter me up for a favor."

"No!" I exclaimed quickly, hesitation being the enemy of sincerity in a conversation like this. "It's a tough situation, Adam, and we've gotten ourselves in a bind." I explained what had happened with the Cormicks and their inability, and unwillingness, to free the souls they harvested from Purgatory. "I was hoping you'd have a suggestion on how to track them down."

Adam nodded and took off his glasses to clean them as he spoke. "You didn't tell me anything about this before. The statues, I mean. That's weird, for sure."

"I know. When we were here with Cole, we didn't have enough time to bring you up to speed. But you're a data guy. Do you have anything that might help?"

He tapped one arm of his glasses against his chin, then put them on again and swiveled to face his monitor. He gestured for me to come around the desk, so I situated myself to watch over his shoulder as he loaded a spreadsheet.

"There are fewer archivists than agents, so we tend to work together. Once I noticed a pattern of requests coming in without accompanying targets in Hell, I reached out to my network and started compiling data."

"Which led to you feeding us the files about the missing souls?"

"It did, eventually. But until then, I was just collating and analyzing the data."

He scrolled through the file, but it didn't make any sense to me. "What am I looking at?"

"Oh, right, hold on."

He switched to a different tab showing a map of the United States. Markers lay in different cities, and a heat map showed the concentrations of pins. Most were lightly spread across the country, with a few in Canada and Mexico, but the majority of them were in New England. Unsurprisingly, the largest population was in the tri-state area—Connecticut, New Jersey, and New York.

I whistled. "You weren't kidding about how many there were."

"This isn't going to help you figure out where the statues are. Not exactly. But it'll give you an idea of where to look. I have names and addresses for all the requestors, at the time of their submission."

"It's like tracking down the worst letters to Santa I've ever heard of. This is going to take a while..."

Adam laughed. "Better you than me. It's why I sit behind a desk!"

CHAPTER 27

NICK

I wasn't able to sleep for much longer after Amy left. Odin startled me awake when he decided my torso was a springboard for chasing a sunbeam or something equally ridiculous, and I had the air pressed out of me in a kind of "whargh" sound. I eyed him as I waited for my heart rate to return to normal. He sat contritely and licked his nose, which was enough of an apology for me.

I lied in bed, trying to recapture the moment between sleeping and wakefulness, but gave up after five minutes as my long shot plan from the night before crept into my consciousness. It was nearly impossible to stop my train of thought from rolling down the tracks once it got going. I wanted to give Rob more time to spend with Lester before getting back on the case, but we didn't have a moment to waste.

We texted while I made my morning coffee. The aromatherapy seeped into my brain before the liquid hit my stomach. By the end of my first cup, I was feeling human enough to join society. A wave of relief washed over me when Rob told me Lester was okay. Hell's New Haven office manager had to be made of stronger stuff, but he wasn't a field agent, so I didn't know what to expect. Rob was comfortable taking vague direction, so I set him in motion for the day and prepared my own agenda. I donned a summer weight suit, which Dominic, my quasi-immortal tailor, had suggested the last time I was in his shop. I needed the armor and the luck from my favorite red tie.

I was overdue for a visit to my friend, spiritual advisor, and now client, Walter Prospect. Despite the renovations, I expected he would be in the office as he was most days. He wasn't much of a texter, but never seemed to mind my random drop-ins, so I made my way over to the church on Broadway Street.

All the changes since the last time I was there struck me as soon as I arrived. My last visit had to have been at least a month prior. Scaffolding surrounded the outside, providing work crews access to the facade and stained-glass windows. They had replaced most of the old panes, and the new pieces were gorgeous. Multiple scenes from the Bible graced the exterior, but the largest was one of Lucifer being cast into Hell. I guessed Angel Co. project management couldn't help themselves and made a suggestion to not-so-subtly stick it to the Devil. I couldn't blame Walt for agreeing. The piece was beautiful, but I chuckled just the same as I walked through the front doors.

No flames, burns, or sulfur? Check. It was a game I played with myself, wondering if *this* was the time I spontaneously combusted from strolling into a church. I found Walt where I usually did, stuck behind a desk covered in an ever-shifting sea of letters, invoices, and office supplies.

"Nick, my boy!" He jumped up and came around the desk to shake my hand before pulling me into a hug. "It's a little bright eyed and bushy-tailed for you, isn't it?"

Everyone had my number this morning. But it occurred to me I had never come early in the day unless I was working in the soup kitchen. "Good morning to you, too, Walt."

"That wasn't very neighborly of me, but I think we've known each other for long enough that I can tease a little. What can I do for you? You haven't had a crisis in, what, months now? It's a new record." He had a wicked gleam in his eye, and I bet he was enjoying himself. He eased up for a minute, heading to his refreshment nook to brew some tea.

Tea was a bit of a ritual for us, and I wasn't going to argue against it. I wandered over to his increasingly threadbare wingback chairs and moved piles of paper from each onto the floor below them, careful to not disrupt whatever vertical filing system Walt was going for.

"Pardon the appearance!" he called over his shoulder.

"Not a problem in the least. It's good to see all the work is going to plan."

"Yes!" He navigated other piles of paperwork and church supplies, which someone had clearly stashed in his office during the pandemonium of all the contractors, and set the tray on the small side table. "It threw dear Olivia—you've met the project manager? She's a delight.—It threw her for a loop when I insisted on keeping the church's soup kitchen open during construction."

"Did her eye twitch? Sounds like an involuntary eye-twitch kind of request."

Walt laughed hard enough to rattle the cups in their saucers. "I expect it did. Enough about me tormenting the poor woman. What can I do for you?"

"What do you know about Purgatory?"

Walt blinked at me, then frowned and picked up his tea. "Well...I'm Episcopalian, mind. Purgatory was more of a Roman Catholic invention, but we discussed it in seminary."

"So you don't believe in it?"

Walt had taken a sip of tea, but he swallowed it with a grimace and a cough. "I didn't say that. A man needs to wet his whistle before accepting an opportunity to pontificate about doctrine like the gem you've given me."

I chuckled and raised my hand in surrender. "Sorry, jumping to conclusions. It's one of my many flaws."

"It's alright, Nick. Many in my denomination don't believe in it at all, so you have a decent chance of being right. A particular passage stayed with me when we were comparing different interpretations. 'Besides all this, between you and us a great chasm has been fixed, so that those who might want to pass from here to you cannot do so, and no one can cross from there to us.'"

"Have you memorized the entire Bible?"

Walt blushed. "I have few talents in this life, Nick. Remembering scripture happens to be one of them. Now, I never liked the idea of an impenetrable Limbo. It's restrictive, with no concept of redemption. My opinion hasn't changed since I was in school. If there is an in-between place where souls go when they haven't passed into either Heaven or Hell, it's got to serve a purpose. So I believe in it, even if only as an allegory for the journey of the soul. But I have a feeling yours isn't an idle question. Why don't you get to the point where you dash my preconceived notions to the pavement?"

I hid my smile by drinking my own tea. "I've got good news and bad news. The good news? Today, the Episcopalians are right."

Walt pumped his fist in the air with a whoop. "It's about time. What's the bad news?"

"It's a lot more complicated," I said, and filled him in on my problem. By the time I finished, he was rubbing his beard in contemplation.

"So you've got any number of lost souls who would be released back into Purgatory and then lose their minds? What would that even look like?"

"I think the local mediums would have a field day but also lose a lot of sleep for a while. Honestly? I don't know. It sounds bad, and I'm not looking forward to the idea of finding out. That's why I'm here. I have an idea, and I need a sanity check."

Walt beamed. "You've got a complement of professionals at your beck and call. It's kind of you to still want my opinion."

"I'm going to level with you. I don't have a lot of impartial people in my life, so I value your advice and counsel."

Walt reached across and patted my knee in a fatherly gesture. "You keep me on my toes, that's for sure. I wouldn't call myself impartial though. I am a godly man."

"I don't need you to be an atheist to be a neutral party."

"Fair point, and enough mutual backslapping. What's your idea?"

I set my cup down, then squared my shoulders. "I think Heaven and Hell should take the souls in."

Walt nodded thoughtfully. "I agree."

I blinked, "That's it?"

"You didn't ask for a sermon, Nick." Walt chuckled, leaning back and resting clasped hands over his stomach. "There's a psalm, 'The Lord is near to the brokenhearted and saves the crushed in spirit.' It sounds, to me, like these people apply. I don't know what the Devil's stake in these souls would be, but if it were up to me? God should gather all the lost sheep in."

"I think if it were one or two, it might be an easier sell. But the last number thrown at me was the potential of 'thousands,' so I'm preparing for a negotiation. I'll need to find a neutral location, though."

Walt leaned forward, a glint in his eye. "May I offer a slightly distressed church? I find no greater symbolism than a place being made new again by the grace of God, spurred by the efforts of the Devil."

"And you might get to meet them in person," I teased.

The pout that grew on Walt's face was the least likely expression I had ever seen on him. "While it wasn't my goal, it would be an interesting experience. You can't blame a holy man for trying, given what I know now."

"Not in the slightest, and it's a brilliant suggestion. I've got my people on it, and I'll reach out when I have a day and time."

I rose and Walt followed suit, shaking my hand and pulling me in for another hug.

"He isn't what you think he is, Walt. If he accepts any of these trapped spirits, they'll be taken care of."

"I believe you, my boy. You haven't let me down yet, so no reason to imagine you would start now."

We parted ways, and I headed straight for a caffeinated oasis. I was full of nervous energy, and the ease with which I had Walt on my side didn't give me an outlet for it. The only answer was to add more legal stimulants and hope everything leveled out. This strategy had worked for me in the past, and I was going to ride my wave of intuition.

I stood in line at The Fix, waiting to place my order with one of the newer, less glassy-eyed baristas Mark had hired, when I received a text. It wasn't from a number I expected to see.

LESTER:

> Hey, Nick. I know you asked Rob to rope me in on whatever your little scheme is, but I think I need a "me day."

NICK:

> Honestly, I didn't expect you to be conscious. It took me a while to get back to any kind of equilibrium, so take all the time you need. I'll handle the conversation with Lu.

LESTER:

> Thanks. I'm doing okay, but I'm having vision problems.

I chuckled and pocketed my phone. Maybe being terminally sarcastic was a kind of mental armor. On reflection, it had worked for me until it didn't. Either way, it seemed like Lester would be okay, and I suddenly knew what I was doing with part of my day.

I was one customer away from the counter when a hot breath steamed across the back of my neck. I squirmed and did my best to glance over my shoulder without calling too much attention to myself.

The asura's smile was wide and sharp, the storms dancing in his eyes similar to the last time I encountered him. "Good to see you, Nick."

I opened my mouth to answer, but the patron ahead of me moved out of the line, so I stepped deftly to the counter. I placed my order and turned to Gaja. "What are you having? They make a decent Turkish coffee."

They really did. During my first go-round with Angel Co., one of their agents, Hazem, had lamented about there being no good

Turkish coffee around here. His comment confused the hell out of me once I had time to contemplate it. I frequented a fantastic Mediterranean place, and theirs was a delight. No pun intended. So, I finally settled on Hazem being a bit of a coffee snob himself. Typical.

Gaja seemed taken aback by my question but recovered. "I'll have a chai latte."

"Great." I returned my attention to the person behind the counter and added his drink to my order, stepping aside and motioning for him to step up.

He eyed me quizzically until understanding dawned in those tempestuous eyes. His wide smile turned into a smirk. He took a very normal-looking wallet out of his pocket and paid for the beverages, then widened his eyes at me as if to say "Happy?"

I would have given decent money to know why no one else in the building cared about Gaja's appearance, but I took for granted that powerful figures might appear differently to others. Maybe being god-touched let me see things for what they really were.

We waited in silence until "Nick" was called and moved ourselves outside to one of the more remote bistro tables. Gaja was taking my insolence in stride, so I was pretty sure what this was about.

"Are you here to gloat?" I asked.

"Not at all. Why would I do that?"

"It's what villains do when they win," I grumbled, sucking angrily at the straw of my iced latte, if that was possible.

Gaja sighed and stirred sugar into his chai. "You wound me, Nick. Don't you have a boss who's been misunderstood for millennia? I'd think you were more open-minded by now."

"As much as the next guy who works for the Devil, but I'm confident you're not the good guy in this situation."

"Why do you say that? I was going to offer you another job, but it sounds like you've made up your mind about me."

"I haven't known the guys at Elephas for very long, but I trust them. You? Not so much." I plucked a piece of information Amy had provided about Gaja's father from what floated around in my head. "You haven't learned humility like your father—"

Lighting crashed inside his pupils, and red heat glowed in his mouth as he slammed his fist on the table. "Do not *dare* speak to me of my father, you impudent man."

I tutted at him, pressing my luck. "There's that temper."

He reeled himself back, like the first time we had spoken, squaring his shoulders and picking up his cup. The liquid hissed in his mouth, turning to steam as he drank, which was more than a little disconcerting when he exhaled through his nose like a dragon.

"Believe it or not, I wanted to thank you."

"I believe it. I just don't need any applause for failing to do my job."

"You succeeded, Nick, just not in a way you'll recognize. You were pragmatic and suggested a course of action, which gives her a chance to consider her options more fully."

"And you get the next three generations under your thumb. Did she already sign?"

"Not yet, but she will."

Anger rose white-hot in my belly, though no steam came from my lips. "I can't decide for her, but she's making a mistake."

"It's hers to make."

"Yes," I said through gritted teeth. "I thought you weren't here to gloat."

"I'm not, but you can't blame a winner for celebrating a bit, can you?"

If I was tired of higher powers fucking with me before, I was one hundred percent over it now. "Let me tell you what I'm planning to do, Gaja. I'm going to help Meghna's family, and their descendants, escape your clutches. It's going to be a side project of mine.

I'll work on it off the side of my desk, just because you couldn't take the win and leave it alone."

"What do you think you're capable of, little—"

"Call me little one more time." I leaned forward until I was halfway across the table and into his personal space.

He chuckled, then as quick as the bolts flashing in his eyes, his index finger was hooked painfully under my chin. His nails were razor sharp, and my skin tickled as a drop of blood slowly oozed down my neck.

"Know that I will rip your throat out before you ruin my plans, mortal. But..." He released me, flicking his fingernail to the side in distaste. "I can respect someone willing to stand up to a god."

I grabbed a napkin from the table to dab my throat before the blood reached my shirt. "What can I say? I'm stupid like that."

He drained his cup, then rose to leave. "Don't make it a habit. It's bad for your health."

I arrived at Devil Co.'s offices after my visit with Gaja, fuming with anger. My goal was to engage Lu with my plan, given Lester's rightful abdication of his professional responsibilities for the day. But as soon as I stepped into his office, I launched into a tirade about my most recent conversation.

When I finally wound down, Lu paused before asking me a simple question. "You did what?" His face was a study in control. I was positive he was both impressed and horrified by the encounter, and as I described it, the expressions in his eyebrows warring with the ones on his mouth.

"He was gloating, Lu. You know I can't stand it when powerful people gloat. It hits me right in the gut. So I stood up to him."

"Sounds like you goaded him pretty hard for him to threaten your life."

The adrenaline had waned by the time I hit the office, but it got a bump when I spun myself back up for the retelling. It was on the decline again, and an ache grew behind my eyes. I rubbed my temples to relieve the growing pressure radiating through them.

"Can we put a pin in this topic? I'll admit I started it, but I came here for a reason other than complaining to you about my poor choices in arguments."

Lu waved his hand. "Of course. What can I do for you?"

I gave an exaggerated sigh to reset myself. I hadn't updated Lu since meeting with the living Cormicks. "There's some aftermath to the Lee situation, and I need to drag you into it."

"Tell me more?"

"I...can't give you all the details yet—"

Lu raised his finger to make a point, so I rushed ahead.

"Because I don't have them yet. It should only be a day or two, but you have to trust me that it's something you'll be interested in."

Lu raised an eyebrow. "You have my attention."

"I was going to get Lester to attend on your behalf, if you weren't available, but he's had a rough few days."

Lu nodded along as I was talking about Lester. "He deserves some time off if he wants it. Regardless, for his sake, I'll agree to your nebulous plan. Can you tell me anything else?"

"Dress to impress."

Lu cracked his knuckles and winked at me. "You bet I will. Oh, and one thing before you go."

"What's that?"

"It was pretty gutsy, standing up to Gaja, but unless you've got a death wish, you should probably tone it down a little."

"Why do you say that, Lu? I thought my contract had some kind of death or dismemberment clause."

"You and I both know it doesn't stop you from getting in trouble." Lu grimaced.

"But it should keep me on the right side of the dirt."

There weren't any crickets in the building, but they were chirping somewhere. I cleared my throat nervously. "Right?"

Lu chuckled uncomfortably. "Not exactly. With mortals? Yes, absolutely. Otherwise, I couldn't have interfered with Rob when he tried to kill you that one time. But..."

"There's a but?" The back of my neck broke out in a cold sweat.

"*But* you need to be more careful with, uh, 'beings' I guess I'll call them. Gods, demigods, those kinds of people. If they belong to a pantheon, I can't be sure I'd be able to protect you from them."

"It would have been nice if you told me that *before* I tweaked an asura's nose, Lu."

"I thought you had more common sense than that, otherwise I might have mentioned it earlier. I'm sure it'll be fine. Just keep it in mind going forward?"

"Yeah, will do," I said, heading to the door of his office. My brain was stuck in a fog, contemplating my misunderstood near-death experience.

I spent some time sitting on a bench on the Green after wandering out of the office, my head swimming. Amy texted about an evening walk she was taking after work to investigate something, so I stayed on standby with my thoughts. Eventually, after I heard from her that she was heading home, I decided to grab noodle soup to surprise her with. At least nothing else was likely to go wrong that night.

CHAPTER 28

AMY

Nick was kneeling next to me, calling my name, when I cracked my eyes open. I couldn't tell if it had been minutes or hours, but my hand was on fire, and my joints were screaming. I tried to raise myself onto an elbow, but my limbs were jelly. Pins and needles radiated through my arms and legs.

"Wuh—" I tried to speak, but my tongue was thick. I swallowed painfully, willing the words to come. "What happened?"

"Amy, thank God." Nick helped me sit up. "We were asleep on the couch and then you were walking around like you weren't in control of your body. You were—"

"Possessed," I said, completing his sentence. I was on the floor of the kitchen, and I was slowly recalling how I got there. My hand ached, and a large round burn was prominent on my palm. I was getting feeling back in my extremities, so I searched the floor until I found the pendant. The white stone attached to it was completely black. Not pretty, like onyx, but burned-out like coal trapped inside a marble.

I held it up for Nick to see, and his mouth dropped open. He said something about a first aid kit and rushed out of the room. I shook my head to clear it and tried to stand for the first time since waking. My legs were still wobbly, but I made it upright.

I dropped into a kitchen chair when I took in what was on the table. I was still staring at it when Nick returned, holding a small white plastic box with a red cross on it and a wet washcloth.

"I, uh, brought you this to clean up with," he said, handing me the towel and gesturing at my face.

I had been so distracted by the map on the table I hadn't even noticed the bitter taste filling my mouth until he mentioned cleaning it. I touched my lips, and my fingers came away dark with ink. After surveying the floor, I convinced myself most of the ink had ended up on the linoleum, rather than something I accidentally swallowed. I might take a hit on my security deposit when I eventually moved, but at least I didn't need to do an internet search for "is ink toxic and can I drink it?"

I dabbed at my mouth, dyeing part of the washcloth deep navy. Nick sat next to me at the table and gently turned my burned hand this way and that, then retrieved burn gel from the kit. We talked as he treated and bandaged my hand.

"Do you remember anything?" he asked.

"It's coming back to me, but in flashes. I knew something was wrong as soon as I woke up, but then my body was moving, and I couldn't do anything except fight it from inside."

"That sounds terrifying."

"It wasn't fun. I'll tell you that much." I picked the collar up from where I had tossed it onto the table. "Siobhan must have gotten this onto one of my fingers, but I'm not sure how—" I paused, staring at Pants, who was asleep in the living room on the coffee table.

"What is it?"

"The sneaky bitch! She'd been practicing. I found the statue of the golfer on the floor with the collar on it. I assumed Pants still hated collars and tugged it off."

Nick put the last piece of tape on the wrap, holding some gauze in place on my palm. "Any idea why she did it?"

I gestured to the map and waited for Nick's eyes to widen, as if on cue, as soon as his gaze moved to the wildly scribbled circle. "Whoa."

"Ever the poet." I patted his cheek affectionately. I was feeling in control enough to not accidentally slap him instead, but it was a close thing.

"Isn't this what you were looking for?" He folded the paper until it showed the portion of downtown with the markings on it.

Siobhan had clumsily circled the port authority on the eastern side of the New Haven Harbor. It was also on the opposite side of the area I had scribed earlier while dowsing. Despite the migraine I was developing, she had saved me a lot of time searching for a needle in a watery haystack.

I stood experimentally and found I was steady on my feet again, then rummaged around in my junk drawer until I came away with two flashlights. Clicking them on and off to ensure they had some battery life left, I handed one to Nick.

"Are we going somewhere?" he asked.

"Investigating."

Waterfront Street was a desolate place in the middle of the night. It was around one in the morning when we made it over the Q Bridge and into the industrial portion of the city hugging the shore. It was uninhabited, not even inviting to the homeless searching for a comfortable squat for the night.

We parked on a connecting side street and walked to the entrance. A tall fence surrounded the port authority, with a wide gate secured by a heavy padlock.

"What, exactly, are you expecting to find here in the middle of the night?" Nick asked, while examining the lock.

"I'm not sure, but I think I'll know it when I see it—" The bright glow of headlights grew to my right, approaching our position. "Shit, a car's coming."

"Ok—"

Nick yelped as I grabbed his hand and hauled him with me toward a nearby dumpster, ducking behind it before a car pulled into view. It rolled up to the gate, and a stocky figure got out and made his way to the padlock, which he opened with a key. He swung the gate wide, drove through, and repeated the process to lock it behind him. I glanced at Nick, and he was staring with his mouth agape.

"You know him," I said.

"That's Cole. He works for the Cormicks. What the hell is he doing here?"

The car retreated further into the dockyard, and we exited our hiding place to approach the fence once more.

"Do you think he's got something to do with Manannán's problem?"

"I'm starting to wonder whether there are any coincidences."

"I think I can get us in," I said, taking my purse off my shoulder.

"Do you have a magic key in there?"

"Something like that." I swung my bag around once and threw it over the fence. "Oh no, my purse. I guess we'll just have to go and get it." Grabbing the chain-link fence and hoisting myself up, I glanced down to catch a priceless look on Nick's face. It was mostly pride, but mixed with a touch of disappointment.

"That's your magic power? Breaking and entering?"

"Are you coming or not?" I continued climbing until I could swing a leg over the top and scale to the ground. I gave silent thanks that the yard wasn't protected with barbed or razor wire.

Nick heaved an exaggerated sigh, but followed my lead. In short order, we were slinking through the lanes between buildings, heading toward the docks. I didn't know where Cole's car had gone, but we stayed silent and pursued the echoing sounds of a closing door and shuffling feet.

It wasn't a full moon, but enough lights in the yard made the flashlights unnecessary. We rounded a corner and caught a glimpse of Cole carrying a crate into a building. A quick visual reconnaissance showed a metal stairway leading to a steel door above us. I gestured to Nick, and we crept up the stairs one at a time, taking care to walk as silently as possible.

It turned out to be a warehouse. Large windows lined the sides and afforded us a clear view of the interior. *Gods damn it. Siobhan had tried to tell me in the first place,* I thought. *Not WAR, but a WAREHOUSE.* I said a silent apology to the dead girl and returned my attention to the scene unfolding in front of us.

Cole had carried the crate inside and placed it on a long table, covered with other similar boxes. He popped the top off the one in front of him and reached inside, coming back out holding a glass figurine.

We were too far away to see what it was supposed to be, but Nick muttered a low "Fuck me."

"What is it?"

"If I had to guess, those are some of the statues Lee claimed he didn't have in his possession..." Nick trailed off, a pained expression on his face. He was scanning the interior of the warehouse but didn't say anything else.

We continued our impromptu stakeout until Cole finished his business, which consisted of sealing the crate back up and making some notes on a clipboard resting on the table. Afterward, he retraced his steps to the car, presumably driving to the gate and repeating his process for getting out of the lot.

We descended the steps and went to examine the front door. A sign proclaimed the warehouse to be part of "Desai Pvt. Ltd.", which didn't mean anything to me. I tried the door, but found it locked. A quick trip back up the metal staircase proved the emergency exit didn't have an exterior handle, and none of the windows appeared to open.

On our way down, I spied a whiteboard hanging next to the front door, and something about it caught my eye. I took out my phone and used the camera to zoom in on the writing, taking a picture for good measure.

"Find anything useful?"

"It looks like a schedule. There's a note about a final shipment tomorrow."

"It's after midnight. Do you mean 'calendar tomorrow' or 'we're absolutely screwed because it'll be tomorrow after we sleep?' Let me see?"

I handed Nick my phone, and he squinted to read the text, frowning. "That's a problem, but at least it's the former. There are a few of them actually."

"Tell me in the car, we should get out of here in case there's security we've managed to avoid by chance so far. There's one more thing I want to try, though."

I had been running on adrenaline since we arrived and hadn't taken the time to stretch my spiritual muscles. I closed my eyes and grounded myself, placed my hand on the window, and extended my senses.

The wave of unease hit me so hard it nearly knocked me off my feet. It was an oppressive feeling, like being smothered in a heavy blanket trying to press me to the ground. I staggered, and my boots clanged on the steel steps as I stumbled against the wall. Nick grabbed at my arms to keep me upright.

"What the hell happened?" Nick asked.

"It's hard to explain." I did my best to lock my mental defenses back into place, shaking my head to clear it. "It's like a thousand mouths were open in a scream, but no sound came out."

"Well, that's not terrifying at all. Are you okay?"

I grinned at him, determined not to let a little terror from the void dampen our discovery. "I'm fine, more uncomfortable than anything. Let's get out of here."

We made our way back to the entrance and climbed over the fence again, arriving at the car without a greater incident than me ripping my skirt on the way down the second time. If we had to come here again, I would wear pants. Neither of us spoke until we were on the highway going over the bridge toward home.

"Lee told me he didn't have most of the statues in his possession, on top of not being able to free the souls trapped in them."

"Okay, what's the problem?"

"Did you see how many crates and boxes were in there? If even half of them are full of statues, what does that tell you?"

I wracked my brain, which was more than a little soggy from my adventures with possession and burglary. "Uh, there are a lot of them?"

Nick gave me a disappointed stare. "It depends on whether Lee is lying. If what's in the warehouse represents a fraction of what's out in the world? We've got a lot of work ahead of us. It's a rare thing for me to hope for a lie."

"Reasonable, in this case. I have to make a 'call,' since I'm pretty sure of what's going on here. What's your next step?"

Nick closed his eyes and leaned back in the passenger seat. "If those statues are all being moved tomorrow night, we need to get access to them beforehand. Can you free them all if I can get us in there?"

I hadn't considered it fully yet, recalling my experiments with the golfer. The scale of the problem was daunting. "I don't know if I can handle them all at once. It would be...a lot of blood. Let me think about it."

"Okay. I'm going to text Rob while you're doing your thing and see if he's still up. We need to get this negotiation in motion tomorrow."

I nodded and drove us to Long Wharf again. It was later than I would normally consider for a walk on the beach, but I parked near where the food trucks usually were and approached the water. I glanced back to the car, and the light of Nick's phone illuminated his worried face.

Sighing, I pulled the seashell from my pocket and held it to my lips. "Manannán." I breathed into its smooth interior.

I heard him before I saw him. "Ach, I don't think I'll ever get used to that feeling." I turned, and Manannán was sitting on the top of one of the picnic tables, his feet resting on the seat. "It tickles the inside of my ear like mad."

I giggled, despite the serious nature of the night. "I found your problem."

"I didn't imagine you were summoning me to chitchat at three in the morning, darling." He patted the table next to him, so I hopped up and situated myself.

"There's a warehouse across the harbor." I pointed in the general direction of the port authority over the water. "It's full of trapped souls, and when I reached out, the weight of it nearly dragged me to the ground."

His eyes reflected the moon on the water and held a glint of approval. "Good work. It must be acting like some kind of lodestone. The 'gravity' I was telling you about."

"Okay. Now what?"

"What do you mean? Now you free all those souls. Easy peasy." He grinned, looking manic between his smile and the lunar gleam in his eyes.

"Is that something you can help with?"

He sucked his teeth. "The warehouse is *so close* to the water, but..."

"But isn't close enough. You know, for a god you've got some pretty weird limitations."

He shrugged but didn't disagree.

"Alright. They're going to be moved tomorrow." Nick's earlier concern had me suddenly unsure what "tomorrow" meant, given the time. I double-checked the picture on my phone. Thankfully, we had at least thirty-six hours before the cargo would be gone. "Jesus, it's late."

"Tick tock, Amy. Best grab a nap and get a move on. You can all sleep when you're dead."

CHAPTER 29

ROB

I rolled groggily over to turn off my alarm and was dimly aware of an alert waiting for me. The timestamp told me it had arrived after three in the morning, and I was thankful I set my phone to "do not disturb."

> The meeting has to happen today as soon as you can manage it. Text me, and I'll be there.

I groaned, and a wavy mop of hair, half hidden by the comforter, mumbled something unintelligible but with the lilt of a question.

"No rest for the wicked, baby," I said, interpreting Lester's half-conscious babble. "I have to create a miracle. No big deal."

Lester sat bolt upright, any trace of his sleepiness gone. "Excuse me?"

"I need to make the meeting between Heaven and Hell happen this morning. I don't know what changed, but I got a late-night text from Nick...or early, depending on how you look at it."

"And here I was, planning on convincing you to play hooky with me and take the day off. Now I have to go to work too." He huffed, which was adorable.

"You don't have to. Nick said he was taking care of it with Lu."

Lester eyed me as if I were insane. "Honey. I'm traumatized, not dead. You think I'm going to miss this? I've worked for Lu for ten years, and I've never seen representatives from both sides in the same room. The idea of it is delicious, even if I won't even guess what you two have up your sleeves."

"It's part of our charm. We get to be the plucky underdogs who come in at the last minute with some harebrained scheme."

Lester leaned over and pinched my cheek. "Aw, and we love you for it. Everyone in the office is rooting for you two idiots to make a difference."

I rubbed at my cheek, feigning injury. "Hilarious. But, uh, seriously. If you're planning on working today, can you get Lu to Walt's church for 10 a.m.?"

Lester shrugged and picked up his phone from the bedside table, tapping away as I disappeared into the closet and selected an appropriate outfit for the kind of day I was expecting to have. Lester's townhouse had some impressively large walk-in closets, one of the perks of moving in. Nick would almost certainly be in a suit, so I'd need to match intent. Black? It would be a little severe, and the agency was supposed to be neutral.

Did I own a light-colored suit? I dug until I came away with a gray sport coat, paired with some navy pants dark enough they were almost black, and a pink shirt. I was walking back into the bedroom, and Lester was leaning against the headboard with a wide grin.

"You look like you ate the canary," I said, teasing him.

"That's because you've got yourself one Devil. Scheduled for a 10 a.m. meeting, in person, downtown."

I went to his side of the bed and leaned over to kiss him. "Thank you, you're a lifesaver."

"You saved mine. It's the least I could do."

My heart caught in my chest, and I grimaced. "We didn't really—"

Lester held up a hand to stop me. "I put on a brave face, but it was hairy with Cormicks, and I don't just mean their backs." He placed his hand on my arm and drew me down to sit next to him on the bed. "I'm okay, because it's how I deal with things, but you still risked yourself to get me out."

He laid his head on my shoulder, and I kissed his forehead.

"Thank you," I said.

"Sometimes you forget you're one of the good guys now."

We stayed like that, silent, for a few minutes, until I glanced at my phone. It was 8:30 a.m., and I still had preparations to make. My next text was to Elena, asking for an urgent meeting with Leslie at the church. I wouldn't be able to breathe normally until they responded but continued going through the motions. I didn't know how many people were going to be there, so I scheduled an order of bagels and coffee to pick up on the way.

There wasn't any point in texting Nick. Given how late it was when he texted me, I knew he'd be asleep. I dialed, and it went to voicemail. As I was about to leave a message, I received a call back from him. I abandoned the half-spoken greeting and picked up.

I had no idea what the muffled voice on the other side of the line was trying to say, but it came out like "Mrph."

"Good morning to you too, sunshine," I said.

"What time is—oh God, please tell me you're calling about a meeting and not to torture me."

"Sleep deprivation as an interrogation technique is against the Geneva Convention, Nick. When did you go to bed?"

"Four-ish, probably?"

"Then you got enough sleep. This conversation isn't a war crime."

"Ugh, I hate you for knowing that. When's the meeting?"

Nick's pitiful groan was loud enough for Lester to hear it, because he chuckled and rolled his eyes at me as he observed my side of the conversation.

"10:00 a.m.," I said. "I'm getting some snacks together, so we can pretend to be civilized hosts."

"Coffee?" he asked plaintively.

"A river of it."

"Bless you. I'll be there as soon as I can. Suit up."

"Already ahead of you."

I ended the call and checked a notification, which had come in while I was on the phone with Nick. Elena had texted back, and the two of them would be there.

Heaven was apparently full of morning people.

The church was in the exact state Olivia had described. Since Walt had offered it as neutral ground for the negotiation, he was ready to host at the drop of a hat. This was good because we had less than an hour after arriving to prepare, and Walt was already there in his Sunday best. It wasn't Sunday, but you get what I mean.

Tarps of various sizes and material covered most of the furniture while the construction was taking place. We unearthed a folding table and chairs stashed in Walt's office and did our best to establish a seating area. Nick and Amy arrived shortly after we had materialized the table. I hadn't expected Amy to attend, since this was agency business. But she was a consultant on top of being Nick's partner, so her presence wasn't a huge surprise.

Nick looked like death warmed over. His suit was immaculate, but the body inside it had the air of a sentient pile of slept-in clothes. Nick had chosen black, likely without any of the mental anguish I put into my own outfit. We were an interesting contrast in color, perhaps unintentionally embodying the dichotomy between light and dark. If anyone asked, I would claim it was on purpose, of course.

Nick squinted like he had a hangover and poured himself a large cup of coffee from one of the catering boxes I had procured and sat in a folding chair watching the chaos unfold until his eyes came back into focus.

He didn't say anything until we arranged the long folding table and chairs to our liking. "You weren't kidding about this place being a metaphor, Walt."

Walt laughed, and the lack of wall hangings made his voice bounce crazily around the room, loud enough to make Nick flinch. "I hope our guests don't judge the choice too harshly. I am suddenly self-conscious of playing host to the powers that be."

"They're just people, Walt," I said, trying to comfort him. "Okay, maybe they're not *really* people, but you'll get used to it and then one day you'll be swearing at God."

Walt eyed me skeptically. "I highly doubt that will ever occur. For me, anyway."

I shrugged, moving to put out a variety of bagels, pastries, and spreads on the card table where I had set the coffee. It resembled an Alcoholics Anonymous meeting, except it wasn't in the church's basement, and the coffee and donuts were fresh.

As organized as we were likely to be, everyone waited in the lobby for the parties to arrive. I wasn't sure if they were going to use the front door or pop into existence in their seats behind us, but Nick said he had a feeling they were going to follow the laws of physics, given the nature of the meeting. The generals had their mortal adjutants, so teleportation was less likely.

When it finally started, it was as if on cue in a legal drama. Lu and Lester turned into the front path leading up to the church as Leslie and Elena came from the opposite direction. Lu nodded in greeting to Leslie, who returned the gesture. As they walked, Elena and Lester hung back a few paces and clearly either knew each other or were comfortable with introductions on the fly. I envied Lester's ability to make friends out of anyone. I'd seen it happen more than once at the bar.

The stained glass over the entrance must have caught Lu's eye, the one showing Lucifer being cast into Hell. He laughed and made a comment to Leslie, which I couldn't hear given their distance. Then he pointed a finger gun at the window, mouthing "bang" while lowering the hammer. Leslie chuckled along with him, and soon they were all coming through the open front door into the lobby itself.

Nick took point on introductions, and for once, Walter Prospect was speechless. I didn't blame him. God and the Devil were both imposing figures for different reasons. Lu wore a double-breasted, black-and-red, pinstripe suit, and his hair styling was on point. He exuded the energy of a front man or motivational speaker, slick and electric. Leslie was a study in a cozier aesthetic in Their usual soft overalls and boots but radiating a calm just as shocking to the system by its existence alone.

Walt, being a consummate host and all-around nice guy, shook hands with everyone, though he showed clear reverence when he touched Leslie's. I gave silent kudos to him for not showing any reticence to touch Lucifer's or kneeling in front of Leslie.

We moved into the main hall of the church, and thankfully, no one commented on the construction in progress. Lu and Leslie both performed the extremely human task of selecting and preparing a plate for themselves. They then sat at opposite ends of the table, with their office managers perched next to them.

This morning, at least, the Devil preferred everything bagels with smoked salmon cream cheese while God picked sesame seeds and veggie. I filed all this information under things I would never need to remember but couldn't hurt to squirrel away in the recesses of my mind.

I offered to fix coffees while everyone was getting situated and went back and forth a few times, delivering the requested orders. Lu's was black. No surprise there. Leslie preferred tea, which I had been smart enough to bring along with the rest of the goodies. The rest were an assortment of creams and sugars, and I had prepared Lester's often enough to make it blindfolded.

Lester winked at me when I dropped his coffee off in front of him. I widened my eyes and mouthed, "Baby, please" at him. The last thing I needed was my boyfriend throwing off my composure because he was trying to be funny. It was entirely on-brand for him, but I was taking this all seriously despite the casual appearance it had so far.

Nick and I sat opposite each other at the middle of the table. After an eternity of bagel chewing, coffee slurping, and small talk, Nick stood and addressed the room.

"First, I want to thank you all for coming on such short notice. I know we had agreements with each of you, but the sudden change of schedule was entirely my fault. So thank you for accommodating me."

"I'm dying of curiosity, Nick," Lu said.

"We'll sate that in a minute," Nick replied. "I'm not sure how often the two of you meet for conversations like this, but I also wanted to acknowledge the cooperation between Heaven and Hell in working with our agency."

Leslie and Lu both gave a magnanimous nod, but neither said anything in response.

Nick gestured to me. Before everyone had arrived, we'd discussed how to handle the meeting. Since I took point on the investigation into the missing souls, Nick thought it best if I gave the background.

I cleared my throat and stood as Nick took his seat.

"We've had separate conversations with each party about Purgatory and its operation. I hope to make a long story short by asking a simple question. Would it surprise any of you," I waved to encompass both sets of representatives, "to hear there are a large number of souls unaccounted for in transition among Heaven, Hell, and Purgatory?"

Lu leaned forward and steepled his fingers together under his chin. "Would you be a touch more specific?"

"I don't have exact numbers, but I'd venture to say there are well over a thousand souls currently 'missing.'" I made air quotes with my fingers.

Leslie frowned slightly. "This doesn't sound like an enormous problem, in the grand scheme of things. That many people die in this state every month." Their eyes went glassy for a moment. "I mean, someone died just now."

I opened my mouth to reply, but it hung open with no sound until I finally settled on, "That was really dark, Leslie."

God had the good grace to look abashed. "Sorry, not my intention. Please continue."

I shook my head to clear it and pressed on. "I'm hedging, a bit. It was reported to me as 'thousands,' but in reality, we don't have solid numbers. We have two problems ahead of us, which is why we're here today. There is a concentration of trapped souls near the harbor."

"Ah, your statuette problem." Lu smiled broadly.

"Yes. The only reason we were able to find this trove of them is because it's wreaking havoc with another spiritual entity."

Amy's voice cut into the conversation. "People who have died in the city aren't able to travel across the veil. It's acting like a gravitational field, keeping them all on this plane of existence."

Everyone around the table was nodding along with the conversation, which was better than the universal confusion I was afraid of.

"We have a potential solution for freeing them," I said. "But it gets muddier from here. These spirits are in stasis now, but once released, they'll be in a state of suffering. What happened to them has driven them...insane, for lack of a better word." I sat, signaling Nick to take up the discussion.

"Which leaves us with a different problem. We have no idea what unleashing thousands of mad spirits back into Purgatory would do if they even returned there. For all we know, they could stick around and haunt New Haven until someone dealt with them. This is where you both come in."

"I don't see how—" Leslie began, but Nick cut Them off.

"We want you to take them in. Unless there's some Limbo equivalent to group therapy, there's no way to release the spirits and get them sane enough to work their way up or down."

Leslie turned Their sad eyes on us. "I appreciate the request, but there's a reason those people didn't go straight to Heaven or Hell. It's against the rules to—"

"I'll take them all," Lu said, grinning from ear to ear.

"You'll what?" I blurted out in stereo with Leslie.

"If Mx. 'by the book' here is going to stand on ceremony, I'll just take them all."

"Now, wait one minute," Leslie cried, more animated than before.

Walt appeared scandalized and shifted in his seat. Everyone else was staring, seemingly as surprised as I was.

Lu shrugged and held his hands wide. "I didn't hear you offering an alternative."

"I just thought, well, there *are* rules—" Leslie tried to say, but Lu interrupted.

"Which we made up. I don't see a good reason not to bend them in this case."

Leslie stood and paced the short stretch of floor at Their end of the table. "If it's going to come down to one of us adopting these lost souls, my organization would take better care of them. Perhaps we could resolve the issue with their sanity and eventually release them back into Purgatory."

I glanced at Lester, and he was trying to keep a thin smile to himself. He knew Lucifer much better than I did, and this back and forth didn't faze him at all. Nick looked similarly unconcerned, but he was watching the exchange like a tennis match. Something niggled at the back of my mind, but I couldn't put my finger on it.

Lu clucked his tongue, seeming to admonish God. "I don't see why you would want to endanger these poor, mistreated people. No. They can stay on the north shores of Hell for the duration. No catch-and-release program necessary."

Leslie stopped in Their tracks and turned to Lucifer. "You can't say where they would have ended up! I'll give them the benefit of the doubt they would have worked their way to Heaven eventually. They are all welcome through my gates."

Lucifer stood, followed by Leslie, and their bickering escalated. The rest of the room did their best to not call attention to themselves. They argued at volume in a similar vein for the next five minutes. Neither were negotiating in good faith but laying out their respective cases for receiving the entire lot of souls.

The cause of my unease formed in my mind, and a vague sense of disgust settled into my stomach. I watched the proceedings for another minute, observing the tactics and rhetoric each side used to justify their superiority. *Not* why they should be the caretakers, no, but more so why their counterpart *shouldn't* be.

The final straw landed after Lu made a witty dig at Leslie about Their organization losing track of a bunch of souls in the 1960s. Elena chimed in that with so much going on at Woodstock, anyone was bound to lose track of some people, and they had "much better systems" in place since then. Leslie was looking flustered, and Lu took a surreptitious moment to wink at me.

He. Winked. At. Me.

The low-grade disgust I had been experiencing exploded into full-blown rage. "YOU HAVE GOT TO BE FUCKING KID-DING ME!"

The room fell silent, and all eyes were on me, my loud breathing the only sound punctuating the still air.

"Neither of you give a single shit about any of this! It's small potatoes to you. If Lu hadn't jumped at the chance to tweak God's nose, you might have let the cards fall and left us to pick up the pieces afterwards."

Lu raised an eyebrow but nodded slightly, as if acknowledging he was, in fact, only there to antagonize the angelic host.

"Rob—" Nick stood and tried to break in, and to his credit, he did it gently, but I was in no mood to be placated.

"I am not done yet."

Nick held up his hands and sat. No one else took up the task of trying to rein me in.

I breathed deeply and plowed on before I could think too hard about what I was doing. I rounded on Leslie. "And YOU didn't care one bit until Lucifer tried to claim them for himself. Only *then* did you need to have them. Contemplation and penance be damned. You'd have accepted each with open arms."

Leslie looked chagrined but didn't say anything in response.

My vision blurred with sudden unshed tears I hadn't expected, but this tirade was a long time coming. "I don't care who takes the souls in, so long as one of you agrees to, but stop making this a mockery. These people suffered at the hands of the Cormicks, but they haven't done anything to deserve a place in Heaven or Hell. They didn't make better choices or change their ways. There wasn't any introspection or self-improvement." My voice broke on the last sentence, a plaintive noise coming from my throat.

Lester raised his hand as if to reach out to me, but I waved him back.

"I wouldn't have cared, you know? Not if you had kept it simple and haggled a little before agreeing to split them down the middle. But this?" I waved my arms to encompass the room. "This just reminds me I'm going to end up in Purgatory. Despite everything I've done to be a good person. I didn't do it to get into Heaven or stay out of Hell. I did it for me because it's the right thing to do. What you're doing is insulting to anyone who's tried to make themselves better."

I flexed my hands and joints cracked from the tension I was holding myself under. Bitterness flooded my mouth, reminiscent of bile. "We've got a lot of souls to free tonight, and you're wasting time. Fuck you both."

I turned and stormed out of the church, shouldering the door open so hard it crashed into the wall. I found a patch of shade under a tree in front of the building and sat on the curb, breathing heavily until I regained my equilibrium.

Nick was the first to come find me, ten minutes later. He eased himself down onto the concrete with a heavy sigh.

"So," he said. "That was one way to get them to compromise."

"Having a tantrum?"

Nick laughed and patted me on the shoulder. "No, reminding them who they're dealing with. Humanity and not whatever cosmic bet neither of them will admit to having."

I chuckled along with him, the tension broken. "What now?"

"Oh, they're going to split the lot fifty-fifty, like you alluded to."

"Imagine that, a simple solution."

"Indeed." Nick took his phone out and checked the clock. "And we've got plenty of time to get ready for an evening trip to the harbor."

"I live to serve."

Nick eyed me and pursed his lips. "This has been weighing on you really heavily, hasn't it?"

"Like an albatross."

He nodded, considering. "I asked them to reconsider your case, as part of the deal with the agency."

I shook my head. "You didn't have to do that."

"I know. But I did it anyway. You were right. It wasn't fair. Maybe we can suggest some changes to whatever system is running Purgatory in the future. It sure as hell isn't operating well."

"Thanks, Nick. I appreciate it. Maybe we can give that a shot."

"Oh, one more thing." Nick had a wicked gleam in his eye.

I perked up. "What?"

"Walt is probably going to need some therapy, hearing you chew out God and the Devil."

"He should have his illusions shattered anyway. I know I said they were only people..." I leaned my head back against the tree and closed my eyes with a sigh.

"But..." Nick prodded.

I didn't bother to open my eyes. "He got to see that sometimes they're also just assholes."

CHAPTER 30

NICK

No one stuck around for long after the negotiations concluded. Rob had done more than he realized with his rant. He wasn't there to see it, but a lot of chagrin went around the room. Each of the bosses had a consultation with their respective office manager, and we settled on the fifty-fifty split shortly thereafter. I tried to fetch Rob, but he wasn't interested in closing statements, so I left him on the curb while we wrapped up inside.

Walt, once again the perfect host, shook everyone's hand as they exited the church, and I followed them all outside. As Lu walked away, he looked back at me when he neared the corner, then winked and glanced toward the church's new stained glass.

My head swiveled as I tracked his gaze. It took me more time to figure out what he was trying to bring to my attention than I wanted to admit. One tiny detail had changed since I had last paid attention to the piece. The largest window, with God casting Lucifer into Hell, now depicted a smile on the Devil's face. Nothing else was different, just one miniscule shift. I turned my eyes back to Lu, who saluted me with two fingers before disappearing toward wherever he had parked, assuming he drove at all.

I laughed and shook my head, heading back into the church to regroup and debrief with the team. Walt sat, stunned, amidst the breakfast detritus with a half-smile plastered on his face.

I patted him on the shoulder. "Was it everything you hoped for?"

The physical contact broke his reverie, and he shook his head as if to clear it. "My boy, it was an experience unlike anything I could have expected."

"We just call that Thursday." I laughed.

"I'm not sure how you do it. I'm not sure I ever want to again."

"Believe it or not, you get used to it. We'll clean up and take it from here." I offered Walt my hand and hauled him to his feet. "You can get back to church business. Thanks for the space."

Walt nodded, a bit absentmindedly, and wandered off in the direction of his office. I assumed it would be a minute before he recovered from the morning's escapades.

Rob came back inside after the two parties had left, so I gestured for him and Amy to sit at the table. I poured myself the dregs of one of the paper carafes and threw some creamer in for good measure. It wasn't quality coffee, but beggars couldn't be choosers, and I needed all the mental acuity I could get.

I landed heavily next to Amy and placed my hand over hers with a wan smile. Time was against us. The warehouse full of contentious souls was due to be emptied tomorrow, and if we didn't want to confront a yard full of workers, we were going to have to take care of it tonight.

"Tell me if I get this right. First, we need to sneak back into the port authority. It shouldn't be too hard, given the lack of security we encountered yesterday. Second, we need to break into the warehouse. Third, we deal with the statues."

"We're going to have to deal with them on-site," Amy said, idly lining up empty cups like toy soldiers.

I nodded and sipped my coffee, which I immediately regretted. "I can't imagine the three of us moving ten crates by ourselves, let alone the entire inventory, so I agree with you there."

"We still haven't tested the actual release of a soul yet, have we?" Rob asked.

In response, Amy took the golfer figurine out of her bag and placed it on the table. "Now that we know where the souls are going, no time like the present?"

Rob looked at me, and I shrugged, I didn't have any better suggestion, and he was right. We needed to confirm whether we had a solution in hand. I nodded to Amy, then she produced a small sewing kit and liberated a needle from it.

She scanned the room and pointed at something with her chin. "Nick, can you grab a hammer?"

I retrieved a contractor's hammer from where she directed me and brought it back to the table.

"Okay," she said, letting out a steady breath. "Here goes nothing." She lowered her head and began muttering similar words to the chanting I had heard previously but quieter and faster. She pricked her finger with the needle and drew a fat bead of blood from the tip. Amy moved to smear the blood on the chest of the figure, but she moved much quicker than the first experiment she had shown me.

The sound was short and sharp, rather than a growing scream. Once she had drawn a small sigil on the statue with her finger, she nodded to me. I took my cue and let out some of the pent-up energy I had from the morning's meeting in a wide arc, bringing the hammer down on the glass.

It shattered, and a wave of energy rippled outward from the point of impact like a stone thrown into a pond. A sense of relief was palpable in the air as well. Not just what I experienced from Amy's success but something akin to a fading sigh. Amy stood, and her eyes were bright, a radiant smile on her face. I dropped the hammer to the table and rushed over to lift her into the air, giving her a spin and whooping in delight.

Rob's voice cut directly through our joy. "How long is it going to take to do a thousand of those, assuming there aren't more?"

I stopped our rotation and planted Amy firmly back on her feet before turning to Rob. "Buzzkill."

He shrugged and spread his hands. "Someone had to ask the question."

Amy chewed her lip. It was a habit of hers when she was deep in thought. "I've got an idea, but you both need to trust me on this, okay?"

"I don't think we have any other options, but I'd trust you regardless," I said.

Rob nodded. "Whatever it takes."

One trip to the hardware store, two power naps, and three espressos later found us creeping into the harbor yard sometime around midnight. We were as prepared as we were going to be. Rob had a crowbar and small tool kit complete with hammers. Amy and I had baseball bats and smaller pry bars. I expected us to have to jimmy a door open or break a window, but otherwise I assumed it would be a lot of opening crates and smashing crystals. We were all decked out in black ensembles, Amy looking the most natural of the three of us.

"Do you want to tell me anything about your part of the plan?" I asked Amy as we scaled the chain-link fence.

"No," she grunted. "You'll know it when you see it."

As we approached the warehouse, a flicker of movement caught my eye. Something must have crossed a light around the corner, and the shadows blinked momentarily. I held up my hand in a fist to halt our forward progress.

"Did you see that in a movie once?" Rob whispered.

"Shh. Something's up ahead. Might be security." I motioned for them both to stay put and crept along the edge of the building until I could peer around it.

A short, thin figure wearing jeans and a dark hoodie was liberally drenching the foundation of the Desai warehouse with liquid from a red gas can. I couldn't believe my eyes when the building's lights exposed enough of their face for me to recognize the person about to commit arson. I stepped into the circle of illumination from the nearest lamppost.

"Meghna? What the hell are you doing here?"

Her head jerked in my direction as I spoke, the gas can falling to the ground with a thunk. She pulled the hood back to reveal a tear-streaked face, eyes red and puffy. No trace of sadness was in her gaze, however, only steely resolve. That and a growing confusion as she took in my appearance. It passed quickly, and she ran up to me in what was clearly a manic state.

"I'm going to burn it all to the ground, Nick," she said, grabbing me by the arms. "I couldn't do it, give away my future children's souls to the asura."

Her voice caught in a hitch when she spoke about the debt she had planned to lay at her descendant's feet, which explained why she had been crying earlier. The sound of footsteps behind me let me know Amy and Rob had left their hiding spot. They came to stand on either side of Meghna and me.

"I'm glad you decided against taking Gaja's deal," I said. "But it doesn't explain why you're here."

She blinked and looked at my companions, seeming to recognize Rob but not Amy. "Me? This is my family's warehouse. Why are *you* here? And why does Rob have a crowbar?"

A moment of silence passed before the clanging of a large piece of metal skittering across the pavement shattered it to pieces.

"What crowbar?" Rob asked, trying to sound nonchalant.

I gritted my teeth and rolled my eyes at him, then glared in the direction he had thrown the tool.

"Right," he chuckled. "I still need that. I'll just..." he trailed off and went to retrieve his equipment.

I sighed, shook my head, and turned to Meghna. "Let's get back to where you said this was your family's warehouse. It's Desai Private Limited. Desai isn't your last name."

She looked at me like I was an idiot. "Of course it isn't, it's Murthy. But my great-grandfather named the company with a Gujarati surname. It's where so many successful businesspeople come from that it's become a stereotype. He took advantage of it, and here we are."

I blinked rapidly as I processed what was happening. "You never told me what your family deals in."

She tilted her head to one side. "You didn't ask. We're one of the largest cut glass and crystal dealers in the region."

My mouth fell open, and when I shared a look with Amy, hers was in a similar configuration. I had suspected the threads we had been pulling on with our respective efforts were related, but the synchronicity of that moment was about to give me an out-of-body experience.

"You have got to be kidding me," Rob muttered, having rejoined us, holding his crowbar again.

"What is it? Why are you all staring at me like that?" Meghna asked.

I snapped back to reality and pulled myself together. "It's hard to explain, but you have to trust me. We need you to *not* set the building on fire."

Her hand was coming out of her pocket, holding a steel Zippo lighter, when she paused. "Try me?"

"Well, speaking of souls. Your warehouse holds a lot of trapped ones, and we need to free them. Trying to do it while avoiding a structure fire would be more difficult than what we had already planned."

"If I didn't already know about your business, I'd think you were insane." Meghna laughed.

I sighed in relief. "But I'm not. There's a local family who has apparently been funneling crystal statues with spirits locked inside them through your company. The Cormicks."

Meghna's eyes widened. "The man you had in your office that I recognized! I'd seen him dealing with my father once or twice."

I nodded. "We can release the souls, but it's going to require a lot of breaking with a little entering. I, uh, didn't know this was your family's warehouse though. I guess it doesn't change the plan if you were going to burn the place to the ground with everything inside."

"What can I do to help?"

"You don't happen to have a key to the front door, do you?" Rob asked.

Meghna put the lighter back into her pocket and brought out a small key ring instead, jingling it.

"Our night just got easier," Amy said, grinning.

We all approached the entryway, doing our best to avoid any large pools of gasoline. The fumes from the puddles on the ground made my eyes water, and I was grateful to step inside as soon as the door was open.

Our vantage point the night before from the windows near the emergency exit hadn't given us the full scope of what we were getting ourselves into. The building was bigger than it appeared from the outside, with racks on racks lining the walls and making slim corridors throughout the space.

I moved to the table where we had seen Cole place his box and checked what turned out to be a shipping manifest.

"There's twelve hundred statues planned to ship tomorrow, everyone." I called loudly, my voice echoing off the high ceiling. "Looks like...at least one hundred boxes, so this is going to take a while."

"Maybe we can help," said a voice from the doorway. Six women of various sizes, shapes, and outfits had materialized inside the warehouse. I said materialized, but I was so distracted by every-thing going on I probably didn't hear them walk in. The leader of the group stood in the middle and matched every description Amy had given me of Melinda, the owner of the Beehive and head of Amy's new coven. She must have been the one speaking.

Amy nearly flew from her side of the room to the other and crashed into Melinda for a ferocious hug. "You came!"

Melinda's laugh was powerful, amplified by the acoustics of the building. "Like I would have missed this, girlie. Everyone wanted to come, but Sprite couldn't make it. She was having a bad mobili-ty day, but she's an old protest veteran, so she's got a police scanner and is keeping an ear out. She'll text me if things get hairy so we can bolt."

Amy looked from Melinda to me and back again, grinning from ear to ear.

I nodded approvingly, and she took the group into the rear of the warehouse. I assumed they had some distribution of labor to plan. Not being a witch myself, I wasn't going to question the professionals. Within minutes, the sound of pry bars levering open crates and the tinkling of broken glass filled the room. The feeling of relief we experienced earlier spread in waves throughout the building, each smashed statue causing its own ripple. I smiled, satisfied we had at least started the night's work, then turned to Meghna.

She had a pained expression on her face, like someone pulled the rug out from under her, and she wasn't sure what to do next. "I would have done it."

"I know, but why? What changed?"

"If I couldn't convince my father, or the rest of the family, I was going to make the choice for them. I'm the youngest. Normally, it means I'm given the least responsibility. In this case, I was the last hope for our freedom, even if I was the only one who truly understood why."

I nodded. "But you didn't have any guarantees that torching the warehouse would improve anything."

She shook her head sadly. "No, I didn't, but I had to try. We only have a little time left. If this didn't prove to Ganesha how serious I am about divesting our family's cursed fortune, then maybe it would shock my family into action."

Meghna's shoulders slumped. I recognized the look of adrenaline leaving her system. She was slight and small against the backdrop of the warehouse.

"Why don't you go all rage-room with the other ladies over there? We can worry about the rest later," I suggested, hoping the involvement would pick her back up again. I offered her my baseball bat, handle-first like a squire passing his knight a sword.

She nodded, giggling, and took the bat, then ran off to join the coven.

"Swing with your hips!" I called after her. I waited for a few moments until I heard Meghna join the chorus of grunts and cheers as each of the statues met their demise.

A warmth grew in my chest. Was it a sense of pride? The decision she made wasn't a small one. Endangering her family's business to prove her point, and maybe catch the attention of a god, was admirable.

The next hours passed in a blur. The coven had started the destruction immediately. Step one, open the box. Step two, do the magic woo-woo business and draw the souls out. Step three, destruction of property. Those of us who couldn't handle step two helped by making step one easier. Rob and I collected various boxes and crates from every corner of the warehouse, comparing them against the manifest until we had assembled multiple small pyramids across the open space. We levered the tops off crates and fed a steady supply of figurines to Amy and her friends.

Meghna was less inclined to haul heavy things, so helped in step three by releasing her aggression while the witches applied their mojo. Rob and I stacked the empties against the walls, otherwise it would have been even more pandemonium trying to determine how many we had left to do.

Sweat soaked my clothes, and I had splinters in my fingers from handling too many crates with careless hands. I wiped my brow and looked out the large windows. False dawn brightened the sky. We only had a couple hours left until sunrise, and we needed to be out of there before then. I glanced back at our piles, and only the last five boxes remained. We were going to make it.

A faint heat radiated from my pocket. I reached in and pulled out the ornate brass pen Arjun had given me. I had kept both it and the accompanying paperwork folded neatly into a small square in my pocket. Call me an idealist, but I had hoped Meghna would change her mind about Gaja's deal. It took me an embarrassingly long moment to connect the dots. She had done it.

"Meghna, get over here!" I shouted, running to the table. Unfolding the contract, I placed it next to the manifest, smoothing the creases out as much as I could. A wild grin spread across my face as I scanned the document. I hadn't taken the time to study it earlier when I had less hope Meghna would change her mind. My eyes darted back and forth, absorbing the words.

It was a pretty straightforward, if broad, agreement. What it wasn't was a straight up wish fulfillment deal. I cursed Arjun in equal measure as I mentally praised him for how slick this was. The signee agreed to transfer their debt from the named party to "Lord Ganesha's service." That was it. No negotiation, no "to be determined" or even "services as needed," just a simple sentence with a fill-in-the-blank name field and two signature lines. First to be signed by the Elephas Group as Arjun indicated to make the contract viable. Second by the petitioner. Easy peasy.

"You crafty son of a bitch," I muttered to myself as Meghna approached the table.

Her brow was glistening with the same sweat staining her embroidered blouse. She looked elated. She breathed heavily, fanning her face to cool herself. She laid the bat on the table with a wooden clack. "What is it?"

I locked eyes with her, and my mouth split into a manic grin. I must have appeared vaguely insane because instead of matching my energy, her eyes took on a worried cast.

I cleared my throat and stood straight, holding my hand to my heart. "On behalf of the Elephas Group—"

Meghna's eyes shot wide open. She grabbed me by the shoulders and started hopping with apparent joy. Caught up in the moment, I locked my arms with hers, dancing in a circle for a few seconds before settling again. We laughed and caught our breaths while tears streamed down Meghna's face.

She wiped them away as she turned to inspect the contract herself, but her laughter cut off as she read the words. "What the hell is this?"

I grinned a little slyly, understanding her surprise. "It's your wish."

Her mouth fell into a pout. "But I haven't even made it yet!"

A laugh formed in my throat, but I stopped it as her eyes narrowed at me. "You did, though, when you were in our offices. You were praying to Ganesha whenever you sent your thoughts toward getting out of your agreement." She looked scandalized, and this time I didn't stop the laugh from coming. "I'm not saying he can read your mind, but do you really believe a god can't hear you when you pray directly to them?"

She tilted her head in a conciliatory gesture. "I suppose you're right. But..."

"But it isn't what you expected?" I finished for her.

She nodded, though the look on her face wasn't sad, only considering what lay before her. It didn't take long for her to resolve whatever inner conflict she was dealing with, because she broke into a grin again. "It isn't what I expected, but it's what I wanted. I don't know what Lord Ganesha has in store for me and my family, but we'll be free. I was ready to destroy everything to make it happen. I shouldn't consider this gift as anything other than what it is. It's a miracle, Nick! What would Gaja say if he saw this?"

"What *would* Gaja say?" asked a deep voice from the doorway.

How did I keep missing people walking into the building? First it was six witches, and now it was a statuesque demon smiling at us both with his sharp teeth bared in a snarl. My situational awareness was severely lacking, and I could only partially blame it on how late it was. I placed myself between the predator and his prey, narrowing my gaze at the asura.

"You're right, you know," Gaja said, sauntering with a dangerous grace toward us. "You have no clue what you're getting into, working with that long-nosed liar."

Meghna gasped. Apparently insulting the nose of an elephant god wasn't done.

"Her chances are better in a pool of sharks than with you," I said, thrusting my chin forward in defiance.

Gaja chuckled, and it was a low, throaty sound. "Your bravado is adorable, if misplaced. It doesn't matter though. I'm not here to play." He had closed the distance deceptively fast and thrust a claw under my chin, like he had at the coffee shop. Heat emanated from his mouth in waves, like a fire stoked in his belly. "You die first, then the girl. I don't even need her, but she'll still serve me in death."

Time slowed when you were staring at your own mortality, and the human brain quickened even though your body couldn't respond any faster than the synapses traveling to your muscles. I wouldn't be fast enough to dodge out of the way before he cut my throat, and I was *not* ready to wake up on the wrong side of the dirt.

I only had one trick up my sleeve, literally, and it wasn't even the right one. *Or was it*, I thought to myself. With my power from Lucifer, which sounded pretty badass when I considered it, I could be in two places at once. I didn't have time to doubt myself. Instead, I ran down that mental rabbit hole as fast as I could.

Co-location was existing at two geographical points simultaneously, but I'd never tried to push the boundaries on what it could do. If I could place my physical body somewhere else, dragging part of my consciousness along with it...

Gaja's razor sharp nail dragged across my neck, a sharp sting chasing through my nerves. I concentrated on my tattoo and visualized myself about fifty feet behind me on top of the pile of empty crates. The gut-wrenching sideways dislocation of my soul nearly knocked me from my vantage point, but I kept my balance.

"Hey!" I yelled, staring down from a moderate height at...myself. I had never used my ability to be in the same room before, and the experience was dizzying. My ears rang, like feedback from a speaker when you stood too close with a microphone.

The asura's eyes snapped to where I was on the boxes, then back to where he held me in front of him. I gritted my teeth and focused on bringing the rest of my consciousness along, like walking through a door and closing it behind me. Another moment's disorientation blurred my vision and then Gaja stood alone, next to Meghna. I wiped my hand across my throat where the claw had cut me, and it came away red with blood. I didn't have any breathing problems, so I hoped it was only a flesh wound.

Gaja stalked toward me, eyes flashing lightning white, his breath steaming in the air. I had less than ten seconds before he would close the distance. I concentrated on my sigil again, this time maintaining my co-location. Nine. High-ground me flashed Gaja a brilliant smile, taunting him to continue his momentum while the rest of me fumbled in my pocket again for the pen. Eight. I brought it out and signed my name with a shaking hand. Seven. The contract glowed with a golden light. I had guessed correctly, after all. Six—

Gaja apparently didn't care about my tactical advantage, so I never got past six. He exhaled a torrent of fire in my direction, catching the boxes and crates in the blast. I didn't realize he could do that and would have been impressed if it hadn't been so terrifying. I jumped, doing my best parkour impression, and half rolled when I hit the ground, only ten feet away from my adversary. Flames licked around the mountain of boxes I had just stood on.

It was hard doing two things at once, and every time I had to give a significant amount of attention to one location, the other was at a bit of a standstill. I shifted to where Meghna stood, holding out her hand for the pen. I reached out to place it in her palm, but my existence narrowed to a bright spot of pain, and I lost my concentration. Gaja had kicked me in the torso hard enough to send me airborne and returned me to the body on the floor.

My perspective shifted, and Megha stood by herself as I flew backwards into the flaming wreckage of the packaging. A look of surprise and horror froze on her face before cardboard and wood crashed over me, occluding my view.

My chest was throbbing, and I had a hitch in my breathing, agony radiating from inside whenever I inhaled. Probably a broken rib, but nothing I could do for it then. I fought to find purchase with my feet and scrambled out of the detritus. I cried out in shock but still tried to send part of myself back to Meghna. My head exploded in agony, but I fought through it until I was next to the table again, extending the pen. I didn't have more than a split second before I lost concentration again.

Gaja's powerful hand had seized me by the throat, and he lifted until my feet dangled in the air. I gasped and a horrible sound came from my mouth, but no air went back in.

Gaja shook me like a rag doll, and clouds formed at the edges of my vision. "You will never meddle in my affairs again, mortal."

Using the last of my strength, I drew my arm back and launched the pen at Meghna. His eyes went wide, then anger suffused his face.

"Fuck you, Gaja," I croaked with the last of my breath.

The sharp ache of his claws slicing into my belly was the only thing I felt before it all went black.

CHAPTER 31

AMY

I wasn't sure what I expected when Mel and most of the coven showed up, but the deference to whatever my "plan" was, wasn't it. I led the group into the back portion of the warehouse to explain what needed to happen.

"We're going to start with the easiest ones first, anything that doesn't need a crowbar to get into. Move any empty boxes toward the entrance, and we'll make those Nick and Rob's problem." I took a piece of chalk out of my bag and drew three large pentacles on the ground while I explained the rest. "I want to work in pairs. One draws the spirit out, and the other breaks the glass and frees it. Rotate as you need to, as this may get taxing. I don't know how much blood this is going to take, but tell me if you start feeling lightheaded."

Nix raised their hand, and I laughed aloud. "This isn't school, Nix. You don't have to raise your hand."

Their face was pale, and they cleared their throat before they spoke. "I, uh, faint at the sight of my own blood."

"You can be our number one smasher, then." I smiled, and they gave me a wan but grateful smile in return. Pulling a pack of sterilized pins from my purse, I held it out for the first three summoners to take.

"Alright, let me show you how it's done." I pulled a figurine from a nearby box, placed it in one of the circles, and handed my baseball bat to Mel. I pricked my finger, drew the symbol on the glass, and spoke the chant loudly and clearly. As soon as the spirit separated itself enough from the statue, seeking the sympathy of my blood, I nodded to Mel. She brought the bat crashing down on the statue, reducing it to shards. The familiar wave of energy washed over me, and the rest of the coven's eyes lit up with the sensation.

"Ready, ladies?" I asked the group.

"You got it," Mel said and started barking orders like a drill sergeant. Whether she had any military experience was immaterial. No one denied her commands, and the other women seemed used to this type of behavior.

A frenzy of activity followed, but all told it was only ten minutes until we got into a rhythm. Until someone needed to swap out, I found the easiest-to-open crates and brought them to the circles. Within minutes, droplets of sweat ran down my shoulder blades, and I called out to Nick in the main part of the warehouse.

"Nick, my dearest love, be *useful* and get these things ready for us! Please, thank you, make Rob do it too."

He called back, unseen. "On it! I'm checking them off the manifest as we find them, so tell me which ones you're opening."

I grinned to myself as I hauled another box off a shelf. My adorable project manager was going to do his best to make sure we were efficient. I'd never call him that to his face. He'd get so offended.

"I'm an *agent*," he'd whine, but I'd remind him that his good deeds were *projects* he *managed*. All that would earn me was him sulking for five minutes, so I stopped teasing him about it. Sometimes you had to let people have their pride even if they were factually incorrect.

Meghna arrived moments later, holding what could only have been Nick's baseball bat. The energy vibrating off her was intense. She wore an awkward smile as she approached me. "Nick said I should get out some of my aggression."

I wasn't going to turn down the help, having her rounded us out to an even eight. I pulled the chalk from my bag again and drew another pentacle while calling to Nick again. "You and Rob need to bring us all of them now. We've got our hands full!" I winked at Meghna, and she giggled in response.

I set us up to release our first soul, and Meghna needed little prompting to do her part. This was how we spent the next several hours. I checked on the rest of the coven periodically, but after a few false starts, each pair was self-sufficient.

It took a while, but eventually a pattern emerged and drew my attention to the rest of the group. Glowing nimbuses grew around each of the women performing the calling portion of the ritual. There didn't seem to be any uniformity. They tended toward the colors I had observed during our first rite together, but the light was blooming around everyone. Well, maybe everyone. I couldn't tell if it was happening to me or not yet.

"Mel, are you seeing what I'm seeing?"

"You're not imagining it, girlie," she laughed, and it echoed through the warehouse. "I've never seen anything like it!"

All of this was new for me, so I could only guess at what was going on. Magic was a fickle thing, and despite getting a crash course in spirit magic, I was far from an expert. Jaminda was pulling while Alex was breaking, and as the soul escaped at the moment of impact, the glow around Alex brightened a nearly imperceptible amount. Whether it was in thanks or by coincidence, each coven member was absorbing some of the spiritual energy of the soul being released.

I licked my lips, and they crackled slightly like they were charged with static electricity. I stood still, tasting the air for a solid thirty seconds. Meghna looked at me like I wasn't entirely sane, which told me it was invisible to the untrained eye. That was something. I hoped we couldn't overdose on whatever this was.

Time dragged on, and we continued swapping out with each other as everyone got tired. Amanda needed to take a break and alternately sucked her finger and drank a bottle of water. The rest of the group fared better, and we kept going until it was close to morning. The worst casualty was a bout of lightheadedness from Lacey, and she recovered quickly enough to continue.

Rob brought us another opened crate and said we were down to the last few boxes. A triumphant, if exhausted, cheer went up from our section of the warehouse.

"Meghna!" Nick called out. "Get over here!" She shrugged, handed the bat to Rob, and wandered to the front. Rob quirked an eyebrow at me but gave his own shrug and helped out for the rest of our efforts as we all got back to work.

"We're almost there, girls!" Melinda shouted, five minutes later.

That was the moment it all went to hell.

A breeze wafted through the building, and I sniffed the air. "Do you smell smoke?"

Every eye turned toward the entrance as gray smoke rolled along the ceiling toward the outer walls.

"Everybody out!" I screamed, pointing at an emergency exit close to where we had been working.

Like the orders from Melinda, no one questioned mine. We dropped our tools where we stood and marched to the door. Mel slammed it open, triggering a loud buzzing alarm. I had never pushed an emergency exit crash bar, but it wasn't as loud as I had feared it would be. The police weren't likely to hear something like that. I guessed it was more for alerting the building itself than projecting much beyond it. I was second through the door and stood outside, shepherding the rest of our numbers out.

Rob came last, but as soon as his foot passed the threshold, he stopped dead. "Shit. Nick's probably still in there!"

"Don't be stupid, Rob. We'll meet him on the other side."

His eyes went wide. "The gas!"

I was still in crisis mode and must have looked confused because Rob grabbed me by the shoulders and shook me.

"There was so much gasoline by the front door, there's no chance he could get out that way! I'm going back."

"Rob—"

"No, both he and Meghna might be trapped. Take everyone and see what you can do. If I get them both out, we'll let this place burn. But if I can't? You need to put the fire out." Rob turned to head inside, but I grabbed him by the shirt.

"How the hell am I supposed to do that?"

"If you can't figure anything else out, call 911? We'll all probably go to jail, but at least we'd be alive." He pulled himself out of my grasp, lifted the front of his shirt to cover his mouth, and disappeared back into the smoke.

I stared after him for a moment before shifting to my own problems. I was worried about Nick, but I had to trust he could handle himself. There was an emergency exit near the front where we had originally cased the place. Hopefully he'd get himself out.

I peered around and found Alex, outlined with faerie lights, turning the corner and heading toward the docks. Melinda must have herded them away while I argued with Rob. I sprinted to catch up and met them halfway to the front of the building. I ran to the front, where Mel was leading.

"We need to put the fire out," I panted, leaning over for a second and resting my hands on my knees.

Mel stopped and let me catch my breath, eyeing me. "Do you have another plan?"

"Not exactly." I unfolded myself and motioned for everyone to keep walking. Flames were visible through most of the windows. I didn't know how much of the building was on fire, but no handheld fire extinguishers would be enough even if I found one.

The window behind us was the first to shatter, exploding outward in a shower of broken glass and twisted metal. We all ducked and ran forward as the sound and fury repeated itself. The rest of the coven dashed ahead of me, gathering midway between the building and the docks. Intense heat from the growing inferno made it impossible to stand close, and the threat of more shrapnel from breaking windows was too real. The gasoline pooled in front of the building danced with flames. Rob and Nick weren't getting out that way, and I didn't see them coming down the escape.

I was heading toward the rest of the witches with tears in my eyes from the smoke, blurring my vision to a softer focus. The luminescence around the women blended with the rolling bay behind them. All that water, and what was it good for?

I held my hands up and stared at them, rimed with energy. "Mel?"

"Yeah, hun?" she called, looking back at me from where she was checking on the other girls.

"We're not done yet. I need your help." Without waiting for a response, I grabbed the chalk from my bag again. I must have looked like Nero fiddling while Rome burned, because I caught nervous glances out of the corner of my eyes as I drew on the pavement until the stick I held was a nub. When I finished, a large triple spiral lay in front of us. It was as big as I had chalk for, enough for two people to stand in each of the arms. The shape had three limbs, one of which was pointed at the warehouse. I stood in the center, facing the building.

Melinda had watched my every move until understanding dawned on her face. She nodded at me and yelled for everyone's attention. She directed the women to stand in pairs at each of the spirals. In short order, we arrayed ourselves across the triskele, a symbol of my patron.

I stretched my arms to the sides and cried out, "Hold on to me!"

The two pairs at my sides reached out and grasped my hands, each linking with the other standing with them. The pair in front held hands with each other, one of them placing their palm on my chest, completing the connection.

"Manannán!" I screamed, the power from each connection flowing through me and down into the triskele. "We call you forth, draw you up from the depths!"

As I paused to draw a breath, six voices called out as one, repeating my words. The echo reverberated in my chest, my body thrumming with energy. The water, which had been gently rolling before, was now crashing loudly against the docks.

"We release you from your courses, your carved riverbeds, the settled stone of the harbor which binds you."

The voices of my sisters howled, "We release you!"

The sound of wood creaking, cracking, and breaking cut through the din of the fire and the roar of the waves.

"Answer our call. Extinguish the fire threatening us. Bring your domain upon the land and drown it!"

"DROWN IT," screamed the seven of us, the shout filling our ears as I raised my eyes to the clouds.

A tsunami wave leapt over our heads, wider than the parking lots and taller than the building itself. My ears filled with the roar of the ocean, the crest eclipsing the pre-dawn light and casting us all into shadow. I pulled at the energy dancing through the spiral and drew it into myself, raising my hands, which still clutched those of my companions, then sent it crashing back down through the triskele until it exploded outward in a burst of light.

I collapsed to my knees as the wave crested overhead, rested my palms on the ground, and fell onto my side to stare up at the wall of water hanging over us. And then I knew nothing else for some time.

263

CHAPTER 32

ROB

My eyes burned from the smoke as I stepped back inside the warehouse. Visibility was poor with the haze from the fire filling the building. I coughed, the thin cotton of my shirt not doing much to filter the hot air I was sucking into my lungs.

I knew going back in was stupid, but I had to make sure Nick got out. Why? Because I was a loyal idiot, that was why. I had screwed up my life pretty badly and hurt people I cared about. If it wasn't for Nick, I wouldn't have gotten a second chance or met Lester. I cursed myself as I hunched over and peered through the deepening murk.

It was easy to get turned around. All the rows of shelving looked the same. I oriented myself against the faint glow coming from the open back door and moved farther toward the front entrance.

I could make out the larger area opening up into the main expanse of the building and stepped from a narrow alley into the wider area where Nick and I had been stacking crates. I froze, taking in the scene across the floor before me with immediate horror.

Nick stood toe to toe with a figure straight from Hell, with flames bursting from the crates behind them like a tableau out of Dante's Inferno. I hadn't met him, but Nick had described Meghna's demon to me, and this was surely Gaja. How were they eye to eye? Hadn't Nick said he was tall? How was he—the blood left my face when the hand around Nick's neck registered in my brain. I inhaled to yell, to distract him, to do anything, but it lodged in my throat and wouldn't come out.

"Fuck you, Gaja," Nick croaked, and the brass pen he held aloft was suddenly hurtling toward Meghna.

I followed the arc of his throw, momentarily distracted, but returned my attention to Gaja in time to witness him shove his claws into Nick's stomach. The scream which hadn't come before burst from my chest as I ran toward the pair. "NICK, NO!"

Gaja turned to face not me but Meghna, and stalked forward with the smooth control of a tiger. I ran past him, and he ignored my very existence. My movements were slow, like I was running through syrup, my mind racing faster than my body could comply. In a moment, or an hour, I was kneeling beside my friend. Blood spilled freely from four slits in his abdomen, and his eyes were closed, but flitted back and forth beneath the lids.

"It's okay, Nick. You're in shock and losing a lot of blood." I pressed my hands to his stomach, and he groaned in pain, eyes suddenly wide and staring into mine. I flailed mentally, trying to recall any of the first aid classes I had taken when I was younger, or medical dramas Lester and I liked to watch. Pressure was the only thing I could do until we got help.

I wrenched my head around, looking for something else to hold against the wounds. Gaja was closing the distance between him and Meghna, but Meghna herself wasn't paying attention to the approaching danger. She must have caught the pen because she scribbled furiously at something on the table, then turned to face the asura with the brass implement still in hand.

"It's over, you monster," she cried, pointing with her free hand at the table beside her. "You don't own me or my family anymore."

"Then what," Gaja purred menacingly, "is the point of keeping you alive? I haven't decided if I'm going to kill you first or make you watch as I murder your entire family. *No one* backs out of a deal with me."

Her expression fell for a second, full of fear, but a different fire returned to her eyes. Not fire...but light. Her pupils glowed with a golden hue. Gaja was facing away from me, but his shoulders tensed in surprise. He hesitated for only a moment before lunging forward with a snarl, his claws bared.

Meghna stepped forward instead of reverse, all fear evaporating. It was saying something when what happened next was the most surprising thing I saw that day. The pen in her hand was suddenly not. A pen, I mean. What she held instead, and grasped solidly in two hands, was a golden three-tined spear. I could only intuit Gaja's expression. His body attempted to recoil away from the small woman holding the long weapon, but he was too late. His movement was committed.

Meghna continued her own thrust, standing firm against Gaja's weight, and the middle point of the spear burst from his back, crimson blossoming through his clothes.

I gasped. Nick's eyes opened, and he looked around wildly.

"What's happening?" he asked.

"Um. Meghna. I think she killed Gaja."

"What?" Nick groaned and tried to sit up, but I pushed him gently down to the ground.

"You're bleeding, idiot. Stay still." I spared a glance toward Gaja, and the asura had fallen to his knees, his body kept upright by the spear through his chest. Meghna's eyes were no longer lit with an otherworldly light but brown and scared once again.

"I..." Nick tried to speak, but the color was draining from his face, and he began to shake. "I don't think—"

I didn't let him finish. "Meghna! Get me a cloth or something. And *you*. Don't you *dare* say your last words to me," I said with as much cattiness as I could muster in the circumstances. "You're going to live through this if it kills me." Meghna ran toward us holding a shop towel, which must have been close to hand.

Nick chuckled weakly, staring upward. He furrowed his brow. "What's that?"

I grabbed the towel from Meghna, blood flowing freely again with nothing to dam it, then pressed it firmly into Nick's stomach. He hissed, and his eyes rolled as if he was about to pass out.

"What?" I asked, turning my gaze upward.

Something gray blocked the light coming in through the skylights, but each second brought it closer to the roof.

All I had time to say was, "Oh, shit," before the sky fell. The glass above us rained down as water cascaded through the openings, and I threw myself over Nick's prone form. A torrent of industrial soup battered my back—liquid mixed with glass, metal, and other debris from above. Gashes opened in my back, detritus tearing through my shirt at the same time as it threatened to drown us.

"Get under the table!" I yelled at Meghna, but I doubted she could even hear me. All I could do was shield Nick and suffer the consequences until whatever was happening was over. It lasted for minutes. The fires sizzled and died, quenched by the disgusting slurry around us. I anchored our bodies against it, holding firm as the deluge tried to wash us across the floor.

Eventually it was over, and the water receded, leaving an unholy mess in its wake. Meghna swore and stomped through the puddles, coming toward us.

"Is he going to be okay?" she asked, kneeling in an already soaked dress. Her forearms were cut to hell where she had likely raised them to protect her head, ducking for cover.

"I'm not a doctor but probably not. Call 911."

"I...can hear...you," Nick wheezed, dirty water spilling from his mouth.

"Shut up and don't die."

Meghna frowned, checking her screen. "No signal. This isn't usually a dead zone, but my phone got soaked."

"Shit, mine definitely took a swim too. Let's get him outside." I didn't care if I was strong enough. I lifted Nick into my arms. "Hold the towel against the wound. What about Gaja?"

"He's still breathing last I checked, but he wasn't moving. I don't think his chances are good either," Meghna replied as we awkwardly crab-walked through the front door.

"Still...here," Nick's voice was a whisper now.

We took him outside, where the dawn light rose above the horizon. Everything in the lot was gone or broken—smashed against the surrounding buildings. Meghna's car was missing, but I wasn't going to mention anything. It would distract her from keeping Nick's guts inside his body.

I only managed to carry him halfway to the gaggle of witches lying around on the pavement before I collapsed, setting him down as gently as I could. Meghna kept pressure on the wound as I raised my head and called out for Amy.

Amy's head popped up from the center of the pile at my shout, turning bleary eyes in our direction. She scrambled to her feet and ran, stumbling, toward us. When she got to the middle of the lot her eyes narrowed and she doubled her speed, nearly falling when she reached us.

"No. No, no, no," Amy cried, touching Nick's cheek with her fingers.

His eyes fluttered open and came into focus, staring up at Amy, her face backlit by the dawn light reflected off the clouds. A smile danced briefly on his lips. His voice was thin and tired. "Did we win?"

Amy choked back a sob and leaned forward to kiss Nick tenderly on the forehead. "You wonderful idiot, of course we won. We haven't lost with one of your harebrained plans yet." Her tone was light, but tears shone in her eyes. I knew she had the same fear as I did.

"Oh, good. I need to...to rest for a minute. Just a minute..." Nick trailed off, his head lolling to the side. I held two fingers to his neck and checked for a pulse, then pressed my ear against his chest when I couldn't find one.

I looked up at Amy, whose mouth was open in silent horror, and shook my head. Meghna sat back on her haunches, finally letting go of the bloody towel. My eyes blurred with sudden tears, and a cry broke the silence with a nearly inhuman keening. I blinked to clear my vision, only to find Amy to be the source. I was numb, limbs shaky with shock. My friend wailed for her partner, our friend, and I could only stare.

Amy ran out of breath, and in the sudden silence, the sound of claws clicking on the pavement interrupted our vigil. Had Gaja somehow left the warehouse with a spear embedded in his chest? I jerked around and locked eyes with what could have only been the elephant-headed god Ganesha. Even stranger, he rode on the back of a giant white mouse. Not a rat but a field mouse, except it was easily the size of a donkey.

The man—god...whatever—wore a blue vest and loose white pants, his husky body accentuated by the lack of shirt. As remarkable as his head were his extra set of arms, one pair holding the reins and the other resting on his hips. On his head was an elaborate headdress, heavy with metal accents. The mouse's coat was sleek, and it walked with a stately gait, Ganesha's figure flowing smoothly with it.

They passed us without a second glance and headed directly into the warehouse. I looked from Meghna to Amy, but neither could do more than shrug in confusion. In less than a minute, the elephant god emerged from the building holding the limp form of Gaja in his arms.

He strode calmly to where we were with the mouse following closely behind and laid the asura on the ground about ten feet from us. Ganesha pointed at the body and said something in what I assumed was Hindi to the mouse, who curled protectively around the demigod, its nose resting over his heart.

Ganesha turned and traversed the last few feet to stand above us. Meghna prostrated herself on the ground, arms extended toward the god.

"Ganesha—" I tried to say, but Meghna's hand whipped back without warning and slapped my leg.

"*Lord* Ganesha," she hissed in a low whisper before returning her face to the ground.

"Lord Ganesha," I amended, waiting to be acknowledged.

His gaze traveled across the four of us, and he smiled at Meghna even though she couldn't have seen him. "Rise, child," he said, with a soft, ever so slightly accented voice.

Meghna raised her head and came to a seated position, eyes wide.

Ganesha turned and inclined his head toward me. I tried to clear my throat but nearly began crying again. "Sir," I croaked. "We need your help."

Ganesha knelt in a puddle next to the unmoving body and placed a hand on Nick's chest. Hints of a glow escaped from between his fingers, and he pursed his lips in concentration. "He is not yet dead, otherwise it would be beyond me. But he is far from this place." He glanced at Meghna. "This one has gotten her wish, but you three," he gestured to Amy, Nick, and I, "have done me a service. I will do what I can. Is that your wish?"

CHAPTER 33

NICK

"Nick? Hey, Nick!"

Two fingers snapping in front of my eyes brought me back from wherever my mind had wandered, and I startled in my chair. Wait. When did I sit in a chair? Where was I? My last memory was the warehouse, fire, and...a set of claws.

I patted furiously at my stomach, searching for bloody wounds, but found none. I wasn't even wearing the clothes I had started my day in, but a generic gray suit and white shirt. The chair I sat in was one of three arranged around a square white table, Leslie and Lu each occupying the others.

Lu leaned back, seemingly satisfied I wasn't in a stupor anymore.

"What the hell, Lu?" I stood from my seat and paced behind it, but there was nothing to anchor my perception. It was a dull expanse as far as I could see. I returned to the table. "Where am I?"

"A bit of nowhere," Leslie volunteered.

"Am I dead?" I rolled the concept around in my mind and couldn't feel strongly about it one way or the other, which didn't seem right to me.

Lu barked a laugh. "No. I mean, maybe. Remember our deal? When you die, you can choose between Heaven and Hell, right?"

"So I *am* dead?"

Leslie sighed, eyeing Lu disapprovingly. "You're not helping."

Lu raised his hands, palms out, trying to placate us both. "You're in a bit of *limbo*. Get it?"

"Really?" I asked. "Too soon."

"You're right. Okay, you're only a little dead. If someone doesn't call your soul back to your body soon, you might get deader."

"LU," Leslie cried.

I rested my forehead on the cool surface of the table and spoke to the floor, "So, why are you here?"

"Well, for one you *do* get to pick," Lu said.

"And we wanted to keep you company," Leslie added. "So you weren't alone while you waited."

I lifted my head again and stared at them. "Wait, why can't you go tell Amy and Rob to, uh, 'call my soul'?"

They both looked chagrined, which didn't fill me with confidence.

"This isn't something we're allowed to intervene in, I'm afraid," Lu said, sadness creeping into his voice. "Trust me, I would if I could. You've been doing great things for me. It'd be a shame if we had to stop now."

My face was hot, and my throat was tight. "So, there's no grim reaper?"

Leslie shook Their head, slowly. "Afraid not, though I don't know if he'd be any more comforting than we are."

"You put on one hell of a show though. I told you—"

"Now is not the time for 'I told you so's,' Lu," I said, my voice jumping in pitch.

He opened his mouth to reply but must have thought better of it. "Fair point."

"How does this work?" I asked, flailing for some kind of control.

"We wait," Leslie said simply.

"Can, uh. Can someone please hold my hand?" I asked, trying to keep my voice level. "Challenging the son of a god didn't bother me, but a peaceful death is freaking me out right now."

Leslie smiled and grabbed my left hand, and within moments Lu was holding my right. They were both warm and comforting, but I didn't think there was enough comfort in the world to make up for what was happening.

We sat there in silence for what seemed like hours but might have been moments. Time was meaningless here. My eyes were getting heavy, and it was hard keeping them open. I was fading, and one look at my hands let me know it was literal. My body was becoming translucent. My eyes were wide with shock, and I looked back and forth at my companions, who stared back like I was a hospice patient on his last legs.

"What's happening?" I asked in a small voice.

"It's going to be okay," Leslie said.

Lu smiled at me and squeezed my hand. "We won't make you choose right now."

Then I had the strangest experience of my life or death. The Devil leaned forward and kissed me square on the lips.

Despite my eyes being wide, they shot open, and the face kissing mine was suddenly Amy's. The relief flooding my body was intense, but it warred with the shock of pain reentering my awareness. I sat up and wrapped my arms around her, despite my protesting muscles, breaking the kiss and nestling my face into the crook of her neck.

"You're back," she said, choking the words out around a sob, and clung to me with equal ferocity.

My words were choppy, spoken through chattering teeth. "I'd say...I never left, but I think we know...it isn't true." I pushed back, and we held each other at arm's length as I examined my wounds. The gashes were red and angry but covered with large scabs.

"You will still need time to heal," a voice said to my right. I looked up and took in the form of Ganesha, who eyed me appraisingly as if admiring his handiwork. "But I did what I could. This one," he inclined his head toward Amy, which was a dramatic gesture when you had large ears and a trunk, "did the heavy lifting."

I tried to stand, testing my muscles and finding aches and pains, but not the searing agony I expected. Amy stepped back and offered her hand, helping me to my feet. I almost lost my balance, but Rob was there to grab my shoulders.

"I don't think 'being upright' has been a team sport before." I chuckled uncomfortably.

Ganesha turned and made his way to another prone figure, who had a huge mouse lying on top of them. Where the hell had that come from? My brain wasn't firing on all cylinders, but I recalled the story Amy told me about Gaja's father being turned into a mouse.

I followed with halting steps and found myself staring into the face of my would-be murderer. I didn't know if he was dead, but the blood seeping from a chest wound said something serious had happened while I was unconscious. This must have been what Rob had tried to tell me about. Gaja's face was serene, a world away from the visage which had bored into my soul as his claws ripped into my flesh.

"What happened to him?" I whispered to Rob, who had come up beside me.

"Meghna happened to him," he said.

I let out a low whistle and nodded. "I guess we *did* win."

Ganesha knelt beside the body and laid a hand on the mouse's flank. "What will we do with him, Gajamukhasura?"

The giant rodent looked at him with plaintive eyes, and a small whimper escaped his mouth.

Ganesha nodded. "Very well. I shall give him the same chance I granted you." He leaned over Gaja's body and touched the center of the asura's forehead. It left behind a golden dot of light that pulsed with heartbeat, then grew to cover the entirety of Gaja's form.

The elephant god stood, dusting off his pants. We waited, dumbstruck, as the glow shifted and changed. Eventually, the brilliance faded away and left behind another rodent of unusual size. This one was gray instead of his father's white coat. The chest wound was gone, replaced by three white locks of fur contrasting the rest of his coloring. His eyes opened, bright and curious, but a furious torrent of squeaks erupted from his mouth almost immediately.

"Silence, young one," Ganesha spoke, holding his hand up with the palm out over Gaja's head. The mouse's tirade tapered off, replaced only by the rapid rise and fall of his chest. "You have much to learn. Come." He mounted the white mouse and rode toward the exit of the lot. Gaja followed, looking back at me only once with a glare that wasn't full of hate as much as supreme annoyance.

"You and me both, pal," I muttered to no one in particular.

They disappeared around the corner, and we all stood in silence until Melinda's laugh broke it, cutting through the morning air. "There's something you don't see every day!" The group of witches were picking themselves up off the ground and seemed to be checking on each other. I was going to have to ask Amy what had happened, but from the chalk symbol they were all standing around, I guessed she was responsible for my unexpected bath.

I glanced around our small circle. Meghna smiled at me sheepishly, but her eyes were full of pride.

"You did it," I said, chuckling to myself but regretting it immediately as my abs protested.

"I did," she replied, standing a little straighter.

I turned to Amy. "Are we done here? We hadn't finished all the crates."

She shook her head. "No, but we were down to the last couple. Rob and I can put them in the car to take with us. We need to get out of here before the police show up."

Rob nodded and headed back into the warehouse, Amy following behind. I sat on the ground, already soaked to the bone, so one more puddle wouldn't matter. We waited, listening to the waves lapping against the dock, until they re-emerged with the two remaining crates. Meghna looked around, suddenly concerned.

"Where's my car?"

Amy grinned nervously, placing her crate at her feet. "My guess is it's in the harbor. It probably got washed out when the wave receded."

Meghna just blinked at her uncomprehendingly.

Rob shifted the wooden box on his shoulder. "One more line item for the insurance claim. We'll give you a ride home."

We hobbled to the gate, and thankfully, Meghna still had the key to let us out without me needing to scale the fence again. I didn't think I could have done it to save my life. I would have sat at the base of it and waited for the end to come. Rob and Amy loaded their goods into the trunk, and we were on our way as sirens blared, blocks away. We were a few minutes into the drive, heading toward the bridge, when I caught Meghna staring out the window, back at the harbor yard.

"How does it feel?" I asked. "Being free?"

She tilted her head slightly, considering the question. "About the same, really."

I laughed out loud, then groaned in pain, holding my hands against my stomach. "After all this? 'About the same, really?' That's what I get?"

"I may feel the same, but the future looks a lot brighter to me indeed."

"Much better."

CHAPTER 34

AMY

None of us had slept, but we had an unspoken agreement that we couldn't go to bed until we were one hundred percent finished with our task. Our understanding of what "done" meant changed when Rob told us about the data from Adam and how many statues still existed. I wasn't going to count those against the quota I had to hit before I could pass out in my bed for a few hours. That was a problem for tomorrow-us.

After helping unload those last few boxes of macabre statuary at my place, Rob took himself home to update Lester and get some rest, leaving the two of us to finish up. Despite his injuries, Nick insisted he was capable of swinging a hammer. I wasn't going to stop him. He had some of his own aggression to get out after his latest brush with death.

Nick and I made quick work of destroying the remaining statues, out in the yard by the fire pit. Smashing glass in the apartment would have been messy, and Pants wouldn't have stood for it. I imagined her tail puffed up to three times its size, sticking out from under the couch trying to avoid the calamity.

Nick's movements were steady each time I drew a soul far enough to break their prison. He clearly made the effort to ensure he wasn't going to reinjure himself, but once we had established a rhythm, he was testing his boundaries enough to break a bit of a sweat in the warm morning air. There was no conversation, just the quiet gestures and small motion we needed to convey what was next. There had been enough noise, and we both seemed grateful for the silence punctuated by the tinkling glass.

An hour or so later, with a push broom, dustpan, and a cardboard box to put all the broken pieces in, our work was complete. We walked hand-in-hand up the stairs to my apartment and stripped out of our clothes simultaneously as we plodded to the bathroom, leaving small piles in our wake. The steaming shower sluiced dirt and grime from both of our bodies. Nick's clothes had splinters and pieces of warehouse debris in them, and I gently scrubbed his back when twisting around caused him to groan.

We dressed in comfortable clothes, his from the spares I stored in a drawer at the apartment. Nick was snoring before his head hit the pillow, the light from the doorway cutting across his face, but even a kiss from the sun itself wouldn't have kept him awake. He needed rest, and I was going to join him shortly, but my mind was still racing.

I turned my hands one way and then the other, the familiarity of them warring with the memory of power that had surged through my body earlier. I picked up my phone to message Mel. I hadn't checked in since we had scattered.

AMY:

It's done, for now. Did you all make it home alright?

MEL:

Safe and sound. Don't you worry about us. What do you mean "for now?"

AMY:

I'll explain later. Can you meet me at the preserve in a few hours? I'll text when I'm on heading out.

MEL:

You got it, girlie. Get some rest. You deserve it.

I smiled, set my status to "do not disturb," and curled against Nick's back, resting my arm across his chest. My eyelids were as heavy as the sea, and I drifted away from consciousness.

Amy.

My eyes snapped open, and my vision swam dizzily. I slapped at my nightstand until I came away with my phone to check the time. It had seemed like moments, but I had been asleep for four hours. Not nearly enough, but something had dragged me back from slumber.

Pants galloped into the room and jumped onto the bed, then turned and scampered into the living room like she was chasing something. I swung my feet to the floor and padded after her. She was standing on the coffee table with bright predatory eyes, pouncing at the letters.

Bap...A...Bap...M...Bap...Y.

"Hello to you, too, Siobhan," I said through a wide yawn.

I followed as Pants tapped out the words, working much slower than when Siobhan could possess her directly. It was hard to get cats to do much of anything when you wanted them to, let alone when you needed them to.

They came slowly but steadily. COULDN'T WAIT. THANK YOU.

"I didn't have any proof we had fixed things, so thank you for letting me know. Do you get to cross over now?"

Bap. YES.

"Well, tell Manannán he owes me one."

Bap. GOODBYE.

Then it was over, Pants looking about the room as if searching for an escaped moth. I touched the Ouija board with a sigh, then petted the soft fur on Pants's head. "Good kitty."

I snuck back into the bedroom and leaned over to kiss Nick on the cheek. Small sounds escaped his lips followed by a "Hmm?"

"I have to run an errand. You sleep. I'll catch up with you and Rob later."

"Mmph." It was all the reply I was likely to get. I readied myself and sent a quick text to Nick's phone to remind him of where I had gone. It was unlikely he would remember being woken up. I added a note to Mel for good measure, telling her I would be at the small pier at the nature preserve shortly.

It was early afternoon, and the sun was shining. By the time I made it to the park, I couldn't find any evidence of police across the harbor at the yard. I was the picture of summer with a black sundress, floppy hat, and iced tea rattling in a large plastic cup. No one would mistake me for anything other than a resident taking a moment out of their day to sit and stare at the Sound.

The reality was far stranger when I sat between a sea god and the leader of a witch's coven. Manannán's face held a pleased grin, and he didn't say anything as I set myself down.

I gave a tiny flourish. "Melinda, meet Manannán mac Lir."

Mel's laugh barked out across the water. "I had a feeling it wasn't a coincidence when you showed up on my bench."

Manannán spread his hand. "Guilty. But you're god-touched yourself. I didn't think you'd mind me crashing your party."

I eyed Melinda appraisingly. I wasn't sure if he meant her brush with Lu or something else, but it wasn't the time to pry. "What now?" I asked.

"Well. My little problem is solved, thanks to you and your friends. I'd say you get to rest on your laurels for at least a little while until the next deity or demigod comes along looking for a favor."

"That's the reward?" I asked. "More work?"

"Isn't it always?" Mel replied.

"That being said, you never asked for anything in exchange for your help. Selflessness, in itself, is a reason to give you something." He reached into his pocket and fished out a pendant hanging on a piece of fishing line. It was a piece of sea glass, tumbled smooth by the waves and shore, wrapped in a filigree of silver wire.

I held out my hand, and he placed it gently on my palm.

"What is it?"

"A favor, literally and figuratively."

Mel's mouth dropped open. "Shut up."

Manannán laughed. "It's for you and your girls. I don't deal in wishes, but if you need my assistance, you'll have it."

I swallowed, taken aback at the size of the gesture.

"You're welcome." Manannán winked, then stood and dusted off his pants. "Alright, I'll let you get on with it." He shook hands with Melinda, then touched my shoulder in a parting gesture before wandering back down the pier and onto the beach.

We watched him go, but it wasn't long before Mel broke the silence.

"He's cute."

I rolled my eyes and fixed her with a glare. "Really?"

"What do you want from me? I'm a sucker for an accent."

The pendant was light in my hand, and I tucked it away before anything could happen to it.

"What now?" Mel asked.

"Didn't I just ask that? Shouldn't *you* be telling *me*?"

"I couldn't help it. First, the girls all need about two more days' worth of sleep to recover from all the mojo we channeled. You and I are lucky to be on our feet."

I chewed my lip, staring across the water at the far shore. "I don't know what that was, Mel."

"It was a hell of a show, that's what. Magic is about improvisation, and you were a headlining act."

I nodded, the pride in her eyes rounding the edges of self-doubt off my mood. "Can I tell you a secret?"

She chuckled at me. "If you can't confide in me, then we have to rethink this whole seeker business."

"I was going to say I was out of my depth or it was too much." I took a deep breath and continued. "But it wasn't. It felt natural. *Good*. Is that wrong?"

She scooted closer to me on the bench and patted me on the knee. "You've got a lot of potential, Amy. I saw it the moment I laid eyes on you. I think you're meant to do great things, and this is only the beginning."

I placed my hand over hers and squeezed gently. "Thank you. Has this put anyone off from accepting me into the coven?"

Melinda's laugh rang out, startling a few people walking along the shore. "Girlie, you led them through a whole arcane operation, and everyone came out the other side in one piece. Your stint as a seeker is going to be the shortest in our history."

I laughed along with her, relief flooding my body, then leaned against her shoulder. "Good. I really wanted to stay. I don't know what's going to happen next though."

Melinda put an arm around my shoulder and hugged me warmly. "That's okay. We'll figure it out together."

CHAPTER 35

ROB

I woke to the gentle symphony of pans being manipulated around a gas range. A quick glance around reminded me I was home in our bedroom, despite the crazy dreams trying to convince me I was still inside a towering inferno. If you had asked me how I got to bed, I couldn't have told you if my life depended on it. I shivered and huddled down into the blankets again, drifting briefly until the scent of frying bacon permeated my consciousness.

I donned a robe off the back of the door and headed to the kitchen, my bare feet slapping against the cool tile. A brunch spread to rival our favorite Sunday spot glistened on the kitchen table.

"Good afternoon, sleepyhead," Lester said in a singsong voice. He bustled near the stove, transferring crispy strips of pork to a waiting paper towel.

I came up behind him, stealing a piping hot sliver and popping it into my mouth. The bite crunched perfectly, and my lips lightly coated in fat. I leaned my head back in satisfaction, then kissed Lester on the nape of his neck. "Marry me."

He was still cooking, but the sudden color to his ears said he was blushing furiously. "Keep being a hero, and I'll consider it."

It was my turn to blush. I didn't remember telling any of the story of last night to Lester, but I also didn't recall driving home, so anything was possible. "Did I talk in my sleep?"

"Baby. You gave me the highlights in an exhausted stupor, then passed out with your shoes on as soon as you sat on the bed."

I grinned sheepishly. "Sorry."

He cut the gas and turned to face me, wrapping his arms around my neck to pull me in for a kiss. Then he picked up the plate of bacon and sauntered to the table, motioning for me to join him. "Nothing to be sorry for. You had a hell of a night. I woke up to over a hundred emails about the number of souls hitting the holding area we set up after the meeting with God. I knew something had gone down."

I sat and sipped at a perfect cup of black coffee, then tucked into the meal with abandon. Lester watched me appreciatively for a minute before digging in himself. The morsel of bacon had awakened my appetite. It had been too long since my last meal, with a lot of action in between.

I was mopping up some egg yolks with toast when Lester slid a white envelope toward me.

"It showed up for you this morning," he said with a glint in his eye.

I examined the piece of mail, but it didn't have any postage, address, or information about the sender on it. The only identifying feature was a stamped silver L in a calligraphic font prominent on the front. "Any idea who sent it?"

Lester couldn't keep a knowing smile off his face. "It came from 'upstairs.'"

The hand holding the envelope shook, and I forgot breakfast as I carefully opened it. Inside was a small, monogrammed card with the same silver letter. On the back was a simple sentence.

"Heaven requests the pleasure of a conversation with you about your future. Please visit our office at your earliest convenience."

I whistled, then absentmindedly picked up my fork and returned to my plate, reading and rereading the card.

"Well," Lester asked. "What does it say, hon?"

"Oh." I swallowed a wad of pancakes, suddenly aware I had zoned out. "Leslie wants to talk to me about 'my future' or something."

"I shouldn't say anything, but it looks like you shook things up between Heaven and Hell. Lu texted me a cryptic message to tell him if you don't like Leslie's offer." He shrugged, spearing a piece of fruit and popping it into his mouth with a smirk.

I opened my mouth but didn't have any words. How had this happened so fast? I had barely slept, and I was already getting invitations from God and a back-channel hint at a competing offer from the Devil. For what? There was only one way to find out. My eyes were bigger than my stomach, but I put another dent in my plate and guzzled the last of my coffee before pushing back from the table.

Lester eyed me with concern rather than surprise. "You *could* take a day off before talking to anyone. I don't think they'd fault you for it."

I was familiar with that look. He could tell when I was pushing myself too hard, but this wasn't the time to play hard to get. "I don't know what They're offering, but there's no point in waiting. I've still got a lot of work to do, and I don't want a conversation like this, whatever it is, hanging over my head."

Lester stood at the same time as me and came over to put his arms around my shoulders again, tilting his head up for a kiss. I was more than happy to oblige. He tasted like syrup, and I hoped I was half as delightful.

"Text me if you need any support, but I'm going to head into the office. I told Lu I would be late. I wanted to stay until you got up, so I planned for a half day."

I nodded, my stomach warmed by more than the brunch. "Thank you, baby."

A quick shower was in order, but within twenty minutes, I was ready and heading downtown. Business casual was the best God was going to get. If I deserved a day off, I could at least dress down for comfort.

Parking near the Green, I made my way to Angel Co's offices. I had never expected to see them again, but here I was for the third time in how long? I barely stepped into the lobby before Elena was calling my name.

"Rob! Leslie's expecting you. Come right in." She gestured to the door next to her desk and led me to the same swanky conference room they had stashed Nick and me in when we were last there together. I helped myself to a bottle of water and snagged a protein bar, stuffing it in my pocket for later.

"It's not stealing if it's in a little basket waiting for you to take it," Leslie's voice said from a seat to my left, outside of my peripheral vision.

"If I didn't know better, I'd think you had something against doors."

Leslie chuckled as I turned to face Them. "Hello, Rob."

"Hello, God." They preferred to be called Leslie, but I had to address the elephant in the room. A person didn't usually get summoned to speak with the creator "at their earliest convenience." I was at least a little intimidated by the concept, regardless of my former employment.

Leslie sighed. "I'm not one for titles—"

"But you materialized an invitation on monogrammed cardstock to come have a conversation."

They pouted, slightly. "I sent a courier. I wasn't trying to impress you, but I wanted to make it at least a little formal."

I laughed but not unkindly. Despite running a messy organization, Leslie had treated me well. Until the point where They didn't keep John from firing me, anyway. "What's this about? Are you trying to rehire me?"

"Straight to the point. I can respect that." They smoothed an invisible tablecloth with their hands, not meeting my eyes. "I...wanted you to know I made a mistake."

I tilted my head and quirked an eyebrow but didn't say anything. That was certainly a statement. Without context, it was meaningless, and with the way Leslie was acting, I actually felt like I had the upper hand. I didn't want to waste it.

They must have been hoping I'd pry, but when I didn't, Leslie looked up and met my gaze. "I should have paid closer attention to what happened. They say you have to trust the people you hire, but I may have put too much in some rather than others—"

I couldn't help but interrupt. "It's okay, Leslie. I like my job and being a part of the agency with Nick. I don't want to come work for you again."

They gave me a wan smile. "Oh, I didn't expect you to. I would have offered if I thought you'd consider it seriously. I'm still getting my house in order, but it's why Nick created your agency in the first place. Right?"

"Alright, why don't you spit it out?" I took a drink to fill the silence.

"You've earned your place in Heaven."

I sprayed water from my mouth, covering the table in a fine mist. "What? Now? Am I dying?"

Leslie had the grace to look horrified. "No! Nothing like that. I mean, I didn't need to tell you. You could have just found out in fifty years—"

"I'm only living another fifty years?" I blurted, still wiping water from the table with a napkin.

"No! Heavens, I'm bad at this. It was hyperbole, just a random number in the future. Look, when your soul is eventually homeless—"

"What does *that* mean?"

"I was just trying to find a nicer way of saying 'when you die,' but this clearly isn't working." Leslie sighed and rubbed Their face in exasperation. They placed Their hands on the table and fixed me with what I assumed was supposed to be a comforting stare. "We let you go because you had stolen data to keep your friend safe. Since then, you risked yourself to ensure innocent souls returned to their rightful places. On top of that, you shielded the body of your friend to save him. Yes, I was watching."

The enormity of what Leslie was saying settled in my chest. Lu's own message from Lester made sense now, and it seemed like I was on equal footing with Nick when it came to a choice of where I spent my days in the afterlife.

"I realize this is a lot," Leslie said. "So don't think you have to—"

"Maybe."

They blanched, caught off guard by my quick response. "I'm sorry, what?"

The weight of anxiety and uncertainty regarding the state of my soul left my body. I was light, unfettered, and free. Given the choice, which I now had, I had no idea where I wanted to go when I died. I had the love of my life, who was Hell bound. My best friend and partner had his pick, and *his* partner wasn't even tied to the Christian pantheon at this point. The spiritual world was suddenly my oyster, and the idea of being so grateful to Leslie that I accepted immediately seemed like settling.

"Tell you what," I said, folding my hands on the table and digging in for a negotiation. "Make it a pass for two, and I'll let you know some time in the next fifty years."

Chapter 36

Nick

I respected everyone else's work ethic, but with the way I felt when I woke that first afternoon after my brush with death? I wasn't going to meet with *anyone* until I had lied on the couch for approximately three-point-five days at least. Once I remembered I was the boss, I didn't even have to call out. There were some perks, I guessed.

Amy told me about her errand, and I heard the good news from Rob about his personal escape from Purgatory, but beyond those things, I did absolutely nothing important for the next three days. Besides going to the doctor, that is.

It turned out that a gut wound, even one partially healed by a deity themselves, still needed your average mortal care. Luckily, our health plan vetted the doctors I worked with, and I didn't have to make up a ridiculous story about sneaking into the tiger enclosure at the zoo. They did, however, assure me I didn't have any new internal bleeding to worry about and rest was the best medicine. Next to antibiotics and painkillers, which they also gave me.

Life went on outside the apartment during my self-imposed and physician- approved sick time. I'd say I emerged from my cocoon as a beautiful butterfly, but no such metamorphosis occurred. I did deep clean my apartment on the last day. Odin was starting to knock over old takeout containers in protest for the state of the place. Cats, am I right?

I was starting to feel human again and ran out of shows to binge-watch on the couch when I decided to reenter society. I wasn't one hundred percent. Far from it. A lingering shadow lay in the back of my mind, and I knew I'd need to address it, eventually. But that was a problem for tomorrow.

I had an overdue meeting with the Elephas group on the docket, following the events of the last week. My phone had blown up after the incident, and despite ignoring it, those messages hadn't gone away.

It took less time than I expected to scroll through my texts and schedule a lunch meeting with Arjun. We met at the Oasis again, and I was starting to think he had a sweet tooth only satisfied by their particular baklava recipe. Regardless, I didn't mind the promise of some rose water, and the least they could do was buy me a meal, given the latest circumstances.

I arrived unfashionably early and secured what was becoming "our" table in the courtyard. A beautifully patterned ceramic cup of Turkish coffee was cooling in front of me when Arjun arrived, followed by Chetan. One of my eyebrows raised involuntarily when a third figure followed them both.

I stood to greet them, shaking hands with the first two, but when I got to the third, I clasped her hand with both of mine.

"I didn't expect to see you here, Meghna," I said.

Meghna smiled shyly, brown eyes offset by a golden salwar, which glinted in the sunlight. "It's good to see you, Nick. I was worried about you after, well, everything."

I sat a little stiffly but managed not to groan, and motioned for the rest to join me. "New experiences to check off my bucket list, right? I don't know if I'd recommend them to anyone, but here we are."

Arjun grinned. He was wearing another floral-patterned vest, this time in a deep blue. "I had faith you would keep the pen on you, and it wasn't misplaced."

I eyed Meghna. "I hope she didn't try to give me credit for any of it."

"Only having a fantastic throwing arm," Arjun replied, laughing. "If you ever want to try out for our cricket league, say the word."

"I'll consider it." I winked at Arjun, then turned my attention back to Meghna. "Why are you here, though? I would have expected you to be knee-deep in divesting your family's business."

"About that," Meghna said, clearing her throat. "Lord Ganesha granted my wish in an…interesting way. Other than the lost warehouse, he hasn't made any demands for my family to give up their livelihood."

"Ah, I thought it might have been more complicated. The language in the contract left a lot of room for interpretation." I inclined my head at Arjun respectfully.

He returned the gesture. "It was determined that Meghna will serve a greater purpose, as part of transferring her family's debt. Instead of having three generations until being claimed by the asura, she, and one descendant from each of the next three generations, will serve in the Elephas Group."

I had taken a sip of coffee but swallowed it painfully at this news. "That's a little severe."

Meghna shook her head. "No, Nick. It's fair. At the end of that period, we will have no obligations and can maintain the family business. It may not have been what I originally wanted for a career choice, but I'll be able to do some good for my people."

I couldn't help but chuckle. "Now you sound like me."

The server interrupted us briefly to take our orders. Once they were out of earshot, I eyed Chetan, who had not said anything other than "*shish taouk*" since we sat. "What do you think of this?"

He tilted his head one way and then the other. "I am not one to question Lord Ganesha, but even if I were of a mind to, I would not object to this decision."

"Even better," Arjun added. "Meghna is going to be the official liaison to your agency."

I clapped my hands lightly in applause. "Who better than someone who has already experienced the madhouse? Though I hope this doesn't mean you're expecting a lot of cases to come our way. I may have had my fill for now."

Meghna blushed but looked pleased. "I still need to be trained. I don't know what being an agent of a god means yet."

"If we're any example, you drink a lot of coffee and meet for lunch a fair bit." I grinned, lifting my cup. "But seriously, you'll do fine."

"Oh!" Meghna exclaimed, brightening. "Speaking of coffee..." She trailed off and rummaged in her purse, bringing out a cylinder the size of a soda can wrapped in a white cloth. She placed it on the table in front of me. "A gift from my father."

I opened the parcel, and inside was a shining steel coffee maker like the one he had used when we were trying to convince him of his family's peril. This was one of a smaller, personal size.

"When I told him what you had done, putting yourself in such danger to free our family from the curse, he was so grateful. He would enjoy your company and promised to teach you how to make it the right way."

"Please thank him for me. I'll definitely take him up on his kind offer."

The food finally arrived, and we moved on to smaller talk as we enjoyed the meal. These were good people, and the conversation came easily. I could still feel a cloud in my mind, a light unease, but sunshine and good food pushed it farther away.

We were enjoying some of the inevitable baklava when Arjun veered to more serious topics.

"One more thing. I know Lord Ganesha granted a wish for you and your friends—"

I nearly spit out the last sip of coffee. "A what?"

Arjun grimaced, but Chetan answered my question with a wry smile. "To bring you back from the other side. Well spent, in my opinion, but I like you. Arjun said they should have wished for a new boss."

Arjun glared at Chetan, pursing his lips, but I laughed at the audacity of the joke. Chetan was hiding a sense of humor in his lanky frame.

"Very funny," I said. "They didn't mention that part, but I guess I'd have done the same if it were either of them."

Arjun cleared his throat, pulling our attention to him. "What I was going to say was Lord Ganesha offers you a boon. Call it hazard pay. It won't reach as far as a wish, but it's not without merit."

I already had thoughts of what to do with a favor from a god, but I filed them away for later. It was nice to have something like that in my pocket, but it was always a toss-up between the greater good and more selfish pursuits. *Maybe I could combine the two for once.*

Arjun seemed to read something in my face and moved back to more casual topics. "So, what's next for you, Nick?"

"I haven't exactly decided yet. There's a lot of work to be done, tracking down the remaining souls, which Meghna's family unintentionally scattered to the wind. Then there's the original purpose I established the agency for."

"Ah," Arjun punctuated his exclamation, waving his fork in the air. "We so rarely get to do what we intended. Fighting fires, as always."

"Quite literally, in this case," Meghna added.

I took a contemplative bite of my pastry, letting the buttery dough melt in my mouth. "If I have my way, we're going to spend a lot of time getting into the details. But God, and the Devil in this case, only knows if it's going to happen."

"Well, it is my solemn hope you get to do your job in peace for a while," Arjun said and raised his cup in toast.

I laughed and raised my own. "From your lips to their ears."

I sat at a table outside Cafe 126, sharing a meal with the Devil. It wasn't an uncommon occurrence, but we hadn't been to this particular restaurant in years. Since the beginning, once I thought of it.

"I was really dead, wasn't I?" I asked.

Lu sipped demurely from a demitasse and only quirked a manicured eyebrow. He let the question lie in silence as he set the cup down on its saucer. "You never were one for small talk, were you?"

I grinned, recalling our first conversation at this very restaurant. "No, I guess not."

He took another drink, inserting a pause I was dying to fill with something, but I resisted the impulse. "Do you want the truth, or do you want comfort? The fact is, you're still alive, so you get to choose how many existential crises to experience."

I chewed a mouthful of lettuce, giving myself a moment to consider. I had been through a lot in the past few years, but the most recent peril was an escalation I hadn't expected. Regardless, I tried not to shy away from the reality of my situation, even if I sometimes wore rose-colored glasses. I settled on what I hoped was the healthiest choice. "Truth."

"Not to put too fine a point on it. Yes."

I winced, but the revelation didn't hold any actual pain. Like when you stubbed your toe but not hard enough to hurt and said "ouch" anyway. I tilted my head, trying to "feel my feelings" like my therapist would ask me to do the next time I met with her. The check in with the various parts of my body lasted less than three seconds, and the only thing I experienced was a gurgle from my stomach asking for more of my fancy duck salad. I shrugged and picked up another forkful.

"Well, that was a fascinating display of your mental process," Lu said, chuckling. "But I'm happy to not drop you into a well of despair."

"Nothing has been normal for years now, Lu. Turns out dying didn't change anything."

Lu gave me a golf clap. "Bravo, now you're thinking like a man who knows there's an afterlife."

"I'm not being fatalistic, Lu," I scoffed.

"Neither am I. All I'm saying is I'm proud of you for looking at the bigger picture. Speaking of which, what's next?"

"Everyone wants to know 'what's next' today. I didn't bring a five-year plan with me to dinner."

"No, not that serious. I'm mostly curious whether you'll be taking a break after everything."

"Is that in my contract? I didn't even know it was an option."

"You don't work for me anymore, not exactly. If you closed up shop for a month to travel and clear your head, I wouldn't think twice about it."

I had three days on the couch to consider the topic and answered without burning any additional brain cells on it. "No, I'm good. There's too much to do. If we can't figure out how to handle it remotely, someone will have to go on assignment to find those remaining souls. I also expect we're going to have more clients on top of the audits we've barely started."

"You sound sure of yourself."

"The reward for a job well done is more work," I shot back.

"I'll admit, you did well. Maybe a little less tweaking the noses of the demigods you deal with, if you're expecting more of those kinds of cases."

"'I told you so' doesn't look good on anyone, the Devil included."

Lu held his hands up in surrender. "I'm protecting my assets. It's just business."

"About that. What was with the kiss? Unless I imagined it because my brain was shutting down or hypoxia, or something." This was something I had been chewing on during my convalescence.

"Ah. That." Lu...blushed. I made the Devil blush. "You were pretty far gone. Someone had to act as the conduit for Amy's connection to allow you to return."

I imagined sitting alone in the blank waiting room, fading out of existence, without anyone to make a bridge. It made me shiver. "That makes sense, I guess. But why you and not Leslie? Is it because you held my contract first?"

"No." His blush deepened if anything. "We, ah, drew straws."

I was scraping the last bit of duck off my plate, and the tines screeched against the ceramic. "Come again?"

"We drew straws," he repeated.

My mouth gaped like a fish as I collected my thoughts but could only focus on one detail. "Was it the winner or the loser who had to kiss me?"

"Nick," Lu said, with a cluck of his tongue. "Some things are best left a mystery."

Epilogue

Nick

It was December again, and the chill of the air followed me through the hall as I doffed my coat and hung it on the rack outside the agency door. I picked our daily copy of the *New Haven Register* off the side table before walking into the office.

"Morning, Nick," Rob said from his desk. He didn't look up from his laptop but gave me a distracted wave. He had taken point on what we dubbed the "soul recovery initiative" and had been coming in earlier than me most days. The reception he received from clients, once they found out their dearly departed family members were free from the Cormick's scam, was enough to keep him at it despite the challenges we faced tracking them down.

We settled on hiring some Angel and Devil Co. vetted private investigators to be our eyes and ears in the field. Rob was loath to leave Lester for prolonged periods of travel, and I couldn't say I was any more enthusiastic about the idea. It also justified a budget increase, which both sides were more than happy to approve.

"Don't forget we've got an interview in about thirty minutes," I said, my own arrival cutting the schedule a bit fine.

"For an admin?" he asked. "We're overdue for one. The phone's been ringing constantly."

"Who knew we'd be opening a can of worms, getting involved in inter-pantheon politics?"

Rob grumbled. "I'm sure *someone* knew and neglected to tell us."

"That sounds like Lu and Leslie."

I let the subject drop and took some time to ease into my morning with what little of it I had. I fixed myself a cup of espresso from our new super automatic machine, checked my emails, and reviewed the resume of our applicant.

All those mundane tasks aside, I shook out the paper to check the headlines. I was scanning the top stories when the front door cracked open, and a head poked inside.

"Is this The Devil's in the Details?" the man asked. He was medium height with dark skin and short cropped hair. The applications didn't have photos attached because it was a recipe for introducing bias, but it was safe to assume this was our nine o'clock.

I stood and moved to meet him, offering my hand. "Derrone?" He had a light handshake without being floppy, which would have been my only complaint when it came to the standard greeting.

"Yes, and you must be Nick?"

"Guilty. We're getting ourselves settled. Why don't you take a seat in our conference area, and we'll be right over. Coffee?"

"I'm more of a tea guy."

Strike one, but I wouldn't hold it against him. Not too much anyway. "We've got that too. Let me put the kettle on."

I led him the twenty feet to our "meeting room," which, in an open office plan, wasn't much more than a nice table and chairs in clear view of the rest of the space. I popped the hot pot on and passed back to my desk. My laptop lay under the newspaper, and as I picked the paper up to excavate it, a bold headline caught my eye.

"Tech giant Bryan Albescu indicted by federal grand jury on multiple criminal counts..."

An involuntary smile played across my lips. It was going to be a good day after all. I scooped my laptop from where it lay on my desk and motioned for Rob to join us. One pit stop at the coffee counter to grab a mug and tea bag, pour the boiling water, and we were sitting across from our guest.

"So, Deronne," I said, settling into my chair. "Tell me what you think of the Devil."

I didn't know if he was expecting a more softball question to start, but he chewed his lip before answering. "I don't have a strong opinion, but I'd say he's probably a bit misunderstood. The whole dichotomy of God and the Devil is a black-and-white construct which doesn't leave room for much gray area."

Rob and I shared a glance, and he gave me a slight nod and the ghost of a smile.

I grinned and took a sip of my coffee. "Why don't we talk about our goals for the Agency over the next five years, and where you would fit into it? You could have a bright future here."

Acknowledgements

If you had asked me a year ago whether I'd have published a trilogy by the end of 2024, I'd have called you insane. Turns out I'm the crazy one. I couldn't have done this without the support of my partner, Katya. They glared at me every time I read them a chapter I hadn't finished, urging me to "write more."

As always, thanks to the local authors in our little collective: Ashton Bush, David Niemitz, Tal Good, and Laurie Neilsen for supporting each other in making art on a daily basis.

This book was a culmination of a long road, so the beta readers who gave me important early feedback were critical to its success. Laurie Neilsen and David Huffman, you both helped make this a great story.

Thanks also to my editor, Katherine McIntyre, for another great job massaging my draft.

Finally, thank you, dear reader. Without you, this book would just be a story lost to time. I hope you enjoyed reading it as much as I enjoyed writing it.

ABOUT THE AUTHOR

Ben Schenkman likes many things in his life: his 20-pound Maine coon cat, his family, his coffee, and his eclectic hobbies—not necessarily in that order.

Ben also likes to play devil's advocate in his urban fantasy books by exploring the gray areas of good and evil with questions like, "Does the end really justify the means? Or is it all simply black and white?" Ben leaves these questions lingering in the ether to challenge readers' conventional thinking and delve into the complexities of moral dilemmas.

As a writer and a native of Connecticut, Ben draws inspiration from his upbringing and college years in New Haven, where his urban fantasy novels take place. On the days he wants to escape being a writer, he's a massive foodie who goes on daring gastronomic adventures, an overachiever who collects degrees in Theater, Nuclear Engineering, and an MBA, or the manager-slash-performer of the fire dance troupe, "HVBRIS"—you know, the basics. No big deal.

To learn more about Ben Schenkman and his work, or if you simply want to invite him for a coffee and talk about cats, visit https://benschenkman.com today.

Thank you for reading! If you enjoyed this book, please consider leaving an honest review on your favorite platform. What's next for our intrepid author?

Coming in 2025

Let Sleeping Gods Lie

New characters, new story, new magic, New Haven.